Bistro Nights

BY DAVID BENJAMIN

LAST KID BOOKS

Last Kid Books
309 W. Washington Avenue
Madison, WI 53703

First Edition
August 2023

Printed in Wisconsin, United States of America

For more information or to order books:
visit www.lastkidbooks.com

Library of Congress Control Number: 2023938843

ISBN-13: 979-8-9876144-2-6

A NOTE ON THE TYPE

This book was set in Athelas, a serif typeface designed by Veronika
Burian and Jose Scaglione and intended for use in body text.[1] Released
by the company TypeTogether in 2008, Burian and Scaglione described
Athelas as inspired by British fine book printing.

Printed and bound by Park Printing Solutions
Verona, Wisconsin

Designed by Kristin Mitchell, Little Creek Press and Book Design
Mineral Point, Wisconsin

For Léa Delebarre
who insisted on it

JUNE

CHAPTER 1

Le Petit St.-Benoit

The thick-shelled snail described a shallow arc against a bright evening sky and the pale gold of the limestone buildings before bouncing on the cobblestones of rue St.-Benoit and clattering off the granite curb. One of Paris' lurking crows swooped to the street and nabbed the shell. Ahead of an encroaching electric scooter, the thief took flight, ascending toward a rooftop where it could extract undisturbed the rubbery molluskcrustacean's mortal coil.

"Brendan!" came a woman's voice coincident with the crow's visit. "You don't *throw* your food!"

In response, the small American wrinkled his nose and gagged theatrically.

"Ew!" He said. "Those things aren't food!"

This exchange passed loudly enough to capture the notice of several nearby diners. Brendan's bleat drew a brief, hooded glance from the waitress.

His mother assumed an air of pedagogical patience, smiling tightly.

"They're called *bulots*," she said, careful not to articulate the "t" and the "s." "It's a kind of snail."

"SNAILS!?" cried the small American's slightly larger sister.

Encouraged by a rare moment of solidarity with his sibling,

Brendan pointed at a small metal bowl beside the pile of *bulots*. "What's that stuff?" he demanded.

The mother sighed.

It was a sunny evening in June, shortly after most schools in the United States had set their pupils loose for summer vacation.

"They're back," said Steve Knight. He was two tables away from the tourist family at a rustic bistro, Le Petit St.-Benoit. He was American. His companion, Mie Nishimura, was a Tokyo girl. She had—about a year before—evolved from Steve's assistant to his sweetheart. Their relationship was now, in Steve's word, "evolving."

"Well, they come every year," Mie noted.

The sightseer influx to Paris begins benignly with a flood of well-behaved Golden Week shoppers and shutterbugs from Japan. Italians and Spaniards, less couth but amiable, followed by barbarian hordes from Germany and Russia, begin their summer invasion swiftly thereafter. Americans, loud, demanding, ill-schooled and inclined to wear shorts for all occasions, add to the melting pot. The Chinese, of course, are everywhere, like locusts.

"It's just mayonnaise," the mother said to Brendan. "You see, you pull the snail out of its shell with this little fork and then you dip—"

"YECCH!" barked Brendan, who then tossed another snail. This one ricocheted off a parked bicycle and settled in a crack between cobblestones. It drew no immediate crow. The waitress, who had only just delivered the *bulots* to the table, took interest. She approached Brendan, his mother and the little girl.

She stood near the table, silent, vigilant, scrupulously nonjudgmental.

The little girl decided to contribute to the discourse. "Mom,

I'm not eating that crap."

The mother sighed. "Bethany, don't say 'crap.'"

Brendan, prompted by his mother's suggestion, had resorted to surgery. He held up, impaled on the tiny fork, the body of a *bulot,* ripped from its shell.

"Mom," crowed Brendan, "it is crap. Look, this part here!" He pointed. "That's shit, Mom. Snail shit."

"Oh my God," said the mother.

"I hate myself for this," said Steve to Mie, his voice low, "but I'm sort of enjoying this."

"I wish it were over," replied Mie. She had her face in her hands but was peeking between her fingers.

The waitress took one almost imperceptible step toward Brendan, Bethany and their mother.

"Perhaps," she said softly.

The mother turned and looked up, her face betraying both pique and supplication.

The waitress, her English measured, with just the faint trace of an accent, suggested, "A plate of *frites*?"

"Freet?" asked the mother, alarmed at the prospect of a dish more disastrous than *bulots*.

The waitress' smile was both kind and mirthless. "Fries," she said. "Like McDonald's."

The mother slumped in surrender. "Oh, yes. Could you?"

"Bien sur," said the waitress. "Of course."

She backed off, about to turn away.

Steve whispered to Mie. "This isn't over."

"Please, God. Make it end."

"No, wait," said Steve.

The waitress suspended her retreat. She spoke, almost intimately, to the mother. "Or," she said.

"Or?" asked the mother.

"Ma," whined Brendan. "This chair is hard!"

Mother and waitress ignored Brendan.

"Up the street here," said the solicitous *serveuse*, "and to the right, not far, a pizzeria. Pizza Roma."

She paused.

"Perhaps?" said the waitress.

The mother leaned close to the waitress. "I hate to give up," she said.

The upturn of the waitress' lips denoted sympathy.

"But you're right," said the mother, bestowing a scowl on her offspring.

The waitress stood erect again and backed away.

"The check, I guess," said the mother, sighing. "Um, *l'addition*?"

"Oh, no," said the waitress. "you've had nothing."

"But the snai—*bulots.*"

The waitress did a French thing, filling her cheeks with air and blowing out gently, dismissively.

"Well, thank you. Thank you so much," said the mother, as she grabbed Brendan by the scruff and yanked him from the chair of his discontent.

"Come, Bethany," said the mother despondently, "we're having pizza ... again."

"Aw jeez ma," nasaled Brendan, "the pizza here isn't the same."

As the American mother and kids departed, wrestling their way toward blvd. St.-Germain, the waitress vanished from the scene of Brendan's crime, along with the basin of *bulots*, its accompanying mayonnaise, tableware, water carafe and glasses.

Steve said, "So. Where do you think they came from."

"No idea. Who cares?" said Mie. "They're all over Paris now, all the same, like lice. But that guy ... "

"What guy?"

Steve had to twist in his seat.

The Petit St.-Benoit, situated near a corner with rue Jacob, is an epitome of simple dining, with a polished-wood facade beneath a long red awning, tables arrayed in twos along the narrow sidewalk, leaving barely a path for pedestrians to tiptoe and sidle through the bistro clientele carving their *souris d'agneau*, spooning up their *pot au feu* and forking their *escargots*. The interior is all woodwork and rickety tables under paper tablecloths whereon the waiters scribble orders and calculate *l'addition*. The interior is tight enough that everyone, customers and workers, walks sideways. A wall of little cubicles like post office boxes houses the personal napkins of regular customers. The kitchen is a small inferno.

Having turned in the direction where Mie could look without contorting her body, Steve asked again, "What guy?"

"Steve, don't stare. He's at the far table."

Steve, trying not to look as though he was looking, peered peripherally. He beheld a rumpled male, shy of his fifties, neither tall nor short, fat nor thin, bearded but not hairy, and blatantly despondent. He wore a plain off-white Perma Press shirt with collar, no tie, blue jeans and sandals without socks. A blue twill jacket, with lapels, hung on the chair behind him. He seemed to be studying, intently and disapprovingly, a glass of wine in his hand that held barely a swallow of remaining fluid.

"There," said Mie, as Steve untwisted and faced her again, "is a story."

It had become a pastime for Steve and Mie, since their first encounter in Tokyo, to make up stories about strangers they saw in bars, restaurants, parks and mass transit.

Steve looked up into his brain, paused for a beat and began his tale of the sad character at the far table: "He had a cat. Calico. Very affectionate, like a dog. He thought he would outlive the cat. But it died. He can't deal—"

"No, no, no," said Mie. She made an "X" sign with her hands. "We've sworn off cat tragedies. Remember?"

"But I'm good at—"

"Hm, look at him now," said Mie.

"I wish I could," said Steve. "The guy's behind me."

Mie provided play-by-play. "The waitress just brought the sad guy more wine. They're talking now. Like they know each other."

"How do you know that?"

"Their faces are too close for them to be strangers," said Mie.

"Really?"

"And they're talking too long. She's not just telling him today's specials."

"Broiled *merlu* and roast chicken."

"Hush, you."

Mie watched silently. Steve waited, watching her. Mie was his favorite thing to look at.

"Somebody broke his heart," said Mie finally.

"Not his cat."

"No cats."

CHAPTER 2

Le Pré aux Clercs

The waiter at Le Pré aux Clercs, just around the corner from the Petit St.-Benoit, had sussed out Steve's American accent after two syllables and assumed an attitude of accusatory *hauteur*. He nevertheless delivered Steve's cognac and Mie's port both swiftly and cordially. He was a pro.

"He doesn't like us," said Steve.

"He doesn't know us," said Mie decisively.

They lifted their glasses and gazed into each other's eyes. Despite the chilly waiter, the corner café felt warm and protective. Steve and Mie had taken a table on the fringe of the interior, overlooking the jumble of tables and canopies that narrowed the sidewalk and diverted pedestrians onto rue Bonaparte. The interior lights, strategically weak, lent Le Pré aux Clercs a slightly illicit golden haze. At night, from sunset 'til the wee hours, the place stayed crowded, not so much for its cuisine, which was bistro basic—onion soup, *steak frites, steak tartare, confit de canard, tartines* and pseudo-hamburgers— but because the drinks were good, the service brisk and the clientele fashionable. Most of the couples on the *terrasse* were married but not to each other. Steve and Mie liked the joint because every summer solstice, during the all-night *fête de la musique*, Le Pré aux Clercs serenaded its patrons with sophisticated French jazz played by gifted young musicians.

"Okay," said Steve. "I've got it."

"Got what?"

"The true story of the sad guy."

"Sad guy?"

"Over at the Petit St.-Benoit."

"Oh, Steve. That again?"

"No, no, I've figured it out. This is a good one."

Mie narrowed her eyes. "I'll be the judge of that."

When they spun yarns about strangers at nearby tables, Steve and Mie preferred protagonists who conveyed a depth of emotion—bright or dark, joy or pathos—that could be felt from a distance. The lonely drinker at Le Petit St.-Benoit fit the profile.

"Tragically ... " Steve began.

Mie rolled her eyes now. "Of course."

"Tragically," said Steve, "the man we saw was once—actually, not very long ago—France's foremost nuclear scientist, a sort of latter-day Pierre Curie."

"You know, Marie Curie did all the hard work," Mie interjected.

Steve let this pass. He continued. "One day, Pierre was on an inspection tour at one of the largest nuclear power stations in France, when an accident happened. Suddenly, radioactive water was gushing from a broken doohickey—"

"Doo-hickey?" asked Mie.

"Yeah, like an atomic faucet," said Steve, "All these power plants have 'em."

"Right."

"Pierre burst into action. He didn't pause to consider the possible consequences. He was terrified at the possibility that La Belle France could, in the blink of an eye, become a second Chernobyl—"

"Or Fukushima."

"Right, yes. Or Fuku-shboom. So, our hero, Pierre, that poor drunk guy at his lonesome table who was once the greatest nuclear mind in all of France, he casts aside all concern for his personal safety. He charges into the contaminated area. He grabs the panicky nuclear workers by the collar of their smocks and pushes them toward safety. Then, he runs over to the atomic faucet that's pouring out gallons and gallons of liquid plutonium. He has only seconds to stop the flood before the nuclear rods are exposed and the reaction reaches critical mass, destroying all of northern France and half of Belgium."

Mie smiled. "Not a bad story so far. Where'd you pick up all that atomic gibberish?"

"Mostly from watching *The China Syndrome*."

"More than once?"

"Love that flick."

"Go on."

Steve nodded. "So, Pierre's up to his ankles in plutonium, but he saves France and Europe. Of course, he's been fatally radiated—like Spock in the dilithium chamber."

"Spock?" scoffed Mie.

Steve raved on. "Despite desperate efforts to flush the poison from his tissues, the doctors give poor Pierre a mere few weeks to live. His career is over and he's unwelcome among the atom smashers who once worshipped him as a mentor. His family is scared to go near him. His friends shun him. He ends up wandering the streets of Paris 'til he arrives at the Petit St.-Benoit, where nobody knows he's a dead man walking. The bistro becomes his hideout. He goes back now, every night, drinking to kill the pain, which gets worse day by day. He drinks 'til he passes out and then the waitress, the pretty one with the Arabian eyes, she pours the miserable wretch into a cab and sends him home."

"Wait," said Mie. "Isn't she in danger? Getting so close to him?"

"No, he's got radiation sickness, but he's not radioactive. He doesn't glow in the dark."

"This story might be better if he did," offered Mie.

Steve settled back, sniffed his Hennessey and took a sip.

"Wait. Go back to the nuclear accident," Mie insisted. "How did it all start?"

Steve was ready. "Funny you should ask," he said with a knowing smirk. "There was a saboteur. He planted a tiny explosive charge that punched a hole in the plutonium tank."

"Plutonium comes in tanks?"

Steve ignored this. "Our hero actually knows the saboteur. Y'see, Pierre wasn't really at the plant to inspect—"

"Of course not," said Mie. "The plot must thicken."

Steve labored on. "Pierre had gone to the nuclear plant to intercept the mad bomber before his diabolical plot succeeded."

"But if Pierre knows who the saboteur is," said Mie, "why—"

"Why, you ask?" said Steve. "Better you should ask how did Pierre know, in the first place, about the plot to blow up the plant and destroy northern France and parts of Belgium!"

"Okay, how—"

"Because they were lovers!"

"Who were lovers?"

"Pierre and the saboteur!" said Steve. "The saboteur talked in his sleep."

"Wait," said Mie. "He's gay? The guy at the Petit St.-Benoit? Pierre is a gay nuclear scientist dying of radiation sickness?"

"That's right. He knew every detail of his secret lover's dastardly plan and tried to stop it. And he did! But he couldn't save himself," said Steve. "Now that the plot has been foiled, Pierre is taking this terrible secret to his grave."

"Oh, Steve, why can't he—"

"Why can't he rat out the saboteur, the only man he's ever truly cared for? Would you squeal on me?"

"Yes," said Mie. "If you were blowing up nuclear power plants."

Steve let this go. "Besides, if he ratted out the saboteur, he would have to admit he was gay."

Mie scoffed. "Oh, come on, Steve. This is France. Everybody's gay."

They paused to taste their drinks.

"This might be true generally," said Steve, recovering the thread, "but not among nuclear scientists. They're infamous for their homophobia."

Mie pondered this. "So, Pierre's dying of radiation but he's not actually radioactive. But, if all the other nuclear guys found out he was gay, then—metaphorically—he would be radioactive to them."

"Well put, honeybunch."

"But, after the accident, they wouldn't come near him anyway."

Steve nodded. "Thus compounding the tragedy."

"No wonder he drinks."

They drank.

"What about the saboteur?"

Steve smiled. "Oh, him?"

"What about him?"

"You mean, the two-faced bisexual terrorist who dropped his gay lover like a hot rock and moved into a garret in Pigalle with a Moulin Rouge chorus girl named Milou?"

"Milou?"

"Yes, it's a nickname."

"It sounds a little too much like my name."

Later that night, taking the long way home to their lodgings on rue du Bac, Steve and Mie passed the Petit St.-Benoit. The lights were still on inside. A few diehard diners were making midnight small talk and killing the last drops from their *carafe d'eau*. At the only outdoor table still occupied, Steve's tragic hero (Pierre) was still working on a bottle of red. The waitress had taken a seat across from him. Their faces were close together. She was talking, he listening.

"Look at that," said Steve.

"Something going on there," said Mie.

CHAPTER 3

Le Petit St.-Benoit

Mireille resisted the impulse to take the man's hand and rub it soothingly. He needed soothing.

Cavendish always needed soothing. If Mireille succumbed to her sympathy, she worried that he would insinuate himself, his troubles, his petty triumphs—and his imminent failure— into her life, pushing aside her own needs, wants, fears and disappointments. He would make trouble. He might even run afoul of Serge.

However, even woozy and mumbling as he eventually became every night, Cavendish was a sweet man. His troubles—which he had told her, in bits and pieces over the last three weeks—were more interesting than the best moments of Mireille's life.

He was American, of course, from some multi-syllable state in the middle of the country. He spoke execrable French and wrote in English. He had published a novel, set in Paris, *Love and Death in the Latin Quarter*, that had spent a month on the *New York Times* bestseller list. He'd been living off the proceeds of that surprise triumph while putting off his editor in New York, who had wanted a new story for the fall list, and then the spring list and then the fall list ...

Cavendish had no new ideas. He couldn't find inspiration

on the romantic streets of Paris, nor in the depths of his imagination, nor in the bottom of a bottle. Eventually, despite the fact that he bought only coffee and a croissant in the morning on rue de l'École-de-Médecine and, in the evening a bottle (or two) of wine and a simple dinner at the Petit St.-Benoit, he was destined to be broke in a year. He envisioned that year, bereft of a narrative spark, stretching out before him like a long eulogy for a dead nobody.

Sighing nightly over that prospect, he had caught the eye of Mireille. She extended a compassion that he absorbed with a mixture of affection and chagrin. Did she actually like him or was this hovering solicitude just pity? He suspected the latter because, he conceded, what was there to like? He was hardly an attractive man. He dressed indifferently. He was mired in middle age, his hair gray and thinning, his beard speckled with white. He was a little lumpy but he didn't eat enough to bloat up or go entirely to seed. His face, usually slack and inexpressive, grew hard and exposed its angles when he was alert. He fended off the occasional onset of alertness by drinking.

But he wasn't a drunk. He didn't think so. He didn't crave it. But it always accompanied his meal, and the bottle—or bottles—steadily went empty.

The waitress, he knew her name—Mireille—filled his glass. Her head bent, he studied her face. It reflected her age. She was perhaps ten years younger than he, slim in the waist and full just above, in a white blouse and black skirt, both impeccably laundered and pressed. Her hair was dark, just shy of black, and her eyes—her eyes, of course, large, dark and exotic, the skin at the edges slightly crinkled, were remarkable. He tried not to stare, but felt the force of her beauty when he did.

To distract himself from the trance he felt coming on—triggered by the wine and the glow of Mireille's gaze—he spoke.

"Hanratty called today."

"Ah," said Mireille, "your, eh, *editeur*."

"No, actually, Hanratty's my agent. The publisher bitches to the editor, the editor bitches to Hanratty, Hanratty bitches to me."

"Bitches," repeated Mireille, smiling. She spoke English well enough to pacify tourists and to empathize with Cavendish. When she heard an interesting word, she would store it in her memory by repeating it.

"Complains," said Cavendish.

"*Oui*, I understand."

"Indeed you do," said Cavendish, dolefully, sipping his Côtes du Rhône.

"*L'editeur*. He wants a new book?"

Cavendish sighed. "I told him I was working on an outline."

"*C'est vrai?*" asked Mireille.

Cavendish shook his head. "I haven't written a whole sentence in a goddamn month," he said. "You know, Mireille, I used to think writer's block was a bourgeois affectation, something that a prima donna author would use to explain why he wasn't getting up, brewing coffee, going to his keyboard and doing his job, every day. Writing, that's my job. I've always done it. But now … Jesus, it's like my mind just drained. I don't know … "

Mireille almost reached out to Cavendish's hand, then pulled back. "Maybe if you went back … "

"What? To Indiana? New York? For some sort of epiphany?"

"Don't you have—"

"What? Family? I have an ex-wife in California. No kids. All the friends I used to have … "

He trailed off and risked looking into Mireille's eyes. "Right now, *chérie*," he said, "you're pretty much all I've got when it comes to friends. And who knows? If I didn't tip you every night … "

The hurt look in Mireille's eyes sent a tremor through Cavendish.

"Shit," he said. "I'm sorry. I didn't mean … "

Mireille, with a little puff of air and a smile, shed the insult. "Please, tell me about the book, *L'Amour et La Mort* …"

Cavendish swallowed a little more wine. He shook his head. "No, that one's behind me. When I've finished a book, a story, whatever, I don't look back. The next story is the most important one I'll ever write, until it's done. And then … "

"Le prochain," said Mireille.

Cavendish nodded and spent a moment swimming in Mireille's eyes.

"What about you?" said Cavendish.

"Me?" Mireille pulled back.

Cavendish mustered the rare smile. "Yeah, what's your story, Mireille?"

"There's no story," she insisted, flatly.

"No story?" Cavendish scowled piercingly. "C'mon. You're no ingenue, Mireille. You're a grown, beautiful woman in the most exciting city in the world. You're cool. You're smart. You've seen so much. I'm sure you've done so much. How do you end up here, waiting on tables in St.-Germain-des-Prés? What came before? Were you a diva? A fashion model? A kickass lady lawyer, maybe, who got sick of defending scumbags and mobsters?"

Mireille laughed. "Scumbags," she repeated. "No, no, Cavendish. No scumbags. There's no story. I am just … *ordinaire*. Normal."

Cavendish eyed her dubiously. "You're lying to me."

Mireille's only response was a tilt of her head.

As much as he tried, he squeezed nothing from Mireille about her history. She got him to talk, though, about a dead brother, about his estranged mother and absent father, about his newspaper days in Illinois, until he could only speak in mumbles and dozed on the tabletop. Around midnight, she helped the driver pour Cavendish into a taxi and gave him an address in the Fifth Arrondissement.

Mireille stood on the cobblestones, hands on hips, watching the cab's taillights and thinking about this thoughtful, forlorn, complicated American. Suddenly, she turned, peering in the other direction, shielding her eyes from the lights. She studied the shadows and watched for movement around the distant corner. But the street was empty.

He wasn't there.

SEPTEMBER

CHAPTER 4

La Quin Cave

Rue Bréa, which connects the Jardin du Luxembourg to the historic sprawl of Montparnasse, was one of Steve and Mie's favorite strolls.

This balmy September evening was only their second night back in Paris after two weeks covering an OECD conference in Berlin and a technology fair in Munich. They were both feeling the fug that comes with long days, short nights and too many Germans. They had forced themselves out of their suite in a funky and economical residential hotel two blocks from the Seine on rue du Bac. Rather than warming soup and eating old cheese at "home," they took the long walk through the Sixth and Fifth Arrondissements to one of their culinary havens, Le Bistrot du Dôme, where the fish was flawless and the service always *très génial*. The bistro also served a *millefeuilles* for dessert that they always ordered, even on a full tummy.

Steve Knight was chief international correspondent for *US Journal*, a weekly magazine that had survived the decline of print news by vastly expanding its digital footprint and conforming to the breathless 24-hour news cycle demanded by internet browsers. That day, closing his coverage of the

Munich event, Steve had dialed, called, emailed and filed copy until just before seven p.m. Mie had labored by his side, speaking into her phone much better French than he could ever achieve. She had arranged interviews the next day at a new technology center housed inside a defunct train depot in east Paris and made sure that Steve would be talking to designers and engineers who spoke English.

Steve had also put in a call to his daughter, Ella, in Massachusetts, who was fifteen and emphatically above average. His divorce had been final for months and there was no reason that he should not marry Mie, who was more than willing. Steve, however, still felt spooked by the rupture with his ex-wife, Eileen, who had wearied of Steve's nomadism and switched her loyalties to a North Shore equestrian named Nickson Talbot.

"He's nice," Ella had told Steve, "but he ain't you, daddy-ou."

By the time they had hiked up blvd. St.-Michel and through the Luxembourg, Steve and Mie were fully revived. They had finished their shop-talk session before turning off the blvd. St.-Germain. Reaching rue Bréa, they were beginning to regain the feel of Paris' back streets as the city came alive for the night's feasting and drinking. Two blocks from their objective, Steve and Mie passed a familiar wine bar called Le Quin Cave. The bar had been founded by a large, florid and gregarious native of Languedoc named Frederick, who had since absented the premises, possibly to cope with an onset of cancer. However, even without Frederick, Le Quin Cave tippled on merrily. It was a spottily lit cavern with walls of wine surrounding tall tables where drinkers shared space, sat close, whispered and guffawed as they swirled glasses of Beziers, St.-Chinian and other husky rural vintages. Often when Steve and Mie dined at Le Bistrot du Dôme, they found that Le Quin Cave had stayed open past its posted closing time, which afforded them an opportunity for a mellow nightcap of Borie de la Vitarelle.

"Hey, what do you know?" said Steve, almost toppling over as his foot slipped off the curb.

Mie saved Steve from falling and said, "What?"

Steve drew Mie away from Le Quin Cave, making distance from the outdoor tables, where couples leaned over their glasses and held hands.

Steve straightened up and turned three quarters away from the facade of the wine bar and its narrow makeshift *terrasse*. Making certain not to look that way, he jerked his head toward one of the tables.

"It's them," he said.

"Who?"

Steve grabbed Mie by the shoulders and prevented her from looking toward "them."

"Don't look," said Steve. "They might remember us."

Mie planted hands on hips. She scowled. "Who might remember us?"

Steve lowered his voice enough that the ambient urban hum made him almost inaudible. "You remember the sad guy at—"

"What? Speak up, Steve."

Steve led Mie to the opposite curb. "Okay, take a look. But be subtle."

Mie sighed, turned and scanned the tables in front of the wine bar. After a moment: "Oh, it's her. The waitress from the Petit St.-Benoit, the knockout with the x-ray eyes."

"Not just her," added Steve. "She's with the sad guy, the one who was sitting alone all night. And then, y'remember, we saw them together, at his table, afterwards."

"Ah, yes. That's right. But the guy—Pierre—he's supposed to be dead by now."

"Dead?"

"From radiation poisoning."

Steve crinkled his forehead. "Radiation poisoning?"

"France's foremost nuclear physicist?"

It dawned. "Oh, right," said Steve. "Yeah, well, I guess that wasn't my best guess."

Surreptitiously, Steve and Mie watched the couple at the table for a moment. They weren't holding hands, nor did they seem intimate. The woman, wearing a simple print dress in soft blues and purples with a loose skirt and a cinched waist, seemed to be talking business. The man—whose outfit hadn't changed at all in the intervening months—was nodding earnestly.

"Something going on there," said Steve.

"Uh huh," said Mie. "But it's not love."

Steve cocked his head. "Really?"

"Not yet."

"Maybe later, when he discovers who she really is, and what she did that night during Carnaval in Rio de Janeiro, with the one-eyed swordsman and the kangaroo."

"Let's not get into that," said Mie, shoving Steve toward blvd. Montparnasse. "Come on. Let's go eat."

Les Deux

Les Deux Mag
9/16/06

CHAPTER 5
Les Deux Magots

Mireille and Cavendish, leaning toward each other over the tall sidewalk table at Le Quin Cave, paid no heed to passersby or the other patrons at the rue Bréa wine bar. They spoke quietly, with an urgency that unnerved Cavendish. He could barely taste the wine.

They had chosen this place for its distance from Mireille's workplace in St.-Germain-des-Prés. They were careful because of what had happened during their last rendezvous.

Beyond sympathy, Mireille had no feelings for this troubled American. She had agreed to see him this night for the same reason they had met weeks before, at Les Deux Magots, the famous café on the blvd. St.-Germain. After that fiasco, Cavendish had begged Mireille again and again for another rendezvous. She had fended off his every plea. However, as time passed and Cavendish's entreaties grew more desperate, Mireille feared what he might do to himself if she did not relent.

Finally, she proposed a Thursday evening—this evening—at Le Quin Cave.

Cavendish had arrived early. She came fifteen minutes late, long enough for Cavendish to think she might have stood him up, which would have served him right. He merited nothing from Mireille but decent service and the pleasure of watching her glide among the tables at Le Petit St.-Benoit.

But here she was, late and lovely. He had poured her wine and ordered an *assiette* of cheeses. Cavendish had begun the conversation by looking around nervously.

"Your ... guy," he asked. "Where is he tonight?"

Mireille lifted a shoulder and sighed. "It's Thursday. His night to play *belote,* lose his money and drink Calvados with his mates in the Nineteenth. I won't see him 'til after dawn."

Cavendish's relief was visible.

"He's not violent. Not really," said Mireille, unconvincingly. "It's just his temper. And he loves me so much."

"I don't think that's love," said Cavendish. "To him, you're property."

Mireille opened her lips to answer, but held back.

Cavendish paused to drink. A young waiter, cheery and brisk, delivered the cheese plate and set down a basket of bread.

"I'm sorry about ... what happened, at the Deux Magots," said Cavendish. "I shouldn't have asked you there, so close to—"

"Don't," said Mireille. "You've apologized how much? So many times. I came. I came there. I sat with you. It was my choice."

"How did he know we were there?"

"He didn't know," said Mireille. "But he watches. If I'm not where he expects, he—what's the word?—he prowls."

It had happened on a weeknight in late August. The traffic at Le Petit St.-Benoit had been light. As usual, the tourists had started dinner early, ate fast, drank little wine and dispersed by ten o'clock. At eleven, Mireille hung up her apron and left the last few customers to the ministrations of Patricia, the other waitress.

Cavendish had remained resolutely sober that evening.

He invited Mireille for a nightcap and proposed Les Deux Magots, a fashionable venue she could rarely afford. Too tired to make excuses and aware of Cavendish's need for a caring listener, she acquiesced.

Cavendish had claimed a table on the *terrasse*, facing rue Bonaparte and the steeple of St.-Germain-des-Prés. Mireille's arrival, and his role as her host, lifted Cavendish from his gloom. He chivvied the waiter in a preposterous mixture of English and fractured French until the waiter—typically stiff and brisk in the Deux Magots tradition—cracked a smile. In return, Cavendish splurged on a bottle of champagne.

Mireille took advantage of Cavendish's sunny mood to ask about his novel. What was the story about? Was it going to be translated into French? How does one go about getting a book published?

"First," said Cavendish, lifting his champagne flute, "you must sell your soul."

A moment later, the waiter was refilling their glasses. Appearing suddenly, a man, lean and electric, in black jeans, black t-shirt and a mane of black hair, seized the waiter's arm. He tossed the waiter aside, sending the bottle skittering across the pavement in a hiss of flying foam.

The intruder pounded on the table, toppling both glasses, and shouted—in words too swift, compacted and foreign for Cavendish to understand even one—into Mireille's face. She backed away in alarm and then staggered up from her seat. Her chair clattered to the ground.

"Hey," said Cavendish, prompting the man to twist toward him. He pressed a fist against Cavendish's nose.

"You, fokkah! You stay out!"

Cavendish caught the guy's drift. He backed away from the fist, but got to his feet, ready to …

Cavendish didn't know what he was ready for, and he was taut with sudden fear. As he rose to his feet, he didn't dare take his eyes off the intruder. He sensed that the entire clientele of Les Deux Magots and lots of people on the street were staring at an unexpectedly entertaining threesome in a locale typically genteel, orderly and dull.

Mireille got the madman's attention by calling him a fool and a savage. In doing so, she spat out his name.

Meaning to mollify, Cavendish, in tones as gentle as he could manage, said, "Serge?"

Without looking or hesitating, Serge turned on Cavendish and swung for his head. Cavendish ducked the blow, throwing Serge off-balance. Serge sprawled across the café table, skidded into another table, regained his feet and growled at the startled occupants. They had been eating. Most of their food had migrated into their laps.

Waiters were beginning to shout. Serge stood erect and faced Mireille, tossing aside table and chairs. He called her several foul names, one of which, *"salope,"* Cavendish recognized. In another few seconds, a pair of waiters were striving to seize Serge. He fended off both. They were reinforced by a third, who led the second assault. This skirmish was in progress when the distinctive klaxon of a police van, joined swiftly by a chorus of several more cop vehicles, split the summer night.

The siren's wail galvanized Serge, who shrugged off the full complement of Deux Magots employees. He directed another evidently profane threat at Mireille and disappeared, in the direction of rue de Rennes, on thin, springy legs that called— to Cavendish's mind—a praying mantis.

"Who the fu—" Cavendish began. "Who the hell was that?"

He did not get an answer that night. The police arrived in a swarm and, in the absence of the actual perpetrator, hauled Mireille and Cavendish into custody. They were questioned for hours and released, uncharged and rumpled, just as the pink haze of dawn was tinting the limestone walls of the Prefecture of Police.

In subsequent evenings, Cavendish haunted Le Petit St.-Benoit, pressing Mireille relentlessly to explain her association with this crazy vandal with the Rasputin eyebrows. But she revealed almost nothing.

"We've known each other," was all she said, "since we were … young."

"How young?" Cavendish kept asking.

"Young," said Mireille, tersely and repeatedly.

Leaning toward Mireille and surveying rue Bréa, Cavendish said, "Now then, there is no Serge in sight. He's far away. We're here. You agreed to talk. Tell me now, please. Who is this man and what is he to you?"

"We've known each other—"

"I know," Cavendish broke in, his voice rising. "Since you were young."

"Oui," said Mireille, denying eye contact.

"I'll ask again," said Cavendish. He lifted Mireille's chin. "How young? When did you meet each other? How long has this been going on?"

Mireille seemed ready to speak when Cavendish continued, "And *what* is going on?"

"We were in school together. *College,*" said Mireille barely audible. "What would be, in America, high school."

"I understand," said Cavendish.

"He … " She hunted for a word. " … pursued me. He was very handsome."

"He still is," said Cavendish.

A tiny smile from Mireille. "He was very exciting."

"I can tell."

"He swooped—no—"

"He swept you off your feet."

A bigger smile. "Ah! *Oui.*"

"Literally?"

Mireille blushed for the first time Cavendish had ever seen this happen. He fell mute as a thought stirred in the back of his mind.

They paused to sip their wine.

Prompted gently by Cavendish, Mireille described a relationship that had waxed and waned, stormed and ebbed for twenty years.

"You're not married to Serge?"

Mireille's eyes widened. "Oh, *mon Dieu!* No, Cavendish! I couldn't imagine!"

"But you love this maniac."

Mireille sank in her seat. "Ah, *oui.* I do."

"Madly?"

"Madly, yes. That's right. Madly. I am mad."

"Yeah, well, talk about mad. You can't hold a candle to that guy. He's fuckin' nuts."

Mireille didn't argue the point. "Fuckin' nuts," she said to herself, absorbing the words.

She drank more wine and explained that, after school, she had gone to work and Serge had gone to sea, training as a merchant sailor. After three months, drummed out of his abortive career after picking fights almost daily with his fellow trainees, Serge showed up at Mireille's one-room flat off the avenue de St.-Ouen. He moved in. They were a couple for almost a year, supported by Mireille's job in a café near Port St.-Denis, until Serge went to jail for the first time.

"He was flirting with a whore. The pimp came along. Serge started banging the pimp's head against a building. The whore tried to stop him. Serge knocked out three of her teeth. The *flics* arrived before Serge could kill the pimp."

"Interesting," said Cavendish. "It didn't bother you that Serge was ... consorting with hookers?"

"Oh yes. I told him we were finished, not to come back," said Mireille.

"But he did."

"Yes, *oui,*" said Mireille. "After, oh, a year?"

"And you let him stay."

Mireille nodded a little sheepishly. "He had a job then.

Lifting things, onto trucks. Off trucks. He's very strong."

"This was evident," said Cavendish.

"Evident," said Mireille, softly.

As Mireille explained, not all the lifting Serge did, on and off trucks, was entirely on the up and up. His first release from jail began a cycle during which he regularly vanished from Mireille's life, then barged back in. Occasionally, he moved on to other girls who had struck his fancy or had more money than Mireille. But the motive that always brought him back to Mireille was his discovery that she had met another man.

"Suddenly, he was there," said Mireille. "Full of rage. Rage you can't imagine. *Une rage terrible.* He was ready to kill. He was going to kill. He swore and he broke things and he reached out to kill. But I was in his way. I said, 'Kill me. Leave him alone.' Serge would not kill me. He could not, because he was in love. Mad with love. And so, I said to the other man, my friend, 'Quickly, go. Goodbye.'"

Mireille relaxed, seemingly finished with her story.

"And then?" Cavendish pressed.

"Serge would ... " Mireille's voice went small. "He would ... punish me, a little."

"He beat you?"

Mireille flinched at the word.

"He beat you?"

"A little, *oui,*" she said. "But then we made love. It was wonderful."

Cavendish sneered. "Yeah, it's nice to fuck after a beating."

"Oh no," said Mireille, shaking her head emphatically. "It wasn't like that. You don't understand."

Another sneer. "Yeah, sure. It's a French thing, right?"

Mireille was puzzled. "French? No," she said. "It's how we love each other."

Cavendish slumped and reached for his glass. "That's not love. It's you, good Mireille, who don't understand."

Mireille, silent, gazing stubbornly into Cavendish's eyes,

shook her head. Uneasily, he noticed himself wishing that she might look at him, just once, the way she looked at her crazy Serge.

Bistrot du Dome

CHAPTER 6

Le Bistrot du Dôme

Jean-Luc, Mie's favorite waiter at Le Bistrot du Dôme, was a heavy perspirer. He was also nimble, efficient, quietly genial and possessed of a faultless memory of the bistro's regular patrons. When he saw Mie in the doorway, he hustled over to her, beaming with welcome. He kissed both of Mie's cheeks and greeted Steve with a handshake firmer than the French norm. Jean-Luc led them to a favorite table in the corner near the window and then melted away, returning first with two glasses of kir and a saucer of olives. He set up a blackboard scrawled with the evening's menu.

"I love this place," said Mie, hinting slightly more affection for the sweaty waiter than for the establishment.

They took a breath, sipped their kir and looked around. Inked in blue on walls of ceramic tile, *les fruits de mer*—cod, octopus, sole, lobsters, rays, bass, herring, barracudas, marlin and dozens of other fish—some larger than life, surrounded them. As they indulged in their aperitif, they studied the blackboard.

To start, they would share the bistro's *encornets*—small squid speared on sticks and sautéed luxuriantly in butter— and a plate of sardines, simply broiled. Mie would eschew the sardine heads, Steve would eat them. When Jean-Luc returned, they ordered their main dish, *St.-Pierre* (John Dory) for Steve and a lightly spiced slab of *lotte* (monkfish) for Mie. The Bistrot du Dôme has a short wine list, each bottle priced the same. Steve chose a Quincy, pale and piquant.

Settled beneath a light fixture designed strangely to resemble a bunch of luminescent grapes, they returned to their consideration of the familiar couple—the sad guy and the waitress—whom they had spotted at Le Quin Cave.

"Y'know what I think? She's a princess," said Steve, "in exile."

Mie's eyebrows went up. "A princess? From where?"

"Er." Steve paused in thought. "Ah. Transylvania."

"Oh no," said Mie. "This is not going to be one of your Igor the Undertaker yarns."

"I thought you liked Igor."

"Once. Not every time."

Steve shrugged. "Well then, San Marino."

"San Marino? That's a place?"

"Oh yeah. I remember it from my stamp collection."

"Hm," said Mie. She tippled her kir.

Steve squinted, concentrating on his story.

"Okay, she's an orphan princess," he said, nodding and pointing a finger upward, "her parents and grandmother were murdered by marauding brigands who climbed the mountain and pillaged their castle. The bastards would've killed her, too—after the rape, of course, but she had a loyal servant named, um … Olga, who hid the princess—"

"What's her name?"

"I just said. Olga."

"No! The princess."

"Um … Jeez, I don' know," said Steve. "How about … " He knitted his brow. "Okay, Anastasia?"

"Don't be ridiculous."

"Well, just Anna then?"

"Anna's good," said Mie. "So, where did Olga hide the

princess Anna from the marauders?"

"In the stable, behind a donkey. Along with her little brother."

"There's a little brother?"

"Why not?"

"Name?"

"You're obsessed with names."

"A story can't have characters who prefer to speak under the condition of anonymity, Steve. It needs names. What's the kid's name?"

"How about, hm, I don' know ... Luigi?"

"So, she has an Italian brother?"

"Yeah. They're Italian. San Marino is surrounded by Italy."

"Really?"

"Yes."

"So, the brigands were Italians."

"No."

"What were they?"

"Does it matter?"

"Yes."

"Okay, they were Slavs."

"What sort of Slavs?"

"No sort. They were generic Slavs. They came and pillaged, they took over the castle. Anna and Luigi had to escape."

"Okay," said Mie, "go on."

"Olga spirited the two children out of San Marino and they wandered around southern Europe for a year. But they ran into trouble at the Bulgarian border."

"They made it all the way to Bulgaria?"

"Yeah, almost. But they were stopped."

"Stopped? Why?"

"Olga had no money to bribe the Bulgarian border guards. The guards took the children and sent Olga away."

"Away? Where'd she go?

"Actually, she didn't go anywhere. She was the only mother

figure the kids had. So, she hid in the woods, waiting for her chance to rescue Anna and Lorenzo."

"Luigi!"

Jean-Luc, the waiter, interrupted Anna's saga by bringing to the table *encornets*, sardines and wine. Steve and Mie tucked in. Steve tried to continue the story, but Mie interrupted with a non sequitur.

"You know, Steve," she said, in the accentless English she had learned after being sent from Tokyo, by her mother, to attend high school in Michigan, "your ex-wife is already remarried."

Steve had to finish gnawing a sardine head before he could look up in puzzlement and ask, "Whud—(crunch, crunch)—What does Eileen's marriage have to do with the plight of the princess Anna and—"

"Not a damn thing," said Mie, neatly slicing a morsel of squid. "It just occurred to me that Eileen seems to be moving faster in the relationship sphere than you ... and me."

"Relationship sphere?"

"Yes," said Mie. "Eileen is forging boldly ahead. We're spinning our wheels."

"Now, just a second!" said Steve, laying down his utensils. "Let's bear in mind that Eileen had a head start. She was canoodling this Nickson guy before—"

"Canoodling?" asked Mie.

"Screwing, okay?"

"I know what canoodling is, Steve."

"All I'm saying is ... " He paused.

"What are you saying?"

Steve sighed, thinking back. His first close encounter with Mie was in the Tokyo offices of *US Journal*. This untimely introduction occurred on the same day that Kuniko, Steve's assistant and Mie's mother, died in a terrorist explosion—in Steve's company—at Shibuya Crossing. Mie had charged into his office and raged at Steve for publishing a ghastly photo of Kuniko lying dead in the Tokyo street. Their second meeting, days later, took place at Takada no Yu, a hot-spring retreat in the Japanese mountains. Steve had fled there to escape the trauma and recriminations of Kuniko's death.

He remembered, almost photographically, the sight of Mie, nude and almost luminous, slipping into the steamy water of a warm hillside pool, beside a lazy waterfall, in a wee hour past midnight. Once submerged, Mie apologized for misunderstanding Steve's role in the photogravure of her mother's torn body. Gradually, she convinced Steve to return to his job and chronicle Tokyo's mysterious outbreak of political terror. When they left the hillside basin and retired to separate *futons* in the mountain inn, Steve was bewildered by Mie, and not just because she was beautiful from head to toe.

His bewilderment had never quite gone away.

And here it came again.

Mie was smiling, waiting for Steve's onset of memory to pass.

He said, "Look, I know guys who get divorced. And they feel guilty, even if it's not their fault. They feel disconnected. They need … "

"A woman," said Mie. "Any woman."

Steve smiled. "Yeah. And they rush into a whole new marriage—"

Mie cut him off. "I'm not any woman."

Steve nodded. He relaxed.

"And Ella," said Mie, referring to Steve's fourteen-year-old daughter, "likes me."

"She loves you," Steve insisted.

Mie smiled.

"As do I," said Steve.

Mie daintily lifted a forkful of sardine to her ostensibly perfect mouth and cocked her head.

"Okay," said Steve. "Soon, you and me're gonna stop living

in planes, trains and residential hotels. I'm thinking about a nice condo maybe overlooking the Seine, or the Charles, or Lake Michigan. And then ... "

"How soon?" Mie asked.

"Um, well ... " Steve thought hard. "Pretty soon?"

Mie narrowed her eyes.

Steve tried again. "Okay, this gig in Europe'll be up in, I guess, a year, two years at the most. Then, I could finally take that editor's job Warren keeps offering me. In Boston."

"And then?"

"We can," said Steve, "you know ... "

Mie nodded, mopping her plate with a sliver of bread. "No, I don't know. But I'll table the matter, for now," she said.

"Can I go on now?"

Mie nodded.

"Shit," said Steve. "Where was I?"

"Anna's at the Bulgarian border. Olga's in the woods."

"Right, yes! So," Steve said, "Princess Anna and the kid brother are imprisoned by the brutish Bulgarian border guards."

"Wait," said Mie. "How old are they?"

"The border guards?"

"No, Anna and Luigi."

"Right. About eight. Yeah, Anna's about eight, Luigi maybe, like, four."

"A veritable tyke."

"Right. And the Bulgarians are hatching these diabolical plans for both the kids. Anna would be sold into bondage to a wealthy pedophile. Little Luigi would be auctioned to rich couples with barren wombs and low sperm counts."

Steve was rolling.

"But before the guards' evil scheme could come to fruition, Anna—who's a feisty little princess—works her way out of her bonds, grabs a lead pipe and whacks one of the guards. Tragically, she can't set her baby brother free, because he's locked in a cage and the other guard—he's outside—he has the key. It breaks her heart to leave little Luca—"

"Luigi."

"Right." Steve pressed on. "Anna promises Luigi she'll be back. She sneaks away, into the woods, where she finds Olga, who's sharpening a branch with her Swiss Army knife. They embrace and cry. And then they start hatching a plot to get Luigi away from the Bulgarians. In the silence of the forest, they can hear his plaintive sobs.

"They come up with a plan. Anna's gonna create a diversion while Olga coldcocks the other guard. It's a good plan. But then, just as Olga is about to burst into the open and whack the guard, a truck appears. It stops by the guard shack. From inside the truck, there emerges a mystery woman. She's young and darkly beautiful but she has snow-white hair. She's dressed in flowing robes and carrying a Kalashnikov."

"Does she have a mole on her nose?"

Steve paused. "If you want a mole, fine."

"I do."

"The mystery woman with the mole is accompanied by a nomadic band of vagabonds in a convoy of trucks and caravans. Suddenly, the vehicles empty out. The guard shack is surrounded by slutty-looking women, filthy urchins, mangy dogs, goats, parrots and huge men with scars and bandoliers of bullets."

"Parrots?" said Mie.

Steve ignored the question. "The vagabonds discover that one guard is just regaining consciousness and that Anna has escaped. They're angry at the Bulgarians for losing the princess. They—"

"Wait," said Mie. "How do they know there's a princess?"

Steve smiled. "Aha, good question, my little chickadee. Do

you remember the Slavs?"

"Of course I do," replied Mie. "They killed Anna's mom and dad."

"And grandmother."

"Right," said Mie.

"Well," said Steve. "It didn't take long for the whole criminal underworld to find out that princess Anna had slipped through the Slavs' fingers. In the international white slavery market, an escaped princess is the Big Kahuna. Every crook and pervert in Europe was looking for the girl. And little prince Luigi? Well, he was the cherry on top of the hot-slave sundae."

Mie winced at the metaphor.

"Anyway, back at the border," Steve went on, "there's a lot of shouting. The vagabonds are pissed off because the guards lost princess Anna. Olga and Anna watch helplessly from hiding as the mole-nosed mystery woman orders Luigi, still in his cage and weeping pathetically, to be loaded onto the truck. Money is exchanged. The guards shout angrily because the money is less than they expected. The mystery woman lifts her Kalashnikov and casually shoots off one of the Bulgarian's ears. The Bulgarians run into their shack and hide. They're nursing their wounds as the convoy of vagabonds pulls away. Anna dashes toward the road but Olga grabs her and holds her back, crying, 'No, no! You can't let them see you, my sweet. They'll take you, too.' They would sell you to diseased old men who will have their way with you, over and over again. And then they'll leave you pregnant in a ditch to die among toads and cockroaches.'"

"Steve, my God. Toads and roaches?" said Mie. "We're eating here."

"Right, yeah, sorry."

The sweaty waiter brought fish, interrupting the saga of the lost Luigi.

CHAPTER 7

Le Quartier Vavin

By eleven, all the patrons of Le Quin Cave had trickled away, prompting Andréa, the handsome proprietress, to pull down the shutter and shoo the last lingerers. Mireille and Cavendish retreated down rue Bréa and found a table outdoors at the Le Quartier Vavin, a postprandial sidewalk resort for Parisians determined to prolong their evening. Slightly woozy with wine, Mireille ordered a Perrier. Cavendish, possessed of a hollow leg, had cognac.

Cavendish had an odd light in his eye. From a pocket of his jacket, he pulled a bent and dog-eared reporter's notebook. He shuffled through two dozen illegibly scribbled pages until he found a blank sheet. He produced a Bic pen, popped the cap with his teeth and stared hard into Mireille's gypsy eyes.

"Tell me more about Serge," he insisted.

Mireille turned her head to look sideways at Cavendish. "No," she said.

Cavendish stirred dramatically. "Oh no. You have to!"

Mireille smiled coyly. "I have to do nothing, *m'sieur*. For you or anyone."

She tasted her Perrier.

Cavendish rolled his eyes and backed off. "No, I don't mean," he said. He stopped and thought. Mireille waited.

Cavendish's conundrum was that Mireille, in almost every aspect, was "definite" in her behavior, self-assured and assertive. But her relationship with Serge was timid. The word "submissive" came to mind, but he didn't want to think of Mireille that way. She was too complicated for psychosexual labels.

He resorted to persuasion.

"Please. This is important. Mireille, I have an idea. For a story, " said Cavendish. "Jesus, you have no idea! In months—months!—my first idea."

Mireille's mind leapt to the evident conclusion. "Cavendish," she said, "you are *not* going to write about *me*. Not about Serge! That would be—"

Cavendish dropped pen and notebook, waving his hands and nearly upsetting his cognac.

"No, no. You don't understand. I'm not a newspaperman. And I don't do biography. Oh, Christ no!" he said. "I tell stories. Every story ... the way it comes to me. It's a tickling in the back of my mind."

Mireille cocked her head.

Cavendish said, "Something you said about Serge set something ... whirring, in my memory. There's a word I can't quite see. It's there, in my head, but ... You see, there's something about you, about the way you are with Serge that put this idea in my mind. This word."

"Lequel mot?" said Mireille.

"I don't know," said Cavendish. He gulped his cognac, noticed that his glass was empty and looked around for a waiter.

"It's there," he said to Mireille after ordering more brandy. "It's like a sneeze that won't quite sneeze."

Mireille smiled.

"You see, this idea that's tickling my ... noggin. It's not about you," Cavendish assured her. "Or Serge. But it's inspired—by you. By the passion and ... and danger of how you love each other."

"Danger? No," Mireille insisted, shaking her head. "Serge is not dangerous."

"Maybe not. I've only seen him that one time," said Cavendish. "But the idea, my idea, the word—if it comes to me—if I sneeze! The idea is dangerous."

Mireille smiled, exuding skepticism.

Cavendish shook his head. "I'm not making sense."

He took a sip and started over.

"The book I wrote," said Cavendish, "it wasn't dangerous. There aren't any dangerous ideas. But there are characters in the story, characters fraught with danger, posing danger to other—innocent—characters. You see, danger sharpens the story. It hunts the characters and haunts the reader."

Mireille nodded. "And this word you can't remember, Cavendish. It's a dangerous word?"

"I think so, yes. If I knew what it was, goddammit."

"Goddammit," Mireille whispered to herself.

The cognac arrived. Cavendish inhaled its fumes and wracked his brain.

Mireille noticed, passing by, strolling toward the Luxembourg Garden, a couple who looked faintly familiar, a lean American with an amiable face. His partner was a striking Asian woman. She had seen them before. At the restaurant? Both looked at Mireille, caught her eye and then quickly averted their eyes. As they hurried away, they talked animatedly, as though something unspoken had passed between them and Mireille.

"Je me demande ... " she said under her breath.

Suddenly, Cavendish shuddered and grabbed both of Mireille's hands. His cognac glass rolled off the table and smashed on the ground.

His eyes were wide. "Comanche!" he said, too loudly.

"Comanche?" Mireille asked, mystified.

Cavendish relaxed, let go of Mireille. He looked around at neighboring tables, occupied by people, staring. He had broken a glass and shouted a word that made sense to none of them, including Mireille.

"Comanche," he repeated, in a normal tone. "That's it ... Wait ... I think."

He tested the word again. Mireille listened, silently.

"Does that mean anything to you?" asked Cavendish. "Comanche. Does it ring a bell?"

"Ring a bell?"

"Wait! What would it be in French? Here!"

He wrote the word in his notebook and showed it to Mireille. She studied it, showing no light of recognition. She said it in French, softening the "a," rendering the "ch" into "sh" and silencing the "e."

Then she said, "It means nothing."

"It should," insisted Cavendish.

He paused to think. "Shit," he said after a moment. "Maybe that's not it."

"This *comanche*," asked Mireille. "It's the wrong word?"

"Maybe."

Steve paused and pondered for a beat.

"Maybe not."

A waiter appeared, stoically cleaning up the broken glass and bestowing a fresh cognac. After a while, alcohol quieted Cavendish's ruminations. Mireille and Cavendish turned to other subjects, she explaining why she had never married, he examining why he had and how he had failed.

Later, they parted at the Vavin Métro stop, Mireille hurrying to catch the last train. As Cavendish walked toward his murky garret in the Fifth, he kept turning the word over on his tongue, in both pronunciations.

"Comanche ... *comanche* ... "

OCTOBER

Café de Flore

172 Blvd St Germain

La Closerie
des Lilas

May 29 2008

CHAPTER 8

La Closerie des Lilas

Steve and Mie were waging a familiar battle against journalistic insomnia by staying up as late as possible. It was October, possibly the best month for strolling, deep into the night, the glowing streets of the Left Bank.

They had arrived on a sleepless overnight train from Barcelona, returning to their sterile but comfortable *pension*. They had unpacked, connecting their laptops and mobile phones to Wi-Fi—a travel ritual that Steve still found vaguely irritating. He was irrationally nostalgic for a time when communicating in Paris required ungainly color-coded telephones with dials and cords, for phone booths that devoured ten-centime coins and chewed up plastic phone cards, beeping suddenly and aborting conversations in midsentence. He missed Minitel.

They had reported their arrival to the *US Journal* office near the Opéra. Then they worked through the morning, typing notes, filing copy and making the evening's restaurant reservation. Near noon, they popped out onto rue du Bac and strolled as slowly as possible into the Sixth Arrondissement, along rue St.-André-des-Arts. They moved slowly because, in Paris, noon is too early for lunch. They window-shopped, peeking into a gallery or two, reading menus, browsing at the yellow-fronted news shop on rue Grégoire-de-Tours and mourning a nearby corner café that had been closed for months. They knew it was dead, rather than just shuttered for renovations, because its walls and windows were plastered with posters and graffiti, a certain sign of permanent abandonment. Paris has its own breed of urban jackals and spray-paint vultures.

After wine, salad and coffee at Le Hibou, a bustling, overpriced café-brasserie on carrefour de l'Odéon, Steve and Mie wove back to the hotel, by way of rue de Seine and the *quai* along the river. They took a two-hour nap and rose, sluggishly and affectionately, in late afternoon. While Mie showered, Steve succeeded in calling daughter Ella, who confessed to acquiring a boyfriend named Riley who came from the wrong side of a town named Hamilton that was too affluent—in Steve's estimation—to have a wrong side. Steve wished Ella luck with Riley and reminded her that he was an old hand at coping with a broken heart.

They dined at a tiny bistro, La Grivoiserie, where the chef toiled in a kitchen barely larger than a broom closet, creating a toothsome handful of nightly specials while the only waitress had to be thin because the corridor between two rows of elbow-to-elbow tables was barely twenty inches wide. Anyone waiting for a late table received glasses of wine, gratis, and stood outdoors, peering through a breath-fogged window, waiting for someone to pay the check and liberate a table.

"I love this place," said Mie.

Rather than moseying back to the Quartier Latin after coffee at La Grivoiserie, Steve and Mie headed for blvd. Montparnasse. They were tempted to find a spot on the *terrasse* at the Select or the Rotonde—where Gertrude Stein and Robert McAlmon had communed with Man Ray and Tsuguharu Foujita—but they decided to prolong the evening with a longer walk to the Hemingway Bar at La Closerie des Lilas.

Steve and Mie snagged a table near the piano and ordered glasses of port, which cost enough to support for at least a week a Chinese family in the Nineteenth Arrondissement. They had a panoramic view of the saloon—mahogany woodwork and brass fittings, colored sconces dimming the glow from 25-watt bulbs, art deco flourishes and the strapless flapper on the wall flanked by champagne bottles. Mellowed by alcohol and train lag, they shed their troubles and started up again with the mystery couple from Le Petit St.-Benoit, about whom neither had spoken for more than six busy weeks.

"Let's see," said Steve, prodding his memory. "She's a princess, right? From Transylvania, who had been bitten by a vampire named Fang—"

"No, no, no," Mie said, making a fist and striking the table. "She was from San Something."

"Francisco?"

Mie flashed a dirty look. Steve relented.

"Okay, okay. San Marino."

"Yes, the postage-stamp country," said Mie. "I should have remembered."

Steve scowled. "Jeez, it's been a while. I forgot where we left off in the story. The princess ... "

"Anna."

"Right. Anna escaped the clutches of the dastardly Igor the Undertaker."

Mie fisted the table again, causing ripples in the port. "Dammit, Steve. This is not an Igor story!"

Steve smiled. "Of course not, sweetie. Let's see now," Steve said, picking up the thread. "Okay. Anna reaches the Bulgarian border, right? With Olga her governess and her little brother ... um. Luigi?"

"Luca ... no! You're right. It's Luigi."

"The guards capture the two kids and send Olga into the woods. Anna manages to break free and join Olga. Just as they're plotting to rescue Luigi, this mysterious woman comes along with a band of no-goodnik vagabonds. Wait!"

"What?"

"Shouldn't this villainess have a name?"

"Absolutely," said Mie. "It's Nicole."

"Nicole?" said Steve, dubiously. "Nicole is a name for a badass bitch?"

Mie said, "What? You never saw Nicole Kidman in *To Die For*?"

Steve exhaled and nodded. "Oh, yeah. She was ... whoa! Yeah. Okay, Nicole. Good name for a dastardly slut. Where was I?"

"Nicole and the vagabonds carrying little Luigi off to sell him into sexual slavery to an Iranian pederast."

"Iranian? Really?"

"Yes," Mie insisted.

"Okay, fine. So, Anna and Olga chase the caravan, but they but can't catch up."

"Right," said Mie. "What happens next?"

"What if—I'm just spitballing here—Igor the Undertaker turns out to be the Iranian pederast?"

"No."

"Okay, no Igor. So, next, as I recall, Olga dies of consumption."

"I don't remember that part."

"Well, she does. She wastes away in a little mountain cabin in the Swiss Alps where Anna spends the entire next winter. Snowbound. Eating nothing but fried spiders, crocus bulbs and tree bark."

"Ew."

"In the spring, Anna buries Olga, puts a little cross over her grave and works her way down the mountain, following a narrow-gauge train track, which leads her to a railroad crew who gang-rape her and leave her for dead."

"Oh, Steve."

"Hey, life is not a bowl of cherries," said Steve. "Especially for exiled princesses. Before they hit the road, these sorts of castle-bound damsels are sheltered, naive and vulnerable. Sitting ducks."

"Okay, she's raped. Yecch. But she doesn't die."

"She couldn't die. She's our protagonist," said Steve. "Besides, we've seen her alive, here, in Paris, a half-dozen times."

"So, what happened?"

"Well, there she is lying naked and bloody on the tracks, her beautiful breasts heaving and trembling. A train is approaching. The engineer doesn't see her alabaster form lying exposed and inert in the path of the speeding train. She will be squished, her body cut in two. But just then, a kindly old switchman emerges from his little clapboard hut. He sees Anna. Risking his life, he rushes onto the tracks, waving and shouting for the train to stop. It comes within inches of killing both Anna and the switchman—"

"Name?"

"Huh?"

"Kindly switchman."

"Oh, right. Hm. Okay. Rutger."

"Like the college in New Jersey?"

"No, like the German actor who was in *Buffy the Vampire Slayer*."

"Oh, that Rutger! But he's not German, you know. Or Swiss."

Steve pressed on. "Rutger, the switchman—who's Swiss in this story."

"The actor is Dutch."

"Thanks," Steve grumbled. "The *Swiss* switchman takes in Anna, wraps her in bearskins and nurses her back to health."

"Oh, good. No sex?"

"No sex. Rutger is old, and kindly."

"And then?"

"Well, Anna gets better. She has to move on. She says goodbye to the kindly switchman. It's a tragic parting because she knows she'll never see him again. To repay his kindness, she tries to give him her royal signet right, encrusted with emeralds and diamonds. But Rutger, of course, refuses. He reminds her that Luigi has an identical ring. It might be years, he tells Anna, before she finds her brother. He'll be grown up. Maybe the only way to recognize him will be the ring on his finger."

"I guess that's true," said Mie. "But wouldn't greedy old nasty Nicole rip that ring off Luigi's finger the first chance she got?"

"Of course," said Steve. "Anna has already figured this out. But she doesn't want to hurt Rutger's feelings. She thanks him and hugs him, and she begins her quest to find Luigi. Her dangerous pilgrimage takes her through every city of Europe. She accepts any job that's offered. We know her as a waitress, but she's also been a laundress, a maid, a bookkeeper. For a while, she was a traveling magician's assistant, stuffing hats full of bunny rabbits and getting sawed in two twice a night. She was a croupier in a casino on the Côte d'Azur, but she also descended into the underworld of crime, drugs, decadence and prostitution, where she hoped to find—"

"Steve! Anna was a whore?"

"Not exactly, but for the sake of her kid brother, she dared not leave any stone unturned, even if under the stone all she could find was a bunch of horny guys with their pants down. She closed her eyes and clenched her teeth, but we gotta face facts, kid. Princess Anna used her luscious snow-white body—yes—to charm information from the panderers and human traffickers who might have forced little Luigi into blow jobs and buggery."

"Aw jeez, Steve, a little boy?" said Mie. "Where's Liam Neeson when you really need him?"

"I ask myself that question every day."

Steve and Mie paused to sip their port, envisioning the epic clash of Liam Neeson and Nicole Kidman.

"Steve, can Luigi be saved?"

"If Anna did not believe he could be saved, she would have given up her quest. She might well have slipped into the bathtub of a cheap hotel in the back streets of Bucharest or Zagreb, slit her ivory wrists and ended it all. This almost happened, you know?"

"It did?" said Mie.

"Yes, the drinking, the drugs, the demoralizing life of petty crime and loveless coitus. Eventually, our soiled princess, refugee from a looted palace in San Marino, she comes to the end of her rope. Rock bottom."

"Rock bottom?"

"Yes."

"Where?"

"Oslo."

"What happened?"

Steve turned at the sound of tinkling keys and the tune of "I'm Confessin' That I Love You."

"Hey, the piano player's back."

Steve paused to listen. "Love this song."

Mie grabbed Steve by the chin. "Steve, what happened in Oslo."

"Oh, right," said Steve, refocusing. "Bjorn happened."

"Bjorn?"

"Ssh. Let's listen." Stave started to sing softly to the tune. *"In your eyes I see such strange things ... But your lips deny they're true ... "*

Mie rolled her eyes, leaned back and let the music flow.

CHAPTER 9

Le Petit St.-Benoit

Loyalty and curiosity brought Steve and Mie back to the Petit St.-Benoit. It was past eleven in the evening. Only a handful of tables were occupied, most of them indoors. An autumn chill had rendered the *terrasse* habitable for only the hardier patrons. Steve and Mie, who preferred to sit outdoors and watch the Parisian parade gliding by, had dressed for October. Recovered from their journey, they were lingering over the last of their wine, a ripe and mellow Côte de Bordeaux. They were pleased to see that the waitress, whom they now regarded as "Princess Anna," was still on the job.

As the waitress stepped out of the doorway, she suddenly froze, staring past Steve and Mie—with obvious alarm—toward rue Jacob.

A strange choreography ensued.

The waitress' eyes remained fixed on the distance as she backed slowly up the sidewalk.

"What's she looking at?" whispered Mie, who had the best angle for observing the waitress.

"Jeez, I don' know," said Steve. He peered down the block, but the view was obstructed by a *ravalement* scaffold mounted against the nearest building.

"Don't see anything."

The waitress, however, had seen something that frightened her.

She stopped retreating when she reached the sad-sack drinker who spent every night at the far table on the *terrasse*.

Their view blocked by the waitress, Steve and Mie couldn't see the man at the table. Mie could not hear, but she could tell that the waitress had spoken to him.

"So, he's not dead," whispered Mie.

"Who's not dead?"

"The guy at the far table. The nuclear physicist who had radiation sickness. Remember?"

Steve shook his head emphatically. "No, no, no. He's not a physicist!"

"He's not?"

"No, he's—"

"Wait," said Mie. "Oh, this is interesting. The waitress is sort of moving sideways. And the guy's behind her. He's *hiding*."

Steve twisted in his chair to join the audience. "Oh, yeah. I see."

"And there he goes," said Mie. "Into that door."

"That's where the toilet is."

Having concealed the sad guy, the waitress brushed the bodice of her apron, straightened up and ambled back toward Steve and Mie. Her gaze remained fixed on a dark space down the street, beyond the scaffold.

"What's she lookin' at?"

Steve peered that way again, but saw nothing.

The waitress stopped, seemingly oblivious to her customers. She stared. "She's waiting for something," said Steve.

"Some*body*," replied Mie.

Nothing happened.

"Hm," mumbled Steve.

"So, what is he?" asked Mie

"What is who?"

"The guy who's not a nuclear physicist who's supposed to

be dead by now from radiation. The guy we saw talking to the waitress on rue Bréa. The guy. Steve, who just ran into the toilet. What is he, really?"

"Oh," said Steve, "he's a private eye."

"A private—"

"Ssh!" hissed Steve.

They heard footsteps beneath the scaffold.

CHAPTER 10
Le Petit St.-Benoit

As he scurried into the cramped toilet at Le Petit St.-Benoit to hide from Serge, Cavendish felt cowardly and humiliated. But Mireille feared a reprise of the scene that had erupted when Serge discovered her with Cavendish at Les Deux Magots. Cavendish had no choice but to slink into hiding.

He crouched inside for fifteen minutes, almost completely deaf to anything happening outside. He knew Serge had made the scene, because once or twice, he'd heard a snatch of Serge's voice, his words muffled, his rage fortissimo.

When Mireille finally freed Cavendish from the WC, she guided him cautiously onto the *terrasse* and motioned him to escape up the block, toward rue Guillaume Apollonaire. As he parted with Mireille, he caught a glimpse of Serge. Mireille had installed him, with a pacifying glass of Lillet, at an outdoor table facing toward rue Jacob—away from Cavendish's retreat.

"Desolé," whispered Mireille.

"Yeah, me, too," replied Cavendish, a little too loud.

A last glance revealed to Cavendish a couple on the *terrasse*, an American with an Asian woman. They were just rising to leave. Cavendish was almost sure he'd seen them before. The American's eyes flitted from Mireille to Serge to Cavendish almost intrusively. The Asian woman, lissom and alluring, clamped the American's arm and dragged him toward rue Jacob.

Something going on there, Cavendish thought.

Cavendish disobeyed Mireille. Up the block, he found a shadowed doorway and began a stakeout. He watched as Mireille delivered checks to her last two tables and ushered her customers into the Paris night. Serge downed glasses of fortified wine in sudden gulps, waving at Mireille for refills. It was past midnight when at last Mireille and Patricia had cleared the premises of customers and closed up. Serge showed no effects from having drunk an entire bottle of Lillet. As Serge led Mireille past him toward the Métro at St.-Germain-des-Prés, Cavendish hurriedly turned his back, pretending to be pissing against the door.

"Cochon," muttered Serge in passing.

Cavendish agreed. One of the few objections he had to Paris was, in certain corners, the pungency of stale urine rising from the pavement.

After Mireille and Serge passed, he waited a few beats and followed. Hurrying underground, they caught one of the last trains. Cavendish slipped onto the train two cars away. They rode the No. 4 line more than a dozen stops north. Cavendish followed them through the Métro tunnels of Marcadet-Poissoniers, toward the No. 12 line. He lurked again in the shadows, more than five minutes, as Mireille and Serge waited for the last train. He watched as Serge alternately rag-dolled Mireille, berating her loudly and incomprehensibly, but then clutched her to his chest, lifting her clear of the floor and kissing her with a violence that—Cavendish thought—must leave her lips bruised and her gums bleeding.

The train came. One stop later, at Métro Jules Joffrin, the couple got off. Cavendish followed them out of the station and onto the streets of the Eighteenth Arrondissement, a fringe of Paris once known for danger, drugs and darkness, now a melting pot where immigrants, vagrants and yuppies coexist incongruously.

Trailing Mireille and her proprietary consort up the unfamiliar pavement of rue de Poteau, Cavendish was tempted to turn back. By following her, he was betraying Mireille's trust, poking into a part of her life where he wasn't welcome. If she saw him, if she found out somehow that he had literally shadowed her home, she might banish him forever from his table at Le Petit St.-Benoit—and from her life. But Mireille—clinging to Serge as he jerked and jostled her along the deserted street—exerted a pull on Cavendish that he felt powerless to oppose.

Mireille and Serge turned to climb several steps into a long tree-lined promenade between rues Belliard and Leibniz. They entered a gravel path, flanked by two dense rows of rampant, unruly greenery, lit weakly by distant lamps and the dull glow of the city. Hiding behind bushes at the foot of the steps, Cavendish noticed that the nearest streetlights were dark, perhaps broken on purpose.

Mireille and Serge, conversing in husky whispers between puddles left by an evening rain, faced each other.

Cavendish heard a rustling nearby, and then a low, lazy growl that might have been human or the stirring of a werewolf. A breeze flowing through the hedges carried a fetid mixture of ammonia, rancid sweat and mildew. Peering into the dark leaves as his eyes adapted to the gloom, Cavendish saw—and heard faintly—that the hedgerow was alive with bodies on sodden mattresses, sprawled on cardboard and plastic sheets. Farther away, a torn and filthy nylon tent barely topped the leaf line.

Cavendish realized he was not alone as witness to the passage of Mireille and Serge. But no one spoke. No one moved. The hedgerow's denizens seemed barely to breathe.

As Cavendish edged into the shadow of the bushes, Serge hissed into Mireille's face and lifted her, by the waist, her toes barely touching the ground. She resisted, pressing against Serge's chest, until he let go abruptly. Her heels plunged into the rain-softened gravel and she staggered to catch her balance. Serge and Mireille exchanged a burst of words, unfamiliar to Cavendish, that might have been curse, come-on, or both. Suddenly, Serge roared once, unleashing a mindless fury that seemed to ricochet off the buildings on both sides of the promenade.

Lights should have gone on in windows. Cavendish looked for a sign of interest, or alarm. But the buildings remained dark.

Serge slapped Mireille, throwing her head back violently. She caught herself and slapped back, raking Serge's cheek with her nails, snarling a word that Cavendish barely heard. It might have been *"bâtard!"* Serge seized Mireille and swung her in a circle, letting her go as she teetered on one heel. Unable to break her momentum, she fell, sliding on the wet ground and halting, on her bottom, in a filmy puddle.

Mireille slumped and sobbed once, triggering fresh anger from Serge. He seized her by the front of her blouse. Cavendish could hear the fabric tearing as Mireille rose helplessly, held by Serge, her legs dangling until he swung his left hand, slapping her again and letting her go. She crumpled back to the path, raking her palms on the gravel. For a moment, they were a tableau, Mireille on the path, bent over her bruised hands, head lowered, hair hanging down to almost touch a slick of dirty water. A dozen eyes peered from the silent jungle. Serge loomed above Mireille, a stark profile against a far-off lamp's glow, shoulders thrown back, his chest heaving, fists clenched, his chin lowered as he glared at his fallen woman.

Cavendish looked around. Was there someone? Would anyone leap from hiding to help him rescue Mireille? Would he himself dare to do so? If he intervened, what would happen to him, against this brute who was younger, stronger, more ferocious? Would Mireille, who had forged an inexplicable union with Serge, even want to be helped?

As Cavendish temporized, Mireille was suddenly on her feet, lifted by one arm and swung in a dizzying arc once, twice, three times around, her head slung back, her hair an ebony swirl against an aureole of city light. Serge pulled Mireille close again, slapping her but more softly this time. She slapped him in return. Serge threw her down with startling violence but caught her wrists, saving her from a fall that would have left her crumpled and stunned. She freed one arm and spun away. He caught her by the waist with one hand, tore away her blouse with the other. He yanked her to his chest.

The couple turned in a swift circle so sudden that Cavendish saw little more than a blur. Mireille broke free from this embrace, running toward open space beyond the sinister hedges. This was the briefest of flights, halted as Serge flicked out a hand, like the head of a snake, snagging Mireille's skirt and reeling her in as the fabric tore away. Suddenly, Mireille was standing on Serge's feet, leaning backward and held by the waist, her hair trailing almost to the ground, eyes closed, her breasts naked and gleaming white against the night. Cavendish's breath caught in his throat. Mireille's body seemed to emanate light and heat. Guiltily, before he could banish the thought, Cavendish beheld a woman he could kill for, or whom he could kill if he could not have her completely and exclusively. The only sound in the silent *allée* was a soprano sigh from Mireille. They held this pose only briefly before Serge lifted Mireille above his head, his mouth pressed against her naked belly. He carried her, weightless, into shadow. Against a faint fog drifting up from the damp earth, Mireille rose in a sinuous silhouette. Cavendish could hear a low keening in her throat and then a gasp as Serge loosened his grip and let her slide down his body, her toes finally touching the ground. Serge marched her across the path, pressing her hard against the smooth, mottled skin of an immense, ancient plane tree, where he reached down tore away the slip of silk between her legs.

She was all but nude now, Serge still dressed. They presented a vision of subjugation that stirred in Cavendish a wordless anger.

Cavendish stood, giving up his concealment in the bushes. He stepped onto the path and stared in horrid fascination as Serge rode himself into Mireille.

She turned her head. She saw Cavendish, her gaze unsurprised, uncaring. There was something dazed and oblivious in her eyes. She looked away abruptly, burying her face in Serge's hair. Cavendish couldn't move. He watched as, gasping and growling, the couple made volcanic love. Mireille was an ivory snake around Serge's hips as he plunged and thrusted. She clawed at his back and gnawed his face. Her hair clung to the tree as she twisted and writhed. Serge's belt buckle, beneath the heap of pants around his ankles, clanked rhythmically as he ground the woman against the tree.

Then they were done—too fast, joylessly, thought Cavendish. With a last shudder, Serge released Mireille, letting her sink to the path, her bare bottom in the mud, as he organized his pants and buttoned up. In a moment, Mireille took a deep breath and stood, her profile—breasts, hips and curving legs—silhouetted again in the city's murky glow. Cavendish slipped back into shadow, fearful now of Serge's fury.

Mireille found her skirt. She arranged enough of her blouse to cover most of herself. As she and Serge walked away arm in arm, leaving Cavendish to watch and ponder, she carried her tattered bra on one hand. Her panties, a mere rag, languished in a greasy puddle.

Cavendish removed himself from hiding, wary of the denizens of the hedge. But no one challenged him, or even stirred, Did they witness scenes like this every night? Cavendish backed away, turning south on rue de Poteau.

He was on strange turf here. But he knew Paris well enough

to find his way back to the Fifth, perhaps an hour or longer. He didn't mind the walk, although he kept an eye peeled for shady characters. There was danger on these streets, but Cavendish had the advantage of looking a little less shabby than most of the locals.

As he skirted Montmartre and steered toward place de l'Opéra, he was stricken by a strange excitement that had nothing to do with spying on a man and woman as they humped against a tree in a homeless encampment. There was a tension—mysterious to Cavendish—in the bond that held Mireille and Serge together while seeming, at the same time, to cleave and lacerate them. They were like spinning magnets, attracting and repulsing each other rhythmically. The tempest of their love was both marvelous and grotesque.

Cavendish wondered what Mireille could possibly see in this abusive thug, but wondered also how any woman could resist him.

Cavendish crossed the Seine at the place de la Concorde, pausing to watch the river flow below. Upstream somewhere, the rain had been heavy, bringing high water and turbulence. The lamps on the bridge turned the churn and swirl of the troubled Seine into a flickering dance of light.

Finally, it came to Cavendish, as it often had, in the flash of a word, in a fleeting association which, if he failed to seize it and fix it in his memory, would vanish like breath on frozen air. The word that had been teasing his memory for weeks was not "Comanche."

He said it to himself, to the river, softly and secretly, but with a sense of triumph: "Apache."

Dangerous, profane, fiery and magnificent, Serge was irresistible to Mireille, because he had reincarnated— unknowingly, thought Cavendish—a breed of outlaws who had died out in Paris at least a half-century before Serge was born. That night, in that alley of the concrete Eighteenth, Cavendish had watched the spontaneous, tuneless and frightening struggle that was called, in French, *"la danse apache."*

Forming tenuously in Cavendish's mind was a story that would explain—no! There was no explaining what went on between Mireille and a raw savage like Serge. If he could find words to express it, Cavendish's "apache dance" would be an exposition, an illumination, a performance by dancers without choreography, driven by hungers and angers beyond their control or understanding, who dance unaware that they're dancing.

Cavendish barely reached the top of his stairs and stumbled through the door before the exhaustion of mind and body overcame him. He collapsed on his couch and slept, for the first time in months, through the night and past the morning.

.

CHAPTER 11

Clamato

A few days later, Steve and Mie steered their way to Clamato, a seafood restaurant far from the tourist regions of Paris that thrived on a clientele of affluent young French people and adventurous foreigners. It straddled the invisible border where rue de Charonne fades from fashionable to proletarian. Seen either from the street or sitting inside, Clamato seemed, to Steve and Mie, to define the raveling fringe between old and new in Paris. Its facade is a classic green storefront with big windows and no sign above to suggest what goes on inside.

Steve and Mie arrived just after noon and claimed a pair of wooden stools—true to the rickety Paris-café style—and planted their elbows on a sleek dashboard over which, through glass and stainless steel, they could watch a crew of nimble young chefs spooning *tarama*, whipping sauces and mincing *maquereau*, all the while bantering among their teammates and the customers. Behind Steve and Mie, the decor was an unthoughtful miscellany of chairs in different styles, tables and benches—none with a tablecloth. The depths of the restaurant expanded into a salon that featured an ancient spiral staircase and, on the back wall, not a mural expressing the artist's grim abstraction of ocean carnage and cetacean extinction but a bay window overlooking a lush, flowery and ill-tended garden. On sunny days, this back room glowed with dappled light tinged in green.

Steve liked ordering from the Clamato waitresses, who eventually came around and asked. Invariably slim and lovely, they spoke English better than his own. Mie loved the imagination of the menu, its inventive variety of raw fish and its reliable presence of crab, a shellfish relatively rare in France. Her mother, Kuniko, had been, when she was alive, a tenacious crab miner who would hunker for an hour over a jumble of legs, shells and tomalley, doggedly digging out infinitesimal shreds of white meat, forming a tiny pile on her plate and, every five minutes or so, pausing to take up chopsticks, trickle *shoyu* onto her hard-fought harvest of crabmeat and eat it with eyes closed, savoring the glow of diligence rewarded.

Every crab, to Mie, was a memorial to Mom.

Besides the obligatory crab, Steve and Mie ordered a bowl of *coques* with an addictive butter sauce that they kept to soak their crabmeat. They had *coquilles St.-Jacques* on a bed of sliced radish with a delicate tincture of oil and wine vinegar, and they added later a *tartare* of trout hidden beneath a thatch of shoestring potatoes. With all this, they killed a bottle of Aligoté, and talked about the strangers they had seen a few nights before.

Mie recalled to Steve the scene they had witnessed at Le Petit St.-Benoit. "Our waitress," she said. "You still think she's an exiled princess from Monte Carlo?"

"San Marino," said Steve.

"Right," said Mie. "But what about the guy we saw at the table? He was talking to the waitress—"

"Princess."

"Yeah, Steve, right." Mie rolled her eyes. "Suddenly, the guy gets up and runs inside, to the toilet. Who is he, and why—"

Steve cut Mie off. "Not yet."

"Not yet what?"

"Before I can tell you about the guy in the toilet," said Steve, "there's the little matter of Krisko Krillkin."

Mie drew back. "Krilko Krispin?"

"No, no. Krisko Krillkin, the greatest, most diabolical literary criminal in Europe. In the world, actually."

"Literary criminal?"

"Exactly."

Mie scoffed, "Come on, Steve."

"No, honest. He's a real guy. And I can't really explain the man in the toilet at the Petit St.-Benoit unless you know a few things about Krillkin."

Mie smiled dubiously. "Krillkin."

"Yes."

"First, please, what the hell is a literary criminal?"

"It's the crux of the whole story. It's what led poor Sherm to his downfall."

Mie almost spilled her champagne. "Sherm?"

"Sherman Shaw, private eye."

"Who—"

"The guy in the toilet," said Steve. "Y'know, Sherm wasn't always a self-pitying Paris drunk."

"He wasn't."

"No," said Steve, lowering his voice. "Sherm Shaw was one of the crack secret agents of the CIA."

"CIA?" scoffed Mie. "That guy? In the toilet?"

"Yeah, hard to believe," said Steve, shaking his head, "unless you know a little bit about Krisko Krillkin."

"Ah, back to Kriplin."

"Krillkin."

"Whatever."

"You see how Krillkin works," Steve pressed.

"Works?" asked Mie. "He's still around?"

"He's always around," said Steve, knowingly. "Some people say he's immortal."

Mie rolled her eyes. "Uh huh. Go on."

Steve swirled his wine, suavely. "How Krillkin works, y'see, is he ferrets his way into a great museum or library, where the oldest, most valuable books in the whole world are kept."

"And he steals them?"

"Ah, y'see? You're catching on."

"This isn't hard, Steve."

"But it's more like a kidnapping," Steve continued, "because Krillkin holds the book for ransom."

"A booknapping."

"Exactly," Steve replied. "And Krillkin's biggest caper ever, the one that held the whole world in thrall for more than a month, was the brilliant theft of a Gutenberg Bible from the National Library in Paris."

"Oh yeah?" Mie didn't sound credulous. "How'd he do that?"

"I'm glad you asked," said Steve. "Once he set his sights on the Gutenberg, Krillkin prowled the slums of Paris for a month, looking for an exceptionally thin child. He finally found an eleven-year-old girl who weighed barely seventy pounds. He snatched her off the street—"

"Name?"

"What?"

"What's her name? The skinny girl?"

Steve sighed. "Right, um, I dunno ..."

"Characters have to have names."

"Right, okay," said Steve. "How 'bout ... hm, Esmerelda?"

"Esmerelda, good. Go on."

"Jesus, where was I?"

"Kropotkin snatched little Esmerelda off the street."

"Okay, but it's Krillkin," said Steve. "He dragged little Esmerelda to his secret headquarters, where he tied her up and put her on intravenous saline solution for two weeks. She shrank down to just over fifty pounds, which made her skinny enough to slip through the ventilation ducts in the library to the room where the Bible was kept."

"Wait a minute," said Mie. "Krillkin gets her inside. But what's the point? She couldn't take a Gutenberg Bible back. It won't fit through the ventilation system."

"You're right about that."

"So?" said Mie.

"She didn't need to take the Gutenberg out," said Steve. "She just took it to the nearest window, broke the glass and handed it to one of the St.-Julien Rollers, who was—"

"Just a second," Mie interrupted. "The St.-Julien who?"

"St.-Julien Rollers," said Steve. "They're the most notorious gang of apaches in the history of Paris."

"Apaches?"

"This is what gang members in Paris were called, going back to the early twentieth century."

"You're kidding."

"Not, it's true. You could look it up."

"Okay, fine," Mie relented. "So, this Roller guy."

"Right, he actually breaks the window, from outside. He's suspended on a window-washer's scaffold."

"A scaffold?"

"Right."

"Oh, well, that's clever, but—"

"The girl hands the Bible over. The Roller goes up to the roof where Krillkin has a helicopter waiting. Krillkin has ample resources for this sort of caper. Scaffolds, helicopters ..."

"But the girl?"

"Well, yes. The police come and arrest Esmerelda. But she's only eleven, she'll end up in reform school. A nice bed and three squares a day. Of course, she knows nothing about the whereabouts of the Bible."

Mie waited for the next chapter. Steve poured Aligoté.

"So, a few hours pass. The National Police get a phone call from Krillkin, asking for an ungodly ransom, millions and millions of euros. Or else he'll put the Bible on a stack of explosives and blow it to Kingdom Come. Well, of course, every law enforcement agency in the world, from Interpol to the FBI—"

"To the CIA?"

"There you go," said Steve. "They all team up to try to save the precious, priceless Bible. And the leader of the whole operation is the best spy in the world, Special Agent Sherman Shaw of the CIA."

"But Krisley outwits him?"

"Right again. Sherm goes undercover. He poses as the chief national librarian of France, desperate to recover the Gutenberg. He agrees to bring the ransom money to a crowded public place, the plaza in front of the statue of St. Michael in place St.-Michel. You know it."

"Steve, we live in Paris half the year."

Steve bobbed his head. "Right." He went on. "Well, the Bible arrives— apparently. It's in a satchel that's carried by Lulu Blue."

"Lulu who?"

"Lulu is Krillkin's beautiful but evil female assistant. She bears an eerie resemblance to Nicole."

"Who?"

"Never mind," said Steve. "The plaza is crawling with cunningly disguised agents from Interpol, the CIA, the National Police, all over the place. Sherm meets Lulu Blue, looks her dead in the eye and shows her a bagful of ransom money—which, of course, he never plans to actually turn over. Lulu's carrying a satchel. But then, as Sherm pulls out his gun and signals for the cops to close in, he lunges for the Bible. But Lulu Blue—poof!—disappears literally in a puff of smoke. With the money. And the satchel."

"How'd she do it?"

"No one ever figured that out."

"And the Bible?"

"It was never in the satchel. It turned up later, safe and sound, sitting on the circulation desk at a little branch library in the Marais."

Mie smiled.

"The heartbreak here is that Sherm Shaw was disgraced," said Steve. "He'd blown the biggest case of his career, of anyone's career. He'd pissed away a million euros. Overnight, he became an international law-enforcement laughingstock. He was drummed out of the CIA. Sherm's reputation was so toxic that he got turned down for a job as a patrolman in the Hoboken Police Department. He fled back to Paris, the site of his downfall. He hung out a shingle as a private detective. He didn't expect anyone to actually hire him, and he was right. No one did. Finally, he settled down to his new career, as a drunk."

"At the Petit St.-Benoit," suggested Mie.

Steve nodded. "Where the princess Anna waited on him, discovered that he was a private dick and asked him, one night, if he could help find her long-lost brother."

"Luigi."

"Right."

"Okay, we've finally tied together the sad guy—"

"Sherm."

"Right. Sherm with the waitress. But how did princess Anna end up in Paris? When last we saw her, wasn't she in Oslo, hitting rock-bottom?"

"Oslo ... um, well, that's another story entirely."

"Aha, I see what's happening here, Steve." Mie smirked. "You forgot about the Oslo part, didn't you? You didn't even *have* an Oslo part."

Steve shrugged, looking sheepish.

Mie brightened. "Wait, wait," she said. "This is my chapter in the story of princess Anna. I know what happened in Oslo."

"You do?"

"Yes."

"Far out," said Steve, breathing easy. "This calls for champagne!"

CHAPTER 12

Upstairs, 22, rue de la Harpe

From the notes of Ray Cavendish:

Title: Apache Dance

NB: Find a Paris history, early 20th century, apache gangs. Try Shakespeare & Co., maybe Galignani ...

Story ... love triangle. Two lovers named ... Fifine and Nicolas. He's known as "Nick." He's an apache (lower case), gang leader, thief, mugger, murderer, violently short-tempered, always angry ... but handsome, long dark greasy hair, eyes like black opals, exudes sex appeal, irresistible to a certain type of woman who needs love & craves danger in her men ...

... Fifine is that sort of girl. Chanteuse, sings tragic heartbreaking torch songs at a cabaret in Pigalle. Or Montmartre? Called ... Les Noctambules ...

Where did I read that name? <u>Find the source</u>.

The "club" is a cellar. Describe. Detail. Fights and stabbings.

... Need a third party in the triangle ... Maxim, Max ... an old rival of Nick on the gang, beaten and lost. No legit life left for him and only the crummy jobs. Lookout. Getaway driver. Only needs money to keep drinking. But his love for Fifine is pure & undying.

We meet Maxim, he's holding down a tiny, wobbly table at Les Noctambules, drinking absinthe (cliché?), waiting for Fifine to sing.

She doesn't take the stage 'til 1 a.m., then sings three or four sets, 'til dawn, to the accompaniment of a sleepy guitar player. Or piano? But her voice is hauntingly beautiful ...

Cavendish paused his hurried scribbling. He could barely read his handwriting. He took a deep breath and puzzled over this creative fever.

"Jesus," he said to himself. "I'm completely empty for months. Suddenly, I'm bubbling over."

Cavendish drew on his cigarette and coughed. He only smoked when he was writing. He never drank on the job. He peered at his notes.

"Where was I?"

... Mad with love for Fifine, Maxim's been coming to Les Noctambules, braving the jealousy of Nick and his apache gang. He's been rousted, hassled, beaten. Keeps coming back. Fifine has seen him, at the same table, night after night. She doesn't know why he keeps coming back ... Fifine is afraid for Maxim, because of Nick. If Max ever gets rough with Fifine and Maxim tries to defend her, kaboom. Poor Max is doomed ... a red stain on the cobblestones ...

... Meanwhile, Max drinks through the night, deadening the pain of his impossible love, listening in sullen rapture to Fifine's angelic voice, staggering home for two or three hours rest. Then ...

... What then?

"Okay," muttered Cavendish, stubbing out a cigarette, "It's a premise. Is it all a cliché?" He shrugged. "Probably."

NOVEMBER

CHAPTER 13

Café de la Nouvelle Mairie

Thursday was the one night when Serge's behavior was predictable. Every week into the wee hours of Friday morning, at a dive off the rue des Solitaires in Belleville, he gambled, drank and played *belote* with friends. Certain of Serge's absence, Cavendish had cajoled the reluctant Mireille into another rendezvous in a wine bar near the Panthéon.

Le Café de la Nouvelle Mairie was ideal for the quiet, probing conversation Cavendish wanted. They were settled into a back corner. As in so many of Paris' tight little bistros, strangers were aligned almost elbow-to-elbow along the walls—banquettes facing out, chairs facing in—yet all were courteously oblivious to their neighbors. A single waiter, bearded and athletic with a red bandanna tied over his hair, loped among the tables. The day's menu was chalked onto a board, delivered by the waiter to each new pair or foursome. It listed four *entrées*, a meat dish or two—tonight it was a *cote d'agneau* and *travers du porc*—and a couple of fish choices, with desserts at the bottom. Wines were posted, also in chalk, on the walls. Near the door, a battered zinc bar separated staff from humanity, with beer taps at hand and rows of bottles behind.

The scuffed floors, the brisk, glib service, the sound of

clinking glass bouncing off smoke-stained walls, the yellow incandescence from the forty-watt fixtures—all evoked a comfy reminder of Le Petit St.-Benoit. Mireille touched Cavendish's hand, gratefully. They started their evening with a plate of *saucisson sec* with *cornichons*, good bread from Eric Kayser and Isigny butter. Cavendish ordered a bottle of Fitou.

Neither spoke for a while. Mireille could sense in Cavendish an agitation she could not quite fathom.

Cavendish wanted to share with Mireille the embryo of his new novel. But he couldn't tell her how the inspiration came to him that night in the damp park, as he watched Mireille pinned and writhing against the tree. She would feel violated.

"I'm writing now, at last. My new story," he said almost inaudibly.

Mireille's eyes sparked. She knew how important this was. "Ah, *oui*. The idea you had, the idea not about me."

"Yeah, that's right. Not about you. But you made me think of it," said Cavendish. "I got this word in my head."

"I remember," said Mireille, brightening. *"Comanche, oui?"*

"Well, yeah, but that was the wrong … tribe." For some reason, Cavendish blushed, like a toastmaster caught with his fly open. "My working title—no! My title, it won't change. It's … *Apache Dance*."

Mireille was puzzled. "It's about red Indians?"

Cavendish laughed softly. As he did, the waiter barged in, depositing sausage, pickles, butter, knives, wine and glasses. *"Voilà,"* he said.

"Merci," said Mireille.

The waiter was gone. Cavendish said, "Oh no. It's about Paris, a hundred or so years ago. About the *apache* gangs." He gave the word its French pronunciation. He added, "Sort of."

"Apache gangs?" asked Mireille, mystified.

For many Parisians, the history of the *apaches* has been buried in the mists of time, overwhelmed by the midcentury chaos of Nazi invasion, Allied liberation, foreign wars in

Vietnam and Algeria, Gaullist arrogance and the jumbled politics that followed. Until he began scouring the web for information about *les apaches*, all Cavendish knew on the subject was a vague memory of a sanitized "Apache dance" he had seen on a TV variety show when he was in grade school.

He knew a little more now. He'd begun reading a funky book by a literary ex-criminal named Netley Lucas, *Criminal Paris,* published in 1926. Cavendish was able to explain to Mireille the underworld of cutthroat free spirits that had thrived in the poorer quarters of Paris more than a century before.

Cavendish, as vaguely as possible, told Mireille that he was composing a love story about an *apache* girl and the two men in her life. "A sort of Pigalle *West Side Story,*" Cavendish ventured.

Mireille sipped her wine and wrinkled her brow. "That sounds ... "

"Thin! You're right. Absolutely," said Cavendish. "All I have now is a premise, an obsolete dance and a lot of disconnected scenes bouncing around in my brain."

"Well, but ... it's good," said Mireille uncertainly.

"Jesus, yeah, I hope so," said Cavendish. "It's been forever since I've wanted to get up in the morning."

"Now you do?"

"Now I do."

Mireille smiled, sending a pang though Cavendish's heart.

They ate and drank for a while, as Cavendish steered the conversation away from the details of *Apache Dance.*

"Listen," he said, "this guy—your, um, boyfriend ... "

"Serge."

"Yeah, Serge. I really wish you could tell me more about him?"

For a moment, Mireille's face turned a darker shade. Then she sighed. Cavendish had the right to know something about a man who had attacked him in public on a café terrace. She said, "He's not ... "

She stopped. Mireille remembered seeing Cavendish in the park, his face gray in the darkness, watching the tempest of Serge as he crushed and impaled her against the tree. Was Cavendish really there, or did she imagine him?

"He's not?" asked Cavendish.

Mireille smiled, looking away from Cavendish.

"Well, he is ... " She searched for the word in English. "... *fougueux*. Like fire? He ... "

"Explodes?"

Mireille nodded. "Ah, *oui*. Boom!"

The *saucisson* had disappeared as they talked. The waiter arrived, sweeping away the empty cutting board. He was back swiftly, with fish for Mireille, a filet of *daurade*, and Cavendish's lamb chops. The break had given Mireille time to think.

"Serge, you see, yes, he's angry. Angry at the world. Angry at stupid people. Angry at Paris, even."

"Angry at you?"

"Oh no, me? No, Serge loves me."

Cavendish almost scoffed, but said, instead, "But you. Mireille, you're closest to him. He can't fight the world. He can't take a swing at Paris. So he takes out his anger on you."

"Oh no, he's kind. He's gentle—"

"He hits you ... gently?"

Mireille slumped in her chair, setting down her knife and fork. "No no, sometimes he gets angry—at me. But not me. Not really. I wish you understood, Cavendish."

"Oh, I think I do."

Mireille rushed on. "And he is always sorry. He holds me, touches me. He kisses where I hurt. He says I'm sorry, I'm sorry ... "

Cavendish was tempted to say that all abusive men are sorry, that apologizing after beating the hell out of a woman absolves their violence and grants permission to beat the hell out of the woman the next time. He wanted to talk about vicious cycles, but he saw in Mireille's lowered head and rigid form that he would be wasting his breath.

After a decent interval, he said, "What does he do? His job?"

Mireille, relieved at the change in subject, brightened. "Oh, now, he paints."

"Really?"

"*Oui.* He's very good."

"Oh, well, that explains a lot," said Cavendish.

"It does?"

"Oh, yes, Mireille," said Cavendish, "The creative process, it's often explosive. For days, weeks, even months, there's nothing to write, nothing to create, nothing to paint. Your head is empty as a tennis ball. And you feel useless, stupid, mad at yourself. But then, boing. It's there, a vision, a flood of ideas. Inspiration!"

"Boing," said Mireille. She studied Cavendish, a little warily.

"So, Serge, he's frustrated. His anger grows. He's a powder keg that finally explodes in a burst of creation, flinging colors at the innocent canvas, smearing it with a pallet knife, clawing with his fingers into pots of paint—"

"Oh no," said Mireille.

"No?"

"He's not that sort of painter, not *artiste* but *peintre*," said Mireille. "He paints houses, walls, rooms."

"Oh."

"He hates it. It's boring, a stupid job. It makes him angry. He drinks so much when he's angry like that. When he's angry, *il perd la tête*. He doesn't know what he's doing. I feel so sorry for him. I wish … "

"Yeah," said Cavendish. "I do a lot of wishing, too. It doesn't help."

Mireille sighed.

"You're in love with him?" Cavendish asked.

"Yes, oh yes."

"And he loves you?"

To this, Mireille wouldn't say.

DECEMBER

TERMINUS
NORD
5/14/07

CHAPTER 14

Le Bon Saint-Pourçain

They were conversing aimlessly. Mie cocked her head.

"You remember that couple, the waitress and the sad guy?" she asked. "From the Petit St.-Benoit?"

"Well, of course," said Steve, tapping his head. "Princess Anna and Sherman Shaw, private eye. You were going to tell me what happened in Sweden. But we got interrupted."

"Sweden?" Mie paused to think. After a moment, her eyes lit up as the thread came back to her. "No. Not Sweden. Norway. Remember? You said the princess hit rock bottom in Oslo."

"Oh," said Steve, vaguely. "Right. Oslo."

"Yes, and I know what happened," said Mie, seizing the narrative. "There was this Norwegian rock star."

"Norway has rock stars?"

"Dozens!"

"Oh."

"This one was named Bjorn."

"Bjorn what?"

Mie said, "Hm. Don't know. Bjornson?"

Steve and Mie were face-to-face at a corner table in an immaculate bistro on the rue Servandoni, not far from the massive church of St.-Sulpice. Behind Mie was a section of the restaurant's original limestone wall, scrubbed blonde by its new proprietors. The Bon Saint-Pourçain had long been the province of an efficient Parisian named François and his busy, amiable wife. They had served hearty meals under weak lights to the sort of loyal neighborhood patrons who tended to give off a faint ambience of damp wool. François had retired and, a few years later, passed away, leaving the bistro to the tender mercies of three artful young men who renovated the interior. The centerpiece of Le Bon Saint-Porçain was now a sleek open kitchen where customers could watch the chef wield his skillets and simmer his sauces. The new owners had also modernized the menu, moving it from printed page to blackboard. The changeable *ardoise* listed each night only three or four slightly exotic specialties, intended by the chef to surprise diners with a melange of trendy flavors that were unusual in Paris bistros but still evocative of French tradition. Mie, for example, had discovered atop her sautéed mackerel filet a garnish of pickled *daikon*. This flourish wafted her back, momentarily, to Tokyo.

Le Bon Saint-Pourçain was barely big enough to hold twenty patrons. But it was airy under new lights. A large mirror on one wall added an illusion of greater space.

Remembering the genial warmth and comfort of the bistro when François was boss, Steve had been leery about the new guys. He was solaced, however, by the attentive service of a waiter named Alexander. Also reassuring: every dish was both recognizable and cleverly unpredictable, delivered without explanation by the *serveur*. Steve thought of New York, where every plate tends to come with a speech.

Alexander brought a bottle of the bistro's namesake, a Saint-Pourçain red called Sein-Pourçeau, bearing a comic label that depicted a mob of country bumpkins milking the teats of a giant sow.

As Alexander withdrew, Mie launched into princess Anna's misadventure with Bjorn. "He was irresistible."

"Who?"

"Bjorn, dummy."

"Oh yeah? How so?"

"Oh God, well, he had long blond hair down to his shoulders. All he wore above his waist was a vest made out of reindeer hide. He had muscles that rippled, skin that was bronze, a dimple on his chin, ice-blue eyes."

"Kind of like me," said brown-eyed Steve, who had no evident muscles.

Mie ignored this. "Well, here was princess Anna, in Oslo, searching for Luigi."

"The long-lost little brother."

"Don't interrupt," said Mie. "One night, the princess goes to one of Bjorn's concerts. She's swept away by his beauty, his muscles, his rock and his roll. He sees her in the audience. He winks at her. She falls in love. He invites her backstage. They make love that very night in his dressing room."

"Or maybe in the alley by the stage door," offered Steve.

"This is my story now. Shut up."

Steve shut up. Mie unraveled the tale of princess Anna becoming Bjorn's fleeting paramour, just long enough to get pregnant. Bjorn offers to pay for an abortion. He has done this before, with countless groupies. But princess Anna refuses. Bjorn expels her, in shame, from his entourage. Princess Anna is heartbroken. She thought Bjorn really loved her. Her only consolation is her baby, a boy she names Misha. The baby boy's birth reminds Anna that her true mission in life is to find her kidnapped kid brother. By this time, she knows Luigi is not in Norway, so she boards a ship to cross the North Sea.

"But the ship," Mie continued, "is attacked by the bloodthirsty pirates of Finland."

"Finland has pirates?"

"Hush," snapped Mie. "The pirates board her ship and find princess Anna hiding on the poop deck. Seven Finnish buccaneers, one after the other, rape her violently and leave her for dead."

"Again she's raped?" said Steve.

"It's a pirate thing," said Mie. "It's in their code."

"Pirates have a code?"

"You bet your Jolly Roger," Mie said. "I read about pirates when I was a little girl. And what they did to the women they captured. For years, I was afraid to go near the water—any water. And if I saw a man in the street with an eye-patch, I'd run away screaming bloody murder."

Steve tried to look sympathetic to Mie's childhood fears. "So," he said, "then what?"

"Then? Well, the Finnish fiends snatch up little Misha and attempt to toss him from the burning deck to their confederates on the pirate ship. But the throw falls short. Misha bounces off the hull and drops into the drink never to be seen again."

"Jesus," said Steve. "Why didn't the dumbass pirates just carry the baby across—"

"Quiet," said Mie. "Baby-tossing is a popular pastime among Finnish pirates. You wouldn't understand."

"This is based on your vast experience with Finnish pirates?"

Mie scowled at Steve before proceeding. "Princess Anna lies in a coma on the crippled ship, which finally makes port in Amsterdam. When, at last, she wakes up in a charity hospital and finds out that her little Misha is sleeping with the fishes, she bursts into inconsolable sobbing, tears her hair, scratches her face. She staggers from the hospital, into the city, where she wanders penniless and homeless. Gradually, she sinks into a life of drugs and prostitution. She loses interest in finding Luigi. She loses interest in everything. As time goes by, she wanders from city to city. Eventually, her travels bring her to Paris. Here, one day, a kindly priest from the *église* Saint-Séverin finds her unconscious on the church steps. Once a princess who snacked on peeled grapes in a mountain castle, she's now a broken-down hag, filthy and almost naked, delirious from cocaine and gonorrhea, begging to be put out of her misery."

"Jeez," said Steve, "does this story get better?"

"Of course, it does," said Mie. "We know it does. We've seen princess Anna, waitressing at the Petit St.-Benoit. She looked great."

"She's beautiful," said Steve. "So, how'd that happen."

"The priest."

"Ah, of course. What's his name?"

"Pére Dominic," said Mie who was ready for the question. "He takes her into his priestly residence. He calls the doctor, pumps her full of black coffee and penicillin. He nurses Anna back to health, praying over her and never laying a finger on her even when he's changing her nightgown. As she recovers, he coaxes from her the story of her flight from San Marino and the abduction of Luigi by the mysterious Nicole at the Bulgarian border. She tells Père Dominic about the death of Olga, the kindly switchman, the endless wandering from country to country, the faithless rock star, the storming of her ship and the murder of Misha, and all the bad shit that came after that."

"And then, what?" said Steve. "The priest gets her a job as a waitress?"

Mie narrowed her eyes. "No, she can get her own job," she said. "Besides, that comes later. What he does, Père Dominic …"

Mie paused.

She said, "What you need to know here is that princess Anna is not the first shattered human being that Père Dominic has pulled from the gutter."

"Wait, wait, I get it," said Steve. "This is where Sherm comes in."

Mie smiled. "Of course. After being dumped by the CIA, Agent Sherm was a wreck. His private-eye business failed. He was evicted from his office. He spiraled down into drunken despair, ending up on the street, eating out of *poubelles*, sleeping under bridges, begging in front of the church of St.-Séverin—which is where Père Dominic finds him, takes him in, cleans him up, dries him out and convinces him to start all over in the private-dick biz. But he still has no clients."

"But then," said Steve, "along comes princess Anna!"

"Exactly" said Mie. "Père Dominic realizes that Anna and Sherm are a match made in Heaven. So, after princess Anna finds the job at the Petit St.-Benoit, the priest takes Sherm out to dinner."

"At the Petit St.-Benoit."

"Of course," said Mie.

"Where Sherm meets the princess, Père Dominic quietly slips away and they fall in love. Right?"

Mie shook her head. "Steve," she said crisply. "You saw them together, twice. Did they look like lovers to you?"

Steve tilted his head. "Not really."

"Right," said Mie. "They were—they *are*—bonded not by passion but by their mutual determination to find little Luigi."

"After all those years," said Steve, "wouldn't he be a fairly large Luigi?"

Mie rolled her eyes.

"So, c'mon," Steve insisted. "Is Sherm gonna track down Luigi?"

Alexander appeared with their main dishes, for Mie a *filet de bar* on a tasty-looking bed of something-or-other, Steve two pink tender slices—accompanied by Japanese potatoes and French turnips—of *quasi de veau*.

"I have no idea, Steve. This is a story-in-progress," replied Mie, regarding her plate hungrily. "Can we eat?"

"Okay, but what about Luigi?"

Mie sighed and set down her knife and fork.

"Steve, this is fun, but—"

"But what?"

Mie said. "Don't you think this particular dumb story has gone on long enough? We haven't seen those two people in ages. We probably never will. I mean, this is a big city. The woman's not really a princess. She's a damn waitress. And the guy's not a detective. And there is no Luigi."

"Jeez," said Steve, crestfallen. "No Luigi?"

"And!" Mie went on. "We never drag out these stupid stories like we have with this one. They come and go. That's the fun of it. Here tonight, gone tomorrow."

"Yeah, but those two, they weren't gone tomorrow. They keep turning up like a bad penny. They're really—"

"Gone, at last. From our lives," said Mie, shutting the door. "They're gone, and we don't know them. How about we eat?"

They stared at their plates.

"And figure out later what happened to Luigi?"

"There is no Luigi," said Mie.

Steve and Mie's bistro nights were a lighthearted series of unfinished fictions that entertained them for the evening but left little trace. Luigi would likewise fade away during another sojourn away from Paris. Steve and Mie were departing the next morning for assignments in Bucharest, Ankara and Istanbul. Then, they were on their way to Christmas with Steve's daughter, Ella, in Massachusetts. Afterward, Steve had meetings and interviews in Cairo and North Africa, Israel and Jordan, returning to Paris almost two months later, by way of Madrid, Lisbon, Bordeaux and Périgueux.

"Mm, this is good," said Steve, lifting a tender rosy slice of beef from its piquant brown sauce. "What's it called again?"

"Quasi de veau," said Mie, looking at her mobile phone screen.

"Quasi?" asked Steve, who understood *veau*.

"On my phone," said Mie, *"quasi de veau* translates as 'almost veal.'"

JANUARY

CHAPTER 15

Le Petit St.-Benoit

Cavendish was comfortable occupying a table near the kitchen door. He had arrived just after ten p.m., while Mireille was scrambling to dispatch the early wave of diners and fill their tables with newcomers. He had settled in patiently, ordering the *pot au feu* and nursing a single glass of Cheverny.

His arrival had set Mireille on edge. If Serge were to come in and see Cavendish there, in close quarters, there was no easy escape. Cavendish could end up beaten to death by the bone in his stew.

Cavendish took a look at the bone. He estimated that it was too small to kill a grown man, or even a cat. Nevertheless, Mireille remained nervous.

As she emerged from the kitchen with two plates, another *pot au feu* and a *suprême de volaille*, she paused to whisper, "It's Tuesday. You shouldn't be here—"

"I have something for you."

She was gone before he finished speaking.

A moment later, as Mireille swept past: "You should go."

Cavendish said, *"Un autre verre du vin, s'il vous plaît?"*

"Merde!"

Despite the lights in the bistro, Cavendish's presence made

Mireille feel cornered in a dark place. Serge had been poking into the restaurant every night for weeks, an hour or so before closing time, to see if Mireille's "boyfriend" was hanging around and making sweet talk, enticing her into his web. In winter, the windows at Le Petit St.-Benoit steamed over. It was impossible to see the street outside. From the outside, however, someone could put his face close to the glass and spy on the indistinct shapes and faces of customers inside.

Tonight, finally, Serge's vigilance was vindicated. There was the American, leaning against the wall, picking at his *os a moelle,* sipping some cheap red wine and looking smug. Serge had to keep a grip on his emotions, lest he barge indoors and shove that stinking *os* down the bastard's throat, choking him on his own dinner.

Instead, Serge retreated to the nearest café. He ordered a *pression* and waited to intercept Mireille—perhaps snuggling arm-in-arm with the ugly American—on her way to the Métro.

The crowd at Le Petit St.-Benoit thinned quickly after eleven. Mireille turned the last customers over to Patricia long enough to sit down with Cavendish.

"What are you doing, Cavendish? Why are you here?"

Cavendish shrugged off Mireille's anxiety.

"Mireille, you've inspired me," he said. "I've told you this. This mad, tempestuous passion between you and Serge has me writing again!"

Mireille's eyes widened with alarm. "You're writing about me?"

"No, I told you. No," said Cavendish, patting her hand. "It's a love story, a triangle, that takes place long ago. My characters are not you and Serge. They're ghosts of you, caricatures, evocations."

"Cavendish, your words are too long."

Cavendish smiled. "Sorry." He dug into a satchel that had

become his inseparable accessory.

"Here," he said, handing Mireille a ragged-edged roll of typewritten paper secured by rubber bands.

Mireille accepted the papers cautiously. *"C'est ... quoi?"*

"It's a very rough draft, my first fifty or so pages. I just rattled it off in a couple of days. It's called *Apache Dance*. It's about this woman—oh, she's beautiful. Like you. A *chanteuse* in a terrible dark cabaret, in another era—but, please, just read it. You'll see. It's very rough. Not the final ... God, I feel ... saved. You saved me, Mireille. Really." He spoke softly. "I'm writing again."

Mireille was nonplussed and troubled. She handled the rumpled manuscript as though it were a poisonous snake.

"I don't know," she said.

"Please, just read it. It couldn't hurt. It's not about you. You're just ... my inspiration."

Mireille repeated the word, pronouncing it in French, smiling tightly. "Not about me."

"No, I promise," said Cavendish. "Listen, I'll be going now. I just wanted you to see this." He patted the manuscript.

Cavendish slipped out of the bistro a moment later and paused on the sidewalk, looking around. He assumed that, somewhere near, in the shadows or ensconced at a bar around the corner, Serge was lurking. Rather than moseying home to the Fifth, Cavendish—just curious—slipped into his own shadowy nook, huddling against the evening's chill.

Sure enough, just past midnight as Mireille left the restaurant, Serge materialized from the direction of rue Jacob. He caught up swiftly with Mireille, gliding like a cheetah on the prowl and taking a hard grip on her arm. As the couple passed, Cavendish heard Serge speaking to Mireille in a big-cat growl.

As he had done before, Cavendish followed at a discreet distance until Serge and Mireille stopped for an espresso at a café still open on the blvd. St.-Germain. Cavendish continued on, entering the Métro and riding all the way north to Marcadet-Poissoniers. He felt a little silly lying in wait, loitering in the corridor between platforms. But he also felt a thrill, like a detective on a stakeout.

Moments before the last train west on the No. 12 line, Cavendish spotted Mireille and Serge hurrying past. He waited, followed, caught the train at the other end of the platform. One stop later, they were all on rue de Poteau again.

Cavendish kept them in sight all the way to what he guessed was Mireille's door, on passage Daunay, a grubby *villa* off avenue de St.-Ouen. He was able to conceal himself there in a litter-strewn pocket park, listening as Serge's voice rose in anger, demanding an explanation from Mireille. He took her by the arms, clutched her close and shook her so hard that Cavendish could hear her teeth clack. Mireille cried out in pain and confusion. Cavendish was close enough to see her face, tears in her eyes, her cheeks flush with fear, her hair tumbling free and framing her face dramatically, beautifully, in the light from a naked bulb above the doorway.

If he had the nerve, Cavendish was close enough to burst from concealment and leap to Mireille's aid, close enough to seize Serge, pull him away and struggle with him—however ineptly—while Mireille slipped to safety inside her apartment.

Cavendish stayed put. He watched, as Serge's violence shook, from inside Mireille's overcoat, Cavendish's manuscript. Serge cried out and snatched the papers from the street. He demanded to know what this was.

Cavendish understood little of the following tirade, but recognized the word *"Americain"* and deciphered *"lettres d'amour"* as "love letters."

"Oh, c'mon, dumbass," Cavendish muttered to himself. "A fifty-page love letter?"

The climax of the contretemps was Serge tearing Cavendish's first draft of *Apache Dance* mightily in two and shoving it into an adjacent garbage can.

"Oh well," whispered Cavendish. "Easy come ... "

The ripping of the papers seemed to pacify Serge. Several windows had lit up in response to the ruckus in the secluded passage. Whispering fiercely at each other, Mireille and Serge retreated into her apartment.

As the door clicked shut and light appeared in the window, Cavendish felt both deflated over his cowardice, and elated— by Serge's behavior. His rage and urge to destroy were a real-life parallel with Nicolas, the character whom Cavendish had modeled after Serge.

As he clambered from his hiding place, Cavendish thought of rescuing his pages from the trash, but left them behind. The chapters were safe in his computer. Besides, after tonight, he realized he had made a false start with *Apache Dance*. The manuscript needed so many changes that it would be better to start afresh. Cavendish was disappointed that Mireille hadn't had the chance to even glance at his prose, but he consoled himself with the knowledge that she would have struggled with his English and probably misunderstood his premise.

Too late for the Métro, he made his way carefully home on foot, staying close to streetlamps and sidestepping the darker alleys.

CHAPTER 16

22, rue de la Harpe

Cavendish lived beneath a cracked and puddled zinc roof in a garret that, three centuries before, had been the quarters of a maid who'd serviced a dozen of the cheap hotel rooms on floors below. Facing north, his dormer windows drew in little sunshine even in the brightest months. In January, the two windows were smudgy squares of matte gray.

He had been inside all day, bent over his keyboard then leaping to his feet as though the keys had burned his fingers. Now, he paced the three meters of floor space available to him, smoking and talking to himself.

"C'mon, man. Why would she?" he asked himself. "Why?"

Cavendish's "she" was Fifine, his "heroine" in *Apache Dance*. He was struggling with a character whose contradictions sent him wandering around the room and thinking out loud. How could he frame, credibly, a woman, seemingly intelligent and sensitive, who had sunk into the dank underworld that the early twentieth-century *apaches* occupied? Willingly, Fifine lived in that bleak realm, did not contrive any effort to escape and accepted a degrading subservience to a sadist who beat, raped, humiliated her. Cavendish, in his reading, had come to understand how a young girl without means could slip into the demimonde. Until he had begun his research, he had no idea how seductive, possessive and adhesive were the haunts of Paris' vast community of thieves, murderers, thugs, muggers, gangsters and malignant *clochards*. Once immersed, one lost sight of the surface from which another world might be visible.

Legend placed the realm of the *apaches* in the lower reaches of Montmartre, around Pigalle, Clichy and place Blanche. But histories written by Luc Santé, Andrew Hussey, Netley Lucas and even Balzac had expanded that dangerous turf to the Left Bank, to the flophouses and shanties that had turned the narrow streets around the church of St.-Séverin into a filthy cowpath clogged with sewage. Not far from the church was a violent skid row that began at place Maubert and stretched uphill toward the Panthéon on rue de Montagne St.-Genevieve, where any bourgeois interloper could be "accosted, sapped, dragged into a doorway and left unconscious in nothing but his skivvies and socks."

Eugene Sue had set his stories of a predatory, criminal Paris in a sinister maze of narrow lanes and alleys between the cathedral of Notre Dame and the Seine. Sue chronicled a city of light where all the gaslights had been snuffed and its denizens groped, fearful of every dark recess, along the damp and sticky walls of hovels, dives and brothels.

In *Criminal Paris*, Netley Lucas had described, with a touch of frightful romance, the typical *apache femme* as a "fearless, sparkling, untrammeled creature who loves and hates where she will, ruling the man of the moment with the point of the knife if need be."

Lucas' description evoked Lady Macbeth, but this was hardly the impression Cavendish wanted for Fifine. He imagined, instead, a soiled Juliet, more worldly wise than Shakespeare's ingenue, but clinging still to faint dreams of chivalrous swains and mad, delirious, fatal love. Cavendish sketched Fifine's Nicolas as the nightmare opposite of her tenuous dream. Why, Cavendish asked himself, would Fifine succumb to a man who would draw his blade against another man—or woman—and slash away without a second thought? Why—and how—could he create a character, a woman, who so irrationally defied her own interests, who disdained the love for which her heart ached?

"Mireille," Cavendish muttered as he stubbed out another cigarette.

Before Cavendish had met Mireille and watched her submit to the brutish allure of Serge, no character as self-victimizing as Fifine would have entered his mind. Fifine's attraction to her demon Romeo, would seem, in Cavendish's mind, too incongruous to believe. But his acquaintance with Mireille and Serge had revealed to Cavendish in real life the malign magnetism of Fifine's passion for Nick.

Cavendish talked to himself as he paced the room. "Yeah, it's possible. It happens. But how do I explain? Why do they attract—this sylph and this satyr—rather than repel? She's sweet and shy. She sings like an angel. She's a poetess in Hell, Eurydice. But he's not Orpheus. He's a clod and a pathological bully. A tinderbox full of impulses. Lust and rage and vengeance, jealousy and savagery. Why doesn't she just run? How do I explain? Why is the woman's hunger stronger than her fear and pain? Is something wrong with her or is there some tremendous, irresistible force within this guy that drives and defines this volatile, destructive—crazy... death wish? Does she want to die?"

Cavendish stopped suddenly.

"Shit," he whispered.

He reached out to the nearby kitchen counter and lit a cigarette with a trembling match.

"Oh, Christ. Fifine, really? C'mon. Listen to yourself, dickhead. You're talking about Mireille. You're afraid for her."

Cavendish stubbed out the cigarette.

"Well, yeah. Her boyfriend is scary. But he's not Nick and she's not Fifine. Can't be. Gotta get my head straight. This story can't be about her," he said.

He wrapped his head in his hands. "But how can it not be?"

He sat down. "Cavendish, are you falling in love? Cavendish, can you fall in love? You're middle-aged and cranky. Cynical. You're probably an alcoholic. Unloved ... "

He smirked. "Unlovable."

He started pacing again. "Okay, I like this girl—woman. She's, well ... yeah. I wouldn't be writing this fucking story if I hadn't met her ... " Cavendish pictured Mireille and Serge waiting for the Métro. "She's not my train. She's the platform. The train leaves without her. What am I writing about?"

Cavendish collapsed back into his chair, tapped his keyboard and scrolled up to the top of his notes. His lead phrase was "fatal attraction."

He shook his head. "No."

He deleted "fatal." He stared at the screen. He said, "The attraction is ... reckless. Impulsive but worse. Dangerous, worse than dangerous. Like the road not taken, but not taken by anyone in their right mind. Like a black hole sucking you in but you're drawn to its edge. Dangerous, aware of the danger but unable to resist, as though possessed. Attraction not fatal, but sinister, sexy, irresistible ... "

Cavendish typed "diabolical."

He had seen the devil in the violence of Serge and in Mireille's submission, but as a voyeur. He'd stood and watched rather than defend her. He would—he must—let that storm run its course, whatever might happen, because whatever might happen in real life could guide Cavendish's storytelling. He had a selfish interest in whatever Serge might do to Mireille. Their fevered romance was kindling for the fictional fire he was building, a blaze that would—somehow, he hadn't figured it out yet—consume his imaginary lovers, Nick and Fifine—along with Maxim, the third point in his triangle.

Writing about imaginary apaches provided Cavendish a shield against his emotions. He had begun to write again.

after so long, partly to distance himself from the living lovers who had revived his imagination, who haunted his thoughts, who monopolized—more and more—his waking hours and restless sleep.

"I won't get dragged in. I can't. I can't stand up to him. There's no reason. She loves him, God knows why," Cavendish said to himself. "She can't say why. How do I explain?"

CHAPTER 17

Belleville

When Cavendish moved to Paris, a realtor led him through a dozen vacant apartments. Most were clean, modern and ready for immediate occupancy. But he was astounded, and fascinated, by those ill-lit dwellings, usually the habitat of ancient women who had lived in the same quarters for the better part of a century, that seemed to have gone unchanged decade upon decade. He walked on paintless floors of soft wood with visible gaps between boards. He looked up at ceilings cobwebbed by eight years of leaks and the shock of long-forgotten violence on the floors above. A kitchen could be an afterthought stuck against a wall, with stains on the floor to indicate where each faulty appliance had stood and spilled its juices, sauces and brines. Or it could be a narrow galley, wide enough for one person, flanked by counters barely wide enough to accommodate a hotplate, with doorless shelves above. One apartment, which had only a tiny water closet, showed signs that its late owner had never showered or used a bathtub, but washed standing in a basin, beside the kitchen sink, like a nude by Degas or Bonnard.

From these impressions, Cavendish composed a mental picture of the hovel occupied by his characters: two rooms, a cramped kitchen without shelves and few utensils, only a gas ring for cooking. There would be a bedsit, with a privy in the hallway, and floors that looked as though they had been clawed by tigers. The furniture would be spare and rickety, the bed a mere cot large enough to sleep one, but used by two uncomfortably. There would be no heat beyond a dangerous kerosene stove and only a few bare bulbs hanging from the ceiling—which would shine erratically in a building that clung but tenuously to the weak power grid in the radical, dissolute and destitute enclave of Belleville.

Apache Dance
by Raymond Cavendish
(From Chapter 2)

... The eggs Fifine was preparing for Nicolas had been bought, dearly, from Mathilde Moreau, who lived across the alley. Through the smeared glass of the window, Fifine could see Tilde now, in her tiny, fenced-in chicken yard, brandishing a hatchet and pursuing a scrawny red hen. Despite the confined space, the hen—sensitive to her fate—was proving nimble and elusive.

"He's after you, the fucking bastard," said Nick. He occupied one of two kitchen chairs. He leaned back, propped against the wall, one leg resting on the battered table where, when they were both here in Nick's flat, the couple ate the simple meals Fifine cooked.

Fifine knew whom Nick was talking about. She concentrated on the eggs and kept an eye on Tilde's adventure with the doomed but plucky hen.

"And you like the fucker, don'tcha?" asked Nick.

Cautiously, Fifine, flicked a glance at Nick. "He's just another drunk."

"Bullshit," snapped Nick.

The hunted hen retreated to a corner between fence and wall. Tilde, scattering the other chickens, lunged. Fifine knew Tilde's rule. A hen stayed out of the pot if she produced at least an egg a day. When Petit Poulet couldn't meet the standard, she became chicken dinner.

Beating her wings furiously, the hen lifted three feet from the ground, dodging Tilde's grasp and scrambling, across her murderous owner's back, to temporary safety. Tilde, smirched with chicken dung, cursed magnificently, her voice echoing up the walls of the Belleville tenements.

"He's there every fucking night," said Nick.

"Nicky," replied Fifine, as she delicately folded the eggs, "you're there every night."

"It's my place, dammit," snapped Nick.

Les Noctambules called itself a cabaret. More accurately, it was a dive that served mainly as a hangout for Nick's gang of apaches, who were neither sufficiently organized nor literate enough to have a title. They were known simply by their affiliation with Nick.

"La Combe would be interested to know that," said Fifine.

Nick growled, "All that fat Boar does is pour rotgut and pay your miserable wages, Fifi. I decide who comes and goes."

Fifine moved the omelette to the center of the skillet, where it could brown on the outside.

"If that's so, you could refuse to let Maxim in."

Nick sighed. "I knew Maxie in school. He's ... "

"Your friend," said Fifine.

"No!"

Fifine took a quick look at the battle in the chicken yard. Tilde had finally captured the hen. Lacking a chopping block, she was pressing the chicken's neck onto a board perched unevenly between two buckets.

"No longer your friend?" said Fifine, watching the scene of execution. "That's more than he has ever been to me. I barely know him."

The hatchet came down. Cleverly, the hen shifted its head. Tilde missed so violently that the board bounced off the buckets and clattered to the ground while the chicken wrenched free and fluttered away.

Another mighty roar from Tilde. Fifine smiled.

"He's there every night," insisted Nick. "He's after you."

Fifine sighed. "I sing, Nicky. Men come to hear me. Sometimes, they mix together loving my song with loving me, for a moment, or a night. It passes, Nicky."

"If he tries—"

"Tries what?" Fifine replied. "He sits and drinks. He's a sad, lonely man. His wife left him. He goes away drunk. He comes back, the next night, sober. He sits and drinks."

"How do you know his wife left him? He talks to you?"

Fifine shook her head. "Everybody knows his story. He gets drunk and tells it. Anyone close enough can listen."

"He talks to you."

"No, he doesn't," Fifine lied.

"I'll kill him."

Fifine slipped the eggs onto a plate and set it on the table, shaking her head.

Before starting another omelette, she looked out the window. Tilde had caught the hen again. The hatchet was on the ground. Tilde wrung the bird's neck. The head went limp while feet and wings flapped and kicked.

Nick was eating.

"You'll kill him, for nothing?"

Fifine spoke with trepidation. Nick's threats were not always mere bluster. She knew the depth of his rage and cruelty. These forces within him drew her. They terrified her.

As though on cue, Nick erupted from his chair, tipping the table and dumping his breakfast on the slivered floor. He seized Fifine by the throat, backing her up to the window. He held her there, his face made livid by a fury Fifine had never been able to fathom. She began to grow dizzy for lack of air. When he finally let go, she sank to the floor, fighting to suppress a cough that might reignite his anger.

He stood over her, working his fists.

"I'll kill him," said Nick, "for you."...

FEBRUARY

CHAPTER 18

Mirama

Consumed by his draft of *Apache Dance*, Cavendish had barely seen Mireille for almost a month. On the evening he finally dropped into Le Petit St.-Benoit, Mireille hastily begged him to leave, fearful that Serge might turn a corner and see them together. But as Cavendish shrugged and turned to go, she said, "Cavendish, you worry me." While pushing him toward the street, she surprised Cavendish by proposing a Thursday night rendezvous. Always eager to sit across a candlelit table looking into Mireille's eyes, Cavendish agreed.

Quickly, Cavendish suggested a favorite spot in his neighborhood, on rue St.-Jacques. Mireille said yes and hurried him on his way.

"I don't know what to think about you," he said.

Mireille puffed dismissively. *"Ne pense pas!"*

As usual, Cavendish had to wait twenty minutes before Mireille, eye-foggingly beautiful in a light blue sweater and short black skirt, with black leggings against the winter, appeared. He sighed as she hung her coat and slid toward him in the narrow space between two rows of tables and bentwood chairs.

Barely noticeable from the street, Mirama is a shotgun

bistro with no concession to interior decor, closely packed tables covered in white paper beneath stark white walls. Operated for decades by its brusque Chinese owners, it thrives on its incomparable *soupe de raviolis aux crevettes avec nouilles*, shrimp dumplings and noodles in an addictive clear stock. Mirama's soup is so popular that its pot, bubbling and steaming just inside the entrance, is big and deep enough to boil a missionary.

The host, thin and mirthless in a rumpled white shirt, had led Cavendish, and then Mireille, to the cellar, whose irregular walls evoked the torrent—and arduous excavation— of mud that had smothered the Left Bank in the flood of 1910. After a quiet twenty minutes, Mireille was finishing her soup. Cavendish had already wolfed his bowl and begun to work on plates of duck and broccoli.

Mireille, saving her last dumpling, sat back and speared Cavendish with her exotic gaze.

"I've been worried," she said. "Not seeing you."

Cavendish took a sip of the simple Muscadet that complemented Mirama's peerless soup.

"You sound like my mother," he said, not smiling.

Mireille scowled.

Cavendish said. "I don't know what to expect from you, Mireille … " He shook his head. "No, no, I expect nothing. But the last thing I would ever need from you is mothering."

Mireille looked hurt. *"Desolé,"* she said softly.

Cavendish touched her hand. "No, I'm sorry. You were worried because I, well, sort of disappeared. But it's good. I've been … busy." He smiled, "You probably pictured me in a bar, drinking myself into a stupor every night."

"Oh no!"

Cavendish stared. Mireille's face was troubled but, after a month, a welcome sight. She called to his mind Meredith Willson's "sadder but wiser girl," the subtle lines beside her mouth and behind her eyes lending emphasis to brilliant onyx eyes and sweet-cream skin.

"Sometimes when I'm working," said Cavendish, "I lose track of days and nights. When I looked up the other day, I realized I hadn't seen you in weeks. All of a sudden, I missed you."

Blushing slightly, Mireille looked away. Cavendish said, "I wondered if you'd read any of the manuscript I gave you."

Mireille looked stricken. She opened her lips to speak.

"No? You didn't?" Cavendish broke in. "Good!"

"Good?" asked Mireille.

"I pretty much trashed all those pages. Started over."

Mireille's alarm turned to relief, then curiosity.

"You see," Cavendish went on. "I have this girl in my story. Fifine. She's a *chanteuse*, remember?—and there are two men fighting over her. At first, I conceived of them both as crooks, gangsters, *apaches*, you know?"

Mireille smiled, "*Apaches,* yes, but not red Indians, *oui*?"

"That's right. But that didn't work. Y'see, I needed a contrast. Fifine has to face a choice, between her lover, the exciting scoundrel—I call him Nick—and the other guy. His rival."

"So, the other man, who loves the girl, but he's not her *amoureux*. He is ... respectable?"

Cavendish considered this, pouring wine for Mireille.

"Well," he said, "he's sort of like me. Not exactly respectable, but ... "

"This other man," said Mireille. "What's his name."

"Maxim."

"So, Maxim. He doesn't quite fit in," said Mireille, "with the bourgeoisie, *oui*?"

"Yes. Right."

"But not with your *apaches*, either. He is, what? *L'étranger*?"

"Not entirely. Maxim knew Nick before, when they were both young, on the streets of Paris," said Cavendish, "They went separate ways. Nick found his place among the apaches. Maxim finished school, got a job, got married. But the marriage didn't last and he couldn't settle down. He felt restless, left out. Wherever he goes, whoever he knows, he doesn't quite belong."

"And he doesn't know why?"

Cavendish smiled and nodded. "Maybe not. Maybe that's his problem."

"Hm. *Peut-être*, this is why he makes this *déviation* in his life with the *chanteuse*, Fifine and her *apaches*?"

Cavendish ate a little duck and reflected.

"Maxim, he's lonely, *oui?*" said Mireille.

"Definitely."

"Please, tell me more about him."

Cavendish paused for a moment. He said, "I was thinking the other day. He's a little like the man who shot Liberty Valance."

"*Liberté Valance?*" Her pronunciation made the name sound romantic. Cavendish smiled.

"There's an American movie," he said, "about a young lawyer—an idealist—who comes to a little cow town in the old West."

"Cowboys and *apaches*?" asked Mireille, grinning.

"No. Well, in this story, there are cowboys but no Apaches. No Indians at all. And the hero, the lawyer, is a peaceful man. He ends up being forced into a gunfight with Liberty Valance, who's the baddest gunslinger in the whole territory."

"*Liberté Valance*. He's the *apache*."

"Exactly," said Cavendish.

"So, he's dangerous. He's cruel. He wins the fight?"

Cavendish raised an eyebrow. "Well," he said, "that's a little complicated. But my character in my story, y'see, Maxim, he's like the lawyer in the movie. He blunders into this dark world, where he doesn't belong. He could be killed any minute, and he's totally ill-equipped to deal with it, but there's a woman. He can't stay away from her. But the longer he stays, the greater the danger."

"From *Liberté Valance*."

"Yes, but in my story, my Liberty Valance is Nicolas. Nick."

"So, Maxim. He should leave. Go away."

"Oh, but he can't," Cavendish said. "He loves Fifine, truly, deeply, madly. Fifine's in danger, too, from Nick. Maxim wants to rescue her."

Mireille tilted her face, fetchingly. "*Oui*, but she's there. She stays, with the other one, *l'apache*. Does she want to be rescued?"

Cavendish struck the table softly with a fist. "Exactly," he said. "What does a woman want?"

They focused for a while on their food, allowing the voices of patrons and the shouting of waiters to wash over them.

"Fifine," said Mireille. "Does she love him?"

"Nick? Well, she's his woman."

"No, no," replied Mireille sharply. "Does she love Maxim?"

"Oh ... no. Not yet. Not as far as I've written."

"But you know what will happen. No?"

Cavendish bobbed his head. "Well, yeah. I guess I have to. It's my story."

"*Oui*. So, *will* she love him?"

Cavendish sank a little in his chair. "Hm. That's a good question," he said. "I think, at some point, she has to love Maxim. His whole project is to win her over, to somehow spirit her away from Nick, without getting beaten to death by Nick's gang. He wants to rescue her from the gutter, before it's too late. But she has to be willing."

Mireille smiled knowingly. "To be willing," she said, "she must love him,"

"Yes," Cavendish agreed.

"More than she loves her Nicky," Mireille added.

Cavendish nodded.

Mireille nibbled a broccoli floret daintily. She said, "And you don't know if she will."

"No. Not yet," Cavendish admitted.

Mireille brightened. "*Peut-être*, you do know, Cavendish. But you will not tell me. Not yet."

Cavendish smiled. "*Peut-être*."

That night, Cavendish volunteered to accompany Mireille all the way back to Marcadet-Poissoniers on the Métro. But she dismissed him with chaste kisses on each cheek and sent him back to his keyboard. The fragrance of her hair stayed with him all the way home and clouded his brain.

All through the evening, they had spoken not a word about Serge, nor did Mireille suggest that she saw the slightest similarity between herself and the beautiful, tragic Fifine. Cavendish considered this with growing unease.

CHAPTER 19

Les Noctambules

A *pache Dance*
   by Raymond Cavendish
   (From Chapter 5)

... Weary and chilled, her clothes damp from the icy rain, Fifine climbed down broken steps and slipped into the broom closet that served both as her dressing room and, often, her only safe dwelling.

Les Noctambules occupied a subcellar beneath a cellar, on the wrong side of Montmartre. Its burly proprietor, François La Combe, known by all his patrons as "Le Sanglier"— "The Boar"—would have been flattering his domain if he had called it a dump. Scarred oak pillars, many showing signs of rot, all of them etched by knives with the names of dead drinkers, held up a ceiling that was too low and weighed down treacherously by a hill that would someday bury the joint, crushing the Boar and all his customers like termites. The ceiling timbers, spaced unevenly and sagging ominously here and there, were blackened by decades of smoke and halitosis. The floor was gapped and splintered, with a coating of sawdust that was veined with filth and dense with the flattened butts of a thousand fags. The tables were bare and ravaged, their legs uneven. Some had rickety chairs, other were flanked by upturned boxes or stumps of wood that La Combe, by and by, would split into firewood for the infernal potbelly that guttered and smoldered near the bar, adding to the poisonous fug that inexorably inked the lungs of Les Noctambules' wretched regulars.

Among them was Maxim, whose domain was a table against the wall, between two decaying pillars, where he could see the stage and behold Fifine's profile as she sang her tragic songs. He was almost safe here. No one could creep up behind him. Anyone who came at him with a knife could be seen, emerging from gray shadow, in time for Maxim, perhaps, to deflect the blade and suffer a less than fatal wound.

The Boar had given up on hiring women to serve his degenerate clientele. The last of them, a cadaverous cokie named Paulette, had been found dead, naked and raped excessively, against the wall of the St.-Vincent cemetery. Since then, La Combe had hired, at a wage twice what he had paid Paulette, a series of aged clochards, cripples and ex-convicts. The latest of these, a "reformed" burglar named Valentin, had forsaken his chosen trade after shattering his shoulder in a fall from a third-story window. In that incident, he had awakened the apartment's owner by tripping over a sleeping dog.

Valentin slid furtively toward Maxim's table, a brimming monsieur of cheap whiskey and water on his tray. Shakily, he set the drink in front of Maxim and snatched away an empty glass.

"Shouldn't be here," he whispered. "Nicky said."

Maxim scowled. "Where else?" he asked.

Valentin's crooked smile formed a crack in his thicket of gray whiskers. "Anywhere but here, mon ami. He don't want you even lookin' at his Fifi."

"Only thing on earth," muttered Maxim as he put the rim of the glass to his lips, "worth looking at."

"You'll die for that," replied Valentin, turning away.

"What else," said Maxim, mostly to himself, "to live for?"

It was almost time for Fifine's first set. Her only accompaniment was a piano whose black keys had long since gone silent. Her "pianist," Gaspard, had been expelled from one of the better brothels on the Île de la Cité for getting playfully drunk and trying to play

Chopin. The Boar paid Gaspard in alcohol and let him sleep in a roach-crawling cubbyhole that once served as a kitchen. Gaspard could carry the tunes that Fifine sang nightly but needed at least a half-liter of brandy before his fingers stopped trembling.

Maxim watched as Gaspard crept onto the tiny stage, bracing himself on the piano stool and setting a glass of brown fluid onto several right-hand keys that he had long ago ceased to use. Gaspard emptied the glass in a convulsive gulp and sat, shivering, as Valentin appeared and set down a fresh drink. After killing it, Gaspard was visibly steadier. A third drink came, Gaspard drank it and, after a moment, began noodling on the keys. The sound of the piano drew Fifine from the shadows. She was dressed in a simple dark shift, cinched at the waist with a crimson scarf and cut to suggest, almost surreptitiously, the shallow cleft between her breasts. She paused to kiss Gaspard's scalp, almost bald but for a wispy ring of white hair. They spoke quietly for a moment before Gaspard began to play and Fifine, in a voice timid and almost inaudible, began to sing one of her melodies of heartsick lament.

She had finished several songs, her voice stronger and richer with each one, when Nick strode into the room, stopping before the stage, staring at Fifine 'til she acknowledged him with a meek nod.

Valentin was quick to brush off Nick's ringside table and set down a drink. But Nick didn't sit. He dropped his hat on the table. Glowering malignantly, he scanned the room. Maxim shrank where he sat, dropping his chin but peering past his eyebrows, ready to bolt.

Nick's gaze passed over Maxim and fell elsewhere. Leaning by the bar, talking under his breath to the Boar, was a lean apache, whose usual hangout was a bar near place Blanche. He was known as "Legs," for his slender, high-waisted figure. His appearance was a deception. His lack of bulk was balanced by a lissom quickness that befuddled his opponents and opened them to blows that were surgical in their accuracy and bloody in their result. In the tightest of spaces, Legs could elude the fists and weapons of a much stronger fighter. He would wear a foe to exhaustion, battering and dazing him with a relentless flurry of slaps, pokes and well-aimed jabs. He was like a flock of crows bedeviling an eagle.

As Gaspard played and Fifine warbled, Nick turned toward Legs. He jerked his head toward the door, issuing an unmistakable order. Legs smirked and shook his head. He swallowed his drink and set the glass sharply on the bar, signaling the Boar for a refill.

As soon as the Boar had poured, Nick was at the bar. He swept the glass away, splashing its contents onto Legs. The thick glass bounced on the floor and settled in a clump of gooey sawdust. Speaking now, Nick ordered Legs to leave, to go back where he belonged. Legs, brushing the spilled hooch from his vest, said softly—but heard by everyone because the music had stopped— that he belonged anywhere he chose to go.

Legs easily eluded Nick's first sudden roundhouse punch, stepping back and tilting his head. He countered with a blow that stung Nick's cheek and triggered a roar of spluttery rage. As the fight progressed, Legs frustrated Nick, evading him like an ice skater and peppering him with lightning punches as he glided among the tables and ducked behind pillars.

On the stage, Fifine held her hand over her mouth, her eyes wide, her body taut. Maxim, frozen in his corner, watched with frightened fascination as Nick lumbered after Legs, took every blow like a bull absorbing the pricks of the picadors. Maxim knew—every drunk, lout and apache who frequented Les Noctambules knew this—that Nick's advantage was that his fury never flagged and his stamina was boundless.

After ten minutes, Nick's florid face was blotched and blood-streaked. In the ill-heated cellar, he was shiny with sweat. Looking cool and imperturbable, Legs stood in the middle of the floor, bouncing on his toes. Though surrounded by Nick's confederates and flunkies, none dared to touch Legs. He was Nick's quarry. Anyone who interfered was next on the menu.

Nick drew his knife, the narrow-bladed tool that a fishmonger would use to fillet a salmon from tail to gills in a single stroke. Legs, unfazed, smiled at Nick's resort to the knife. Others, their eyes white in the shadows surrounding the combatants, murmured ominously. They had all seen what Nick could do with an edged weapon.

Moving more quickly than he had since the moment he had picked the fight, Nick lunged at Legs' chest. Dismayed for the first time, Legs eluded the razor edge by a hair. Nick's second thrust, aimed at a hand Legs had carelessly exposed, plunged the blade two inches deep into a tabletop.

As Nick wrenched the knife free, his opponent picked up a table leg. Stepping forward, he swung the wooden bludgeon as mightily as he could muster, cracking Nick across his skull.

Nick didn't move. Nick didn't shake off the blow or regroup. His head bone, everyone knew, was cast iron. They also knew that Legs, as he delivered what he hoped was a coup de grâce, had gotten too close to Nick's terrible fists. One strike, to Legs' chest, staggered him. A second blow, to the left side of his face, shattered a cheekbone and sent him stumbling uncontrollably until his back crashed against the edge of the bar.

"Your little waltz is over, motherfuck," growled Nick as he closed in. Legs clung to the bar, his elbows holding him up, his misplaced mouth searching for air. It never came. Nick's blade swept below Legs' face. On his throat, a thin red smile suddenly appeared. It lasted barely a few seconds before it overflowed, blood pouring down his neck and into his shirt. Legs' elbows lost their hold and he slid to the filthy floor of the Sanglier's bar.

Nick wiped the knife on the Boar's bar rag and straddled Legs' limp form, releasing a lion's roar.

"Aw, shit," said the Boar.

Nick turned, peering through the smoke to see Fifine, who had fled the stage in terror and ended up clutching the first body that could fold her close and give her shelter. The body turned out to be Maxim.

Nick raised the knife again and took a step toward Maxim.

"Shit," said the Boar again.

Before Nick could close in, Fifine detached herself, as though soiled, from Maxim. Maxim stumbled backward. Fifine rushed to

Nick, evading the knife and wrapping herself around his waist.

"Oh, Nicky, I was so afraid," she said. "Thank God you're safe. He was hurting you, my darling."

"Nothing hurts me," growled Nick.

"Kiss me, kiss me!"

Nick had not taken his eyes off Maxim. But as Fifine's fingers caressed his cheeks, gently explored the cuts there and drew him downward, he looked finally at Fifine's tearful, upturned face.

Given the opening, the Boar—who drew the line at one fatality per night—signaled Valentin, who grabbed Maxim by the arm and dragged him toward the back stairwell. Bewildered by Fifine's sudden embrace and then her flight to Nick's arms, Maxim followed Valentin in numb obedience.

The February chill—as Valentin shoved him him into the night and said, "Stay away, asshole!"—pierced Maxim to the marrow ...

MARCH

les éditeurs

CHAPTER 20

Les Editeurs

Cavendish was leaning against the pedestal of Georges Danton's statue when Mireille emerged from the Métro station at Odéon. He knew that she always walked to work from Odéon, window-shopping along blvd. St.-Germain. He intercepted her, took her by the arm and led her to Les Editeurs, a café-bistro whose picture window overlooks a luxuriant paulownia tree standing sentry on the carrefour de l'Odéon. They pushed through the foyer's heavy curtains, hung as defense against winter, and found a table toward the rear, on a slightly elevated mezzanine.

The café, named for the publishers who allegedly lunch there, has the look of a library. Its walls are bookcases. At one end, an immense clock, five feet in diameter, looms over the tables beneath. Chairs on the floor level are shells upholstered in crimson leather. The kitchen creates its own *croissants* which, at opening, still warm from the oven, glisten with butter. When he was awake early in the morning, either sleepless all night or thrown into wakefulness by nightmare, Cavendish would stagger the six-odd blocks from rue de la Harpe to save his sanity at Les Editeurs with *pain au chocolat* and *café crème*. There were also days when he went whole hog and ordered orange juice.

Prodded by Cavendish, Mireille reluctantly plumped down across the table and glared at him.

"Brute!" she said.

Cavendish laughed. "I thought you liked it rough."

Mireille exhaled explosively and began to get up. Cavendish stopped her and, more gently, guided her back down.

"No. I'm sorry. Please. I have to talk to you."

Mireille looked around warily.

"He follows me," she said. "I never know."

"Just a few minutes," said Cavendish. "I need help."

"Help? With what?"

"This woman."

A dozen impenetrable emotions flashed across Mireille's face. "You have a woman?" she gasped.

Cavendish shook his head. "No, it's not—"

A waiter appeared, looking as though he'd like to hurry away as quickly as possible. Cavendish was never sure of his welcome at Les Editeurs. One waitress doted on him. Another treated him like a *clochard* who had spent the night in the horse barns at Sully. Mireille asked for coffee, Cavendish a glass of *vin chaud*.

"It's ... she's in my book." Cavendish translated the title. "*La Danse Apache.*"

Mireille relaxed. "Fifine, *je sais*," she remembered. "What does a woman want?"

Cavendish leaned close, avoiding Mireille's eyes, almost talking to himself. He said, "Okay, here's my problem, There's this woman, young and beautiful—"

"Young, *oui,* I know," Mireille broke in. "But how young?"

Cavendish looked up, surprised. "Oh, I hadn't ... let's see. Not thirty. Not a girl, though. Twenties."

Cavendish made a mental note to suggest, early in his manuscript, Fifine's approximate age. Why did he leave that out? Did it matter? But it must matter, because Mireille had asked.

"I'll fix that," he said, mainly to himself.

Mireille nodded. Cavendish muddled on. "She's poor. She left home very young. A terrible home, a hovel. Her mother's an addict, she's raped by a stepfather, rats, filth, cold wind blowing through the walls. I haven't written her history yet, but it's in my head. When we meet her, she's singing at Les Noctambules."

Mireille smiled at this. "The sleepwalkers?"

"There was actually a club with that name," said Cavendish. "I found it in a book."

"Yes, I believe that. In Clichy?"

"No, Montmartre. The back slope. The wild side."

"Oui, bien sûr."

"So," said Cavendish. "We have a scene at Les Noctambules, a dark, dirty cellar. Fifine is the singer. She's the lover of Nick, the chief of the apaches."

"I remember," said Mireille. "But there's another, who loves her."

"Yes, Maxim."

Mireille nodded. "Yes, yes," she said, urging Cavendish on.

The waiter arrived, delivering the coffee and wine, retreating briskly.

"Thing is, I don't understand Fifine," said Cavendish. "Men I can write. I know how men think, and react. How they feel. How they explode. But here's this woman. I mean, I know her. She's on my mind all the time. But I can't put my finger on her reasons for … Why does she … "

Mireille lowered her chin, staring, waiting.

"He beats her. He terrorizes her. In one scene, he's at her throat, pressing her against the window, choking her, threatening."

Mireille nodded. "But he can also be gentle, loving," said Mireille. "Exciting. A wonderful lover. He's full of surprises, *oui*?"

Cavendish nodded. "Of course, yeah. I know there are

couples who live like that. But I can't figure her out. Is it worth it? To her? The pain and the fear. He could kill—"

"Oh!" said Mireille, looking out the window. *"Merde!"*

"What is it?"

"He's there! I saw him pass."

"Serge?"

"Oui."

"Jesus Christ."

"You must," began Mireille.

"Hide again?"

"Upstairs, quickly."

"I'm getting fucking tired of this."

"Oh, please!" Mireille's was plaintive, irresistible.

"Did he see us?"

"No, but ... "

Cavendish was already on his feet. Mireille was posed like the Virgin beneath the Cross, holding Cavendish's hand in both of hers, her dark eyes imploring.

"Okay, I'll hide again. But this is the last time. Mireille, I'm only your friend. Not—"

"I know," said Mireille. "Please, hurry. He'll come back. He was waiting. He's looking for me."

"All right." Cavendish detached himself and turned toward the steps. A staircase to the rest rooms was a few feet away.

Mireille stopped him by saying Fifine's name.

Cavendish paused.

Mireille said, "You can't save her, Cavendish. She's mad. *Une femme folle!"*

"Which means what? That I'm crazy to make her up?"

"You couldn't help it, Cavendish. She's in you."

Cavendish turned and went, climbing the staircase 'til it curved. Then he waited, watching for Serge, wondering about the madwoman inside him. After a moment, Serge burst through the doorway curtains, striking a pose like a pirate on the quarterdeck.

Cavendish heard Mireille call out to Serge. He saw her, the tension receding from his body. He disappeared from Cavendish's view. After a moment, Cavendish slunk back down and slipped into the street, turning right so that Mireille's dangerous lover wouldn't spot him through the window.

"Chicken," he said to himself.

CHAPTER 21

La Coccinelle

Their train from Périgueux had arrived at Montparnasse at 5:30. Via the Métro, they had lugged their bags to rue du Bac. They had barely eaten all day. Normally, they would have called ahead, made a reservation somewhere and dined around eight p.m. But they were both famished.

Mie had read about a bistro called La Coccinelle on rue St.-Dominique that was getting raves for its cheap, but excellent *prix fixe* menu—three courses for a mere 21 euros. After a twenty-minute stroll, they arrived there. It was before 7:30, unfashionably early for dinner in Paris. But they were famished.

Steve and Mie were neatly dressed and relatively clean. They stepped into the reception area, a bar on their right. La Coccinnelle proved spacious, with perhaps forty tables on the ground floor and a dozen more arrayed on a gallery above. A wainscoted barrier separated the bistro's dining room from a corridor, on the far left, leading to the kitchen. A staircase at the back accessed the gallery, which was supported by steel pillars, painted rusty red. The floors were dark polished oak. The walls were a soft gold, adorned here and there with artful variations of the common ladybug (*coccinella septempunctata*), the restaurant's namesake. Each table wore a white tablecloth and a bud vase holding a single flower. The chairs were the functional bentwood frames common to Paris bistros.

"Nice place," said Steve.

They took off their coats and scarves and hung them on a rack near the bar.

La Coccinelle was empty, save for an elderly couple seated at a far table, beneath the gallery. Each was sipping a bright green aperitif, a drink Steve had often seen in Paris, but had never dared to order. He didn't know what it was called and he was pretty sure that tasting one would make him wince.

A trim, spidery waiter in a black waistcoat, black pants, black bow tie and blindingly bleached shirt bustled toward Steve and Mie, squinting dubiously.

"*Bonsoir,*" he murmured unconvincingly.

Steve knew how to say good evening in French. He even knew how to navigate to a table and order most of his meal in French. But he was tired from the journey, so he spoke English, forcing the waiter to respond in kind. "Hi," he said.

The waiter's squint deepened. In French, Mie told him that she and Steve would like a table, for dinner.

The waiter straightened, lifted his chin and aimed down his nose at Steve. In English, but pronouncing the last word in French, he asked, "Do you have a *réservation*?"

Steve bobbed and shuffled. "No, actually. We just got into Paris on the train, and—"

"*Oh, m'sieur. Je suis desolé. Nous sommes complét.*"

Steve was puzzled. Mie bristled. "*Complét?*" she replied. "How could you be full. There's nobody here. It's empty."

"Ah, *oui*, madame," said the waiter, rising to his full, but unimposing height. "*Mais—*"

"Oh, come on," Mie pressed. "You must have something. This place is huge."

The waiter sighed. He turned. He cast his gaze over the pristine sea of white tablecloths. He appeared to be peering through a vast throng of invisible diners.

"Ah, peut-être." He turned to Steve, avoiding Mie's eyes. "Come with me."

Rather than leading Steve and Mie into the main room, the waiter veered to the left, to the corridor behind the wall. Following him, they arrived at a small round two-top. One chair was adjacent to the kitchen doors, the other several feet forward from another door that bore the legend, "Toilettes." The waiter politely held one chair for Mie and directed Steve toward the chair that backed up to the W.C. The table had no cloth. Through a hole in the center of the table, a pillar connected the floor to the gallery above.

Nonplussed for a moment, Steve and Mie both, obediently, sat. The waiter dropped menus in front of them and toddled away. Rather than study the bill of fare, Steve stared at the pillar. It was painted a rusty red to match the others. Slowly, as Mie watched, Steve's face darkened. She waited. It came.

"Just a fucking minute!"

Steve stood.

"C'mon. We're outa here."

As he stood, his chair tipped back, clattering on the concrete floor. Mie stood more demurely, but the fire in her eyes mirrored Steve's. Steve punctuated his decision to blow this pop stand by tossing a menu back over his shoulder. It hit the toilet door. He began to storm out of La Coccinelle. Mie, on his arm, joined righteously in tow.

The rumble of Steve's discontent, in the empty restaurant, had had no discernible effect on the waiter who had greeted them. He was far away, hovering solicitously over the aged couple with the green drinks. Steve's commotion caught the attention, however, of another man, wearing a black suit jacket over his waistcoat. Moving swiftly from a vantage point behind the bar, he intercepted Steve and Mie just short of the coatrack.

Steve skidded to a halt. "Excuse me," he growled. "We're leaving."

"But, *m'sieur!*"

The interloper was medium height, with shiny black hair and wire-rimmed glasses. His face was shaven to a baby's-ass smoothness except for a small black, mustache, meticulously trimmed and speckled with gray. His eyes were wide. He looked both alarmed and tentatively sympathetic.

Steve began to sputter. Mie intervened, pointing to the tiny table—speared by a pillar—situated between the swinging kitchen doors and the shithouse. Having learned the American vernacular as an exchange student in Michigan, Mie was fluent in her use of the term "shithouse."

Seeming to understand, the interloper wrinkled his brow in a display of distress. He explained that he was the *maître d'hôtel* and that his colleague had made a *petit erreur,* for which he, the *maître d',* was heartsick and inconsolable.

"Oh yeah?" snapped Steve.

"*M'sieur,* please," said the *maître d',* wringing his hands. "Wait at the bar. Here. Perhaps a glass of wine? There is no charge."

"Oh," said Steve, placated by free alcohol.

"That would be nice," added Mie. *"Merci, m'sieur."*

"Excuse me for a moment," said the *maitre d',* who then dashed over to the waiter and engaged in an animated dialog. Meanwhile, a heavyset bartender, in waistcoat and bow tie, produced two glasses and poured a Chablis that caused Mie to roll her eyes and smile.

"Whoa. This is nice."

"It better be," Steve snarled.

While they sipped at the bar, they watched the *maître d',* who was evidently scolding the waiter. The waiter, clutching an empty tray, leaned toward the *maître d',* so close that their noses almost touched, speaking through clenched teeth and white lips.

"They're both talking at the same time," noted Steve.

"I can't tell who's winning," sad Mie. "You think the waiter'll get fired?"

Steve snorted sarcastically. "Are you kidding? He's the essential Paris waiter. If life was fair, he should've been a professor at the Sorbonne, a chef at Taillevent or a fucking senator. Instead, he's waiting on tables, catering to tourists and getting reamed out by a restaurant host. He's been screwed by the world. His only purpose in life is revenge."

Mie nodded. "I think we should leave, actually. If that guy's our waiter, he's gonna spill something all over us."

"Something really hot."

"But let's finish our wine first."

"You know where we could go," Steve began. He changed his thought.

"Uh oh. Here he comes."

The *maître d'*, after an apparent stalemate with the surly waiter, had disengaged. He was mincing hurriedly toward Steve and Mie.

"Let me show you to your table."

Steve and Mie hesitated. The *maître d'* read their minds. He waved a hand and bent his head toward the waiter, who stood adamantine in the middle of the still empty restaurant, his head high, his feet together, his tray tucked into his armpit.

"*Oh, m'sieur et madame, no.* Hippolyte—him, no, he won't be serving you."

"Oh, well then."

As though on cue, a waitress, dressed identically to the dread Hippolyte, emerged from behind the bar, adjusting her little bow tie. She was short, with clipped brown hair, broad hips and a round face that suggested jollity. The *maître d'* greeted her late arrival with a mixture of disapproval and relief.

"Ah, Giselle," he said. The *maître d'* took Giselle aside and whispered extensively into her ear. Giselle nodded busily, smiling once at Steve.

Suddenly, the *maître d'* broke up the conference and swept an arm toward the dining room. *"M'sieuretdame,"* he said in the jumble of syllables that formed polite address toward a mixed couple or couples in France, "please, follow me."

Their table turned out to be in the rear left of the room, nicely situated for people watching, which was possible when the bistro began to fill a half-hour later. Eventually, three-quarters of the tables were peopled, although Steve and Mie could not determine whether every party had called for a *resérvation*. The pillar-speared two-top by the john remained empty. Giselle proved an able and genial *serveur*. Steve and Mie happily consumed a repast of herring with potatoes, sautéed *cèpes, coq au vin, filet de cabillaud* and a whipped-cream-layered *millefeuilles* pastry for dessert, along with a bottle of Moulin-à-Vent.

After they had been re-seated and Giselle had opened the wine, Steve said, "I was thinking, before the boss so rudely interrupted us, that we could've gone back to Le Petit St.-Benoit. They'd never hassle us over a goddamn reservation."

Mie clinked Steve's glass. "True. But we're here now."

"But we should go back," said Steve. "I wonder if that waitress is still there."

"Princess Anna," said Mie, smiling wryly.

Steve scratched behind an ear. "Y'know, I think the real story of those people—the waitress, the sad guy and that other one—"

"You mean, the good-looking stud who showed up, and then the sad guy hid in the toilet."

"Right. Yeah, that's like a triangle. The girl, her handsome, jealous boyfriend and Jack Lemmon, the sweet, harmless confidant who never gets the girl."

"Wait," said Mie. "You're not making up a whole new story about these total strangers, are you?"

"Oh no," said Steve. "I wouldn't do that now. These people are interesting in real life. There's something going on, a lot more interesting than some dumb yarn about princess Anna and Olga and Sherman Shaw, private dick."

Mie nodded, then looked up as Giselle delivered the *entrées*. She smiled at the waitress, who cocked her head and grinned back. *"Bon ap!"*

"But," said Mie, dipping fork into mushrooms, "we'll never see any of them again."

"Maybe, maybe not. If we go back to the Petit St.-Benoit," said Steve, "she'll probably be there. That's her job. Wait-people in France spend their whole life in the same joint."

"Some do," said Mie. "But princess Anna? I think she'll move on. Maybe she's gone already."

"To someplace better, nicer, fancier?"

Mie thought this over, remembering the woman, her dark, knowing eyes and the fear that flashed in those eyes when the handsome, brutish boyfriend showed up.

"Or worse," said Mie.

Steve held up a forkful of tangy, butter-dripping *hareng*. "I don't understand why you can't get this in an American restaurant."

CHAPTER 22

Les Noctambules

Apache Dance
    by Raymond Cavendish
    (From Chapter 8)

    ... When Fifine was on stage, singing in her brittle soprano about betrayal and heartache, Maxim could not look away. Her voice was his narcotic. She flooded his senses and blinded him to the squalor and clamor of Les Noctambules. Whenever she slipped offstage, often collapsing at a ringside table with a cigarette and a glass of vermouth, Maxim broke from his trance and, anxiously, scanned the room for Nicolas.

    Since Nick had murdered Legs, a crime of which the police were either unaware or simply didn't care, Maxim knew he was crazy to return here. His persistence derived not so much from courage but from an acquaintance that went back to childhood. He had studied Nick. He knew his moods. Nick could explode inexplicably into a rage that sent him casting about wildly for an enemy to destroy. Maxim knew that Nick was jealous of him and that Nick's jealousy was a ticking bomb. But Maxim also understood that Nick's deadly fits were a sometime thing. Somewhere in the depths of Nick's psyche was the memory that he and Maxim had been schoolboys together, one of them quiet and attentive, the other a hellion who terrified his teachers. More than once, Maxim had been lost in one of

Fifine's torchy laments, oblivious to everything but her voice, when Nick suddenly dropped into the chair opposite, banging a bottle on the table, filling two smudgy glasses and saying, "Here, drink with me, pencil-neck. How're ya doin'?"

Nicolas knew—Maxim knew—that Maxim had no chance, no hope, no dream that Fifine would love the meek and moony clerk who sat in the shadows, listening and yearning, drinking himself to sleep before every Paris dawn. Nick could afford to curb his jealousy. He could afford to tease Fifine's lovestruck groupie and call him "pencil-neck" He could retreat for a moment from the war in the streets and hang out with the only harmless person in the room.

Maxim's mortal risk was that Nick's geniality would dissipate in a blink. He could turn from his place at the bar, spot Maxim in the corner and see, through red-rimmed eyes, a rival who hungered and plotted to possess his woman. He could cross the room in three strides, drawing his blade, roaring in bestial fury and descending on Maxim like the three-headed guardian of Hell.

Since Legs' death, Maxim had taken the precaution of retreating to a table beneath a staircase that ascended through a lightless, suffocating tunnel. This corner afforded the only possible quick escape from a sudden attack by Nick. Maxim positioned his chair so that he could see Fifine when she approached the apron of her cramped stage. When she stepped back, she was gone from sight, so that Maxim could close his eyes and melt into a blackness where only the sound of the song could penetrate.

At two a.m. on a night so cold that the draft down the staircase blew across his table and made his fingers hurt, Fifine's voice began. Maxim awoke from a doze. Fifine sang of a woman whose lover had died somewhere in a war. She was reading a letter she had received a month after learning of her darling's death. Without reason to go on living, she was ready to die herself.

The song did not finish.

Suddenly, with a shocking, aborted scream, Fifine went silent. Maxim sat up straight, instantly vigilant. Peering through smoke and shadow, he looked to the stage. Nick stood there, clutching Fifine by the throat, his eyes ablaze with drink and lust. Fifine, her toes barely touching the floor, stared into Nick's face. Her hands were like talons gripping Nick's arms, preventing him from strangling her.

"What is this shit?" Nick growled. He turned his head toward the piano and glared at Gaspard. "Stop playing that."

Gaspard, who had already stopped, nodded diffidently. He had, that night, a fellow accompanist, a mouth harpist known on the street as Deminote. Both musicians remained frozen in silent attention, ready to escape. Nick let go of Fifine so violently that she sank to the floor, her small black skirt askew, her legs crumpled beneath her.

"God damn you, Nick!" shouted the Boar as Nick rampaged through the room, shoving chairs aside and toppling tables. He drove the drinkers, thieves, whores and apaches into the shadows, forced them to huddle against the bar and cower behind splintered timbers. Maxim noticed several of them fingering the hilts of knives or gripping the truncheons hung from their belts.

Suddenly tense and sober, Maxim edged toward the staircase. The floor had been cleared. Bloodshed was imminent.

Nick turned, legs wide, facing the stage. Fifine's face, behind her hair, was invisible, unreadable. But her body trembled. Tossing aside his cigarette, Nick spread his hands, palms outward, from his waist. He shouted.

"Fast! And hard!"

Gaspard looked up from the keyboard. He met Nick's gaze.

"Play it!"

Gaspard looked to Deminote. Tapping his harmonica against his sleeve, Deminote nodded.

Gaspard played hesitantly through the first eight bars of "Careless Love," when Nick roared out, "Faster! Faster! I wanna dance!"

A fresh tremor of fear rippled through Fifine's body, as Gaspard upped his tempo and Deminote joined in, turning his mouth harp into a blue-blowing clarinet. Nick was upon the girl, seizing her arm, snatching her from the stage. He flung her toward the circle of spectators, his hand sliding along her arm and catching her by the wrist. He wrenched her back brutally, until she slammed to his chest, her head snapping back, her long black mane whirling and sparkling in shafts of lantern light.

Here it was, the watchers knew. Nick's apache dance, his only flicker of joy, his moment of release from a self-destroying cycle of drink, danger and death. To dance like this was his ecstasy and Fifine's agony. He had her 'round the waist now, spinning, her legs flailing, her shoes clicking against timbers and toppled chairs. He spread his arms suddenly, letting her go as Gaspard again quickened the tempo, and she landed, on one leg, out of control, pirouetting with her momentum, about to fly into a jumble of tables and broken bottles. A legless beggar on a roller board—denizen of the bar's darkest corner—arrested her fall. With powerful arms, he stood her upright, feeling her ass as he did so, and pushed her back toward Nick ...

... who reached out, snagging her belt, tearing her chemise, white, loose, with nothing beneath. He threw her wild and spinning toward a crash into the bar, where the watchers parted. Her fingers clawing at the beer-slicked zinc, she tried to hold on, but Nick was on her again, nails digging into the flesh of her arm, then tossing her to his shoulder, releasing her to fall, her head plunging toward the floor until, an inch away, he seized her by her thighs, his face between her legs, her hair trailing in a dizzying mad, violent circle.

Gaspard was pounding the keys now, turning a bluesy ballad into a runaway train, Deminote keeping pace frantically, his eyes wide, one foot hammering the floor.

Somehow, a second later, Fifine was upright, gasping for breath, her nose almost touching Nick's. He threw her away again, this time letting go. She caught herself, sliding on the floor, raising to her toes in a pirouette that carried her into the jumble of chairs. She tightroped from chair to table to another table, slipping at last, falling into the arms of a burly apache. As though her body had *struck him with lightning, the huge man—frightened of Nick—discarded her like a soiled rag. Fifine stumbled, spinning toward Nick.*

She tumbled to the floor, its filth and sawdust soiling her legs, her skirt now torn to the waist. She slumped and bowed her head, her hair touching the ragged surface, but only for a breath. She was back in his arms, then tossed outward whirling, slammed back to his chest, and again—three times, four—her breasts bruised, her face wet with tears.

Deminote blew out a pullulating melody of blue-note sobs.

Nick held Fifine cruelly close, his groin grinding into hers, squeezing her breath from her body as he turned and glided to the music, his movement swift and sudden, his grip deathly … "Love, oh love, oh careless love, You fly through my head like wine, You've wrecked the life of a many poor girl, And you nearly spoiled this life of mine … "

Exhausted, Fifine let Nick bend her backward, his hand on her neck, her head pressed against a timber, hungry eyes all around, feasting on her flesh and sweat and fear. Nick shoved her toward the floor, then lifted her by the armpits, holding her as high as he could lift and, with delicate, steps, turning her above his head in circles, guiding her downward, slowly, steadily, straining 'til she could see the blood ready to burst from his temples, until her toes, then her knees dragged on the floor, until—at last—he let go, flinging her like a cigarette butt to be crushed by the feet of the idlers, sluts and thieves at the bar.

And he bowed. The crowd roared with adulation and applause. Gaspard, who in this danse apache had been given rare liberty to play his piano with fire and gusto, ended the song with a flourish, slamming all ten fingers down onto his battered keys and throwing his head back with a drunken grin.

Fifine, beneath a shower of spilled beer, covered her breasts and wept …

APRIL

CHAPTER 23

Le Petit St.-Benoit

Steve and Mie had not been disappointed.

"Cool. She's still here," said Steve, nodding toward the waitress.

"She's always here," replied Mie. "This is her job."

"Yeah, well, you're the one who said she might not—"

"She's beautiful, isn't she?"

"Well, I guess ... "

Mie laughed. "You stare whenever she floats by," she said. "Are you falling in love?"

"Huh? What?"

Her eyes still teasing, Mie changed the subject. "Are you having the *agneau de lait* or the fish?"

"Say what?"

"The blackboard, Steve. They have suckling lamb."

Steve changed the subject. "He's here, too. Look," said Steve. "I saw."

"That little table in the corner," said Mie, peering past Steve. "He's writing something."

"I think I'll have the lamb."

"Oh my God!"

Mie stiffened and stared past Steve, eyes wide, lips forming an "O."

"What?" Steve swung in his seat to see what was happening. He heard a chair bang against the floor.

They saw a man in a leather jacket and black jeans, looming over Cavendish.

Had they seen him before?

In the narrow spaces of Le Petit St.-Benoit, Serge's rear end pressed against the chair of a woman seated opposite Cavendish. Her chest was pinnèd against her table, her bodice impinging on her plate. Another woman, facing her trapped companion, was squeezed into the banquette, struggling ineffectually to extricate herself.

"Who *are* you, fockah!" shouted Serge in semi-English. "S'you fockin' name?"

Inextricably cornered, Cavendish sighed and strove to keep his cool. He laid a pen down beside his notebook and gingerly shifted his wineglass away from Serge, who expanded his chest and hunched his shoulders menacingly.

Cavendish craned his neck slightly forward and looked up past his eyebrows. "Serge," he said soothingly, "we meet again."

"Serge!" whispered Steve. "His name is Serge."

"Sh!"

"How do you know my name?" said Serge, this time in French.

Cavendish's French was still not good, but this much he understood.

"One finds these things out," said Cavendish, in English, still feigning calm. "I'd offer you a seat, *mon ami*, but—"

Serge took another stab at English. "What d'fock are you do here?"

Cavendish lifted his wineglass and cocked his head, managing a tense smile. "A little drink, a little dinner."

Serge clenched his fists and responded with a torrent of French that Cavendish recognized as largely profane. Serge swore with so much animation that the woman behind was pressed even further into her table. She bleated weakly, sucking air.

Finally, Mireille, who had been at the far end of the bistro, swept past Steve and Mie. She was carrying an empty tray. Swinging with all her strength, she hit Serge with the tray. For a few seconds, the air was flecked with crumbs and water droplets. Shocked, Serge swayed, first leaning into Cavendish and spilling wine, then teetering backward, mashing the unfortunate woman into her plate, which contained a filet of *cabillaud* colorfully garnished with a *sauce Provençale*. She moaned in soprano misery.

Mireille began to rage at Serge, slapping at his shoulders and face. Understanding every third or fourth word, Cavendish gradually determined that Serge's intrusion into her workplace was an offense that went beyond Mireille's threshold of tolerance. She was flushed and screaming, pounding at Serge as diners gaped. Several held their hands up defensively, expecting objects to start flying through the bistro.

The two trapped women, spattered with *sauce Provençale*, reached across the table to clutch each other's hands, whimpering and gibbering in consternation.

Mireille was still in mid-attack when, on the far side of Serge, Patricia, Mireille's co-*serveuse*, emerged from the kitchen and swooped toward Serge. She wielded a half-quart stainless-steel ladle, which she began applying to Serge's neck and shoulders while grabbing his sleeve and tugging at him, seemingly to drag him toward the exit.

Flanked and battered, Serge glared at Cavendish and issued a hurried farewell warning. "Ah see you 'gain, ah keel you, mazzafocka!"

"I think he means, 'motherfucker,'" Steve whispered.

"Hush!"

Pushed by Mireille, shouting and livid, and pulled by

Patricia, who had begun to apply the ladle to his head, Serge thumped and bumbled past patrons toward the door and, finally, into the street.

Mireille, breathing heavily, shouted several more purple French paragraphs at a retreating Serge while Patricia, dropping her weapon, rushed to the two women who had been pinned and ravaged. Mireille soon followed, wielding a damp towel. Patricia apologized profusely while clearing the table and promising new plates of food and bottles of free wine. Mireille strove to wipe most of the *sauce Provençale* off the spattered women.

"Well, well," said Mie, settling back.

"Judging by the way she swings that tray," said Steve, "that babe's no princess."

"Definitely something goin' on there," said Mie.

"I wonder," said Steve, "if we should, like, talk to the sad guy?"

Mie pondered Cavendish, who was sopping up spilled wine with his napkin.

"You really want to get involved in that?"

Steve made a sheepish face.

Mie sensed insincerity.

Ten minutes later, tranquility reigned once more. Patricia was delivering to Steve and Mie their starters, a half-dozen *escargots* for Steve and a plate of *asperges vinaigrette* for Mie. Mie watched intently as princess Anna leaned into the face of the sad guy, who looked up from his notebook. She was whispering sharply, in English. Mie strained to hear but gathered only that the maniac in the leather jacket posed an imminent and genuine threat to the sad guy's survival. The beautiful waitress was obviously making this point. Mie observed that the sad guy received the waitress' solicitude with an appreciation that suggested infatuation. She also got the impression that the sad guy was taking the crisis less seriously than was the waitress.

Mie had one other observation.

"Funny," she whispered to Steve. "The sad guy? He doesn't seem as sad as he used to be."

CHAPTER 24

Les Noctambules

A*pache Dance*
by Raymond Cavendish
(From Chapter 10)

... It was a song she sang every night. Maxim knew it so well that it lingered in his mind on his way home as the first glimmer of dawn outlined the roofscapes of Paris.

The blood on my lips
Is my man's love
The ache in my heart
Is his soul in mine
He sees my face
In his every lover
Through every bruise
I smile through tears
His every touch
Though soft, though hard
Reveals a love
He cannot deny
Confesses he's mine
Through pain, through joy
With love and hate

In life and in death
I will be his
He will be mine
In love and death
He will be mine

She sang the last line in a voice fraught and trembling with some hidden remembrance. Gaspard clanked his last careless note and reached for his cigarette. There was no applause. Fifine exhaled heavily and inched to edge of the stage, peering beyond the lights, her anxious eyes searching the shadows, scanning the soaks and slatterns.

Maxim watched her and knew. She was looking for Nick. Tonight, the chief of the bar's apache gang had not yet appeared. Absent his unpredictable nemesis, Maxim had listened rapturously to Fifine. For a while, he had even left his hidden table beneath the stairs to stand at the edge of the tiny stage, gazing up at Fifine's wide, dark, unseeing eyes as she poured out the anguished lyrics of a dozen bleak songs.

Le sang sur mes lèvres
Est l'amour de mon homme
La plaie de mon coeur
Est son âme dans la mienne...

Valentin appeared at Maxim's table, delivering a fresh libation. Maxim always ordered whiskey cut with two parts water, a mixture that enabled him to drink all night without slipping into deep sleep or delirium. Without taking his eyes off Fifine, Maxim paid for the drink. The sullen waiter snatched the coins and slouched back to the bar, muttering over the tip that Maxim had never offered. Stepping down from her stage, Fifine seemed for a moment lost, as though in a strange land that contained no fist to beat her, no claw to choke her. As though answering the call of Maxim's wishful, hungry gaze, she turned, saw her lonely devotee and took a step in his direction.

They had sat together a few times before, barely speaking, always when Nick was away, on a "job." As she approached, Maxim was freshly amazed. For all her suffering, she retained an ineffable grace, her feet not seeming to touch the floor, her eyes—though wary—alight with life. Whatever her trials, despite her indenture to the Boar and her bondage to Nick, there stirred in her form and face a defiance against utter despair.

She slipped into the chair opposite Maxim.

"You persevere, Fifine," he said. "But how?"

"Ah." She smiled weakly. "My times have been worse. They could get better."

"Worse times than this?" said Maxim. "Trapped in this sewer of a tapis-franc, singing so beautifully to an audience of the dead and dying, ground like a flower beneath the heel of that savage, Nick."

She shook her head, lowering her chin. "Don't speak of him."

Maxim sighed. "I'm glad he's not here."

"I worry," whispered Fifine, "when he's away."

"Worry? The world is terrified of him."

"The world maybe, but not les vaches. They would kill him sooner that arrest him."

Maxim almost said that such a fate would be good riddance. But his speaking against Nick always troubled Fifine. Maxim raised his hand to summon Valentin but La Combe, the proprietor, was already on his way, with a dram of his best brandy for Fifine. Although she sang for less than nothing, working off a debt that could never be repaid, she was entitled to a free drink between sets.

"Here you are, chouchou," said the Boar.

Fifine spoke formally, as a slave to her master. "Merci bien, François."

"De rien."

Maxim chose to speak boldly. "You say, Fifine, that your times have been worse. How is that possible? What happened?"

Fifine seemed to slip into reverie. As she sipped her cognac, she cast furtive glances toward Maxim, as though studying him.

"You can trust me," he said. He almost said he loved—adored,

worshipped—her, but bit his tongue, anxious that a declaration so bold would frighten her away, never to return.

"I trust no one."

"Never?"

"Once."

"Who?"

"Maman."

Maxim smiled. "Well, your mother, of course."

But the word, "mère," made Fifine flinch. Maxim said, "What did she do?"

A sigh, then, "She fell in love." Maxim didn't answer. He waited. Fifine spoke. "She called it Uncle. Mon oncle."

Maxim knew the street jargon. It drifted nightly through the fetid air of Les Noctambules. The "uncle" to which Fifine's mother had become lover and slave was opium.

Maxim had urged Fifine before to talk about her life. She had always shrunk away and fallen silent, her eyes blank, as though staring into a lightless shaft. Tonight, perhaps too tired to resist Maxim's supplications, extending him a small measure of trust, she told some of her tale.

A man, she said, a "physician," had promised Fifine's mother, Monique, a remedy for her pain. He was no doctor, simply a sensualist who peddled his poison and plied his women. Named Remy, he stayed with Monique and made her so fully consumed by the drug that, finally, he could drain no more pleasure from her limp and flaccid body. So, he turned to Fifine, young—eleven years old—fresh and firm. When first Remy raped her, on the dirt floor in the basement room where she and her mother lived, Fifine accepted that this was a woman's place in life. Although subject for more than a year to Remy's brutish desire, she refused the drug that had turned her mother into a walking ghost.

Pregnant at twelve, Fifine was too frail to carry the baby to term. It died, barely recognizable as boy or girl, on the same dirt floor where it had been conceived.

No longer able to either help Monique or tolerate Remy's

attentions, Fifine had fled, never to see her mother again. She lived a year or more in the Bois de Boulogne, hiding in the bushes, covered with nothing but rags, freezing in winter, eating scraps from rubbish piles. She earned a meager living singing, in the sweet tones of a child, near a doorway of the Café de la Paix. She would receive a sou or two from the rich and beautiful who attended the opera and then flocked to the famous café for champagne, fois gras and sparkling conversation. Fifine would stare through the windows at them until a waiter eventually burst from inside and drove her away. Inevitably, Fifine's residence in the Parisian forest caught the attention of the pimps, gangsters and wolves who patrolled the Bois. An alpha thug known only as Matraque, promising Fifine a hot meal to eat indoors, drew her into his orbit. He had earned his sinister nickname through the fame of his sledgelike fists. The mere sight of Matraque sent the hardest men in Paris turning corners and slipping into shadows.

She was used more cruelly by Matraque than ever she had been by Remy. But the monster of the Bois wearied of Fifine after a month or so. He turned her over to Mère Dubossie, the madam of a brothel in Batignolles. Mère Dubossie swiftly deemed her a "lousy lay" for her inability to feign pleasure while in pain. The madam thought of sending Fifine back to die in the woods, enslaved to Matraque. But then she discovered that Fifine could "sing like a lone canary in a wicker cage." Mère Dubossie paired Fifine with a Negro piano player named Cates and kept her crooning night after night until cholera swept through the city. Fifine caught the deadly bacterium and would have died in her tiny whorehouse room but for Cates' ministrations. Unable to sing for months, however, she became a drag on Mère Dubossie's bottom line. Fortunately for Fifine's mistress, one of her regulars was a publican, François La Combe, known to his intimates as the Boar. La Combe bought Fifine from Mère Dubossie for an amount he never revealed to the girl except to tell her she would have to recoup his investment, singing for him at Les Noctambules until her debt was paid. Fifine never learned how much she owed, nor how much larger the balance grew as the

Boar charged her for meals and for the windowless room where she was allowed to sleep on the nights she did not—or dared not— spend at Nick's flat in Belleville. If Fifine had any consolation, it was the Boar's apathy toward her as a sex object. He was content to subcontract that part of Fifine's ordeal to Nick.

By freeing her—off and on, according to his mood—from the vermin who infested the Boar's tiny closet, Nick won from Fifine a loyalty she had felt for no one but her mother. She regarded the grubby two rooms overlooking Mathilde Moreau's chicken yard as a sort of palace ...

Cavendish stood up, peering suspiciously at the last two paragraphs on his screen. He muttered to himself. " ... pouring it on too thick? Just too wretched ... too much squalor and melodrama ... ?"

Cavendish worried that he was getting carried away with Fifine's encyclopedia of hardships. He lit a cigarette and paced the short path between doorway and kitchen. Still, as gruesome as he tried to be, nothing in Cavendish's descriptions of the bygone Paris demimonde rivaled those lushly limned by Eugene Sue, who had absorbed the miseries of the most pathetic among Paris' downtrodden and had created immortal images of the enslaved orphan Fleur de Marie, the hellishness of the women's prison at Saint-Lazare, the blinded Schoolmaster locked in a watery dungeon and nibbled by rats.

" ... yeah, well, readers ate up this stuff when Sue wrote it, but today ... ?"

During what he called his Tweed Period, Cavendish had taught literature at a middling liberal-arts college in the Midwest, where most of his academic peers wrote "what they knew," neurotic tales about middle-class married men and women with kids who anguished over whether they really wanted to be middle class, married or have kids. Cavendish was a faculty oddity because he preferred stories that lifted him out of himself and transported his readers into adventures that neither he nor they would ever experience. He wrote, when the urge overtook him, about pirates and pilots, fugitives, murderers, mountain men, lion tamers and hard-hearted vamps. He wished he had been the guy who thought up Jean Valjean and Lara Croft.

Cavendish paused at the dormer that looked out on the 21st-century rooftops of Paris and tried to picture them two hundred years before. From this vantage point in the Latin Quarter, the cityscape would have looked the same (sans satellite dishes). But, back then, there existed none of the social structures that might have protected girls like Fifine from the cruelties of lawless men and the complicity of corrupt police.

He thought about the description, in Eugene Sue's *Les Mystères de Paris*, of the bleak, drafty garret on rue du Temple where Jérome Morel, too poor to feed his children, ruins his health cutting gems for the ultrawealthy. Morel's wife is bedridden on the verge of death, while his infant girl perishes from cold and hunger and his eldest daughter works meekly and hopelessly as her rapist's housekeeper.

A century after Sue, in the time of Fifine, Nick and Maxim, denizens of "the other Paris" had seen little improvement in their lives. Vast reaches of the city were the province of outcasts and predators—from the Île de la Cité to the red-light hellscapes around Montmartre and Clichy, even the fringes of the Champs Elysées where the wretched, the crippled, the discarded and forgotten lived out lives of beggary, thievery, chicanery, lunacy and perversity and died in the same state in which they had been born, on a bed of filth in a lightless hole.

Paris, the world's most beautiful city, stood guiltily on a historic foundation of boundless suffering. Cavendish stared at his keyboard and stubbed out his cigarette. He returned to the story of Fifine ...

... Maxim guessed that Fifine had endured the abuses heaped

upon her since childhood by somehow transporting herself into a sort of Neverland that existed only behind her eyes and only when the pain of reality became too great to bear.

"No," whispered Fifine, smiling enigmatically. "I know the pain. I know little of happiness, or peace. When I feel no pain, I'm … " Fifine paused to find the word she meant. "I'm adrift. That's when I'm most afraid."

Maxim could not answer, or console a woman for whom pain was her boon companion. Fifine seemed almost dreamy as she said, "When Nicky is hurting me, I close my eyes. I concentrate on the greatest pain, the place on my body that hurts the most, and I go there. If he's crushing my breast, squeezing my throat 'til I have no air and my lungs ache, or he's breaking my arm, I bring all of myself there to that pain, until only there do I feel. Only one pain, one deep, piercing pain instead of so many little aches and pricks."

Maxim sighed. Fifine had been miserable so long that, like her mother and her mother's "Uncle," she was addicted. He wondered if it was possible, if he could somehow …

He dared to ask. "If you could leave this life, would you?"

Fifine was puzzled. "Leave? How?"

"With me, with me." Maxim spoke hurriedly, pouring out his thoughts before she could interrupt, before her surprise turned to disdain. "You don't have to hurt, Fifine. You don't need Nicky. You have me. I have a place to live. I have a job. You can be safe. You can start over—"

Her reaction was neither hopeful nor contemptuous. She was simply incredulous. Fifine silenced Maxim with a laugh as soft, cold and ghastly as snow on the stone mascarons of the Pont Neuf …

MAY

La Tartine
3/23/11

CHAPTER 25
La Tartine

Recalling his earliest visits to Paris twenty years before, Cavendish remembered when La Tartine, a bar that poured almost exclusively wine from the valley of the Loire, was an all-girl oasis on the rue de Rivoli. Its *serveuses* were daughters of a gnarled grouch who occasionally roared, waved his cane recklessly and terrorized patrons. Shortly after the turn of the millennium, he finally died—freeing his daughters to sell out and flee the big city, probably to Amboise or Sancerre. New owners had since renovated, scrubbing or painting over a century's worth of grease, grime and nicotine from floors, ceilings, walls and grotty corners. But they left untouched the magnificent mahogany bar and, after messing for a while with the menu, resorted to the bistro's historic bill of Parisian bar fare—*rillettes*, cheeses, butter-smeared *tartines* of *pain de Poilâne*, simple blue-plate specials and desserts. To the trusty Loire vintages, they added a half-dozen *crus* of Beaujolais, a little Burgundy and a few thrifty Bordeaux table wines. After a brief period of turmoil and mild panic among the joint's regular drinkers, life and leisure at La Tartine had settled back into a cozy familiarity.

Cavendish had chosen La Tartine because it had a back parlor with a door that opened onto rue du Roi-de-Sicile, out which he could slip if he saw Serge roaring through the front entrance.

On a Tuesday afternoon,. Cavendish had strolled across the Seine to the Marais, for a rendezvous. Because he wasn't meeting Mireille, Cavendish had no reason to expect Serge nor to need an escape hatch into the back street. Nonetheless, he was on edge. Despite his denials, he had modeled Fifine after Mireille. Gradually, her similarity with Fifine had affected Cavendish's perceptions. His mind, more and more, conflated Mireille with his imaginary *chanteuse*. Worse, Serge and Nicolas had begun to merge. Waking in the morning, he had to spend a moment looking around, peering out his window, reminding himself as he pulled on his socks that, no, these are not Maxim's feet. He was not Maxim. Cavendish was not so needy, not so bewitched by Mireille as was Maxim by Fifine. He was not as mortally threatened by a jealous, violent, barbaric boyfriend as was his tragic imaginary cabaret canary in the lawless Parisian demimonde of a century past.

Still ...

Cavendish could not write lest he identify with his characters, transposing their loves, hates and crises into his own psyche as he crafted his narrative. At first, this mingling happened unconsciously. But one day, he would notice that he was thinking like his protagonist or groping for a solution to the problems of a heroine who existed only on his computer's hard drive. Intimacy with his characters eventually had him talking to himself in their voices, melding their fears and pleasures into his own troubles. Never before, however, had he felt so deeply this demented confusion between life and illusion. Unless he fought to suppress it, Maxim's terror of Nick joined and intensified Cavendish's fear of Serge. Several times, a powerful anxiety had swept over him. He would wake in the wee hours, bolt upright in bed, searching the darkness for the figure of Nick—Serge?—looming over his bed, a dagger poised over his heart. Or seated in a café, Cavendish felt stricken suddenly with horror, afraid to look left or right, because there beside him, he knew—he could feel it—was his jealous murderer, eyes ablaze, hands twitching. He would remember reading what André Warnod had written about the killing tools of the *apaches*, "... their hands, their big thick strangler's hands, their short-fingered hands."

His nightmares had brought Cavendish to La Tartine. Maxim's fictional fear was a fever in his real-life blood.

Early in his Paris days, Cavendish had met, and interviewed, an amiable degenerate named Felix. Curious about the back alleys and dark byways of Paris, Cavendish had frequented the strip clubs of rue St.-Denis and Pigalle. Briefly, he had an affair with one of the girls, named Clementine, whose pimp—Felix— would flash a revolver beneath his purple blazer if a customer seemed reluctant to pay. Since then, although Clementine had slipped out of his life, Cavendish had kept in touch with Felix, whom he saw and valued as a sort of underworld beau ideal, the stereotypical cheap crook. Cavendish had never imagined, however, that, beyond symbolism, Felix would ever be of any use to him.

A furtive figure stepped through the back door of La Tartine. He looked both ways, then fixed his eyes on Cavendish and smiled crookedly.

"*Ah, mon ami, l'ecrivain américain.*"

Cavendish nodded. Felix glided over and sat down.

"*Ça va?*" said Cavendish.

Felix shrugged, raised an eyebrow, cocked his head. "*Eh, ça va.* Life doesn't suck."

A waiter was johnny on the spot. Felix nodded toward Cavendish's glass, which contained a dram of Touraine red, fragrant and mild. The waiter caught the drift and departed.

"*Longtemps,*" said Cavendish, with a note that implied apology.

Felix waved this off.

They settled into a brief bout of small talk, which included news that Clementine had fallen in love with a glass factory manager from Issy. She had fled the notorious Ninth to wed and breed.

"She was a good earner for you," said Cavendish.

"Soft," said Felix. "Dreamy. I knew she wouldn't stay."

"Is she happy?"

"Happy?" said Felix with a smirk. *"C'est mariage."*

The waiter delivered Felix's glass.

He took a sip, frowned acceptingly and asked, "Why am I here, Yank?"

Cavendish paused to choose his word. Finally, "I remember ... "

Another pause, and Felix said, "Remember?"

"You used to carry ... " Cavendish lowered his voice. " ... a gun."

Felix backed away several inches. scowling. "Oh, not here," he said. "Not in the street, where *les flics* ... "

"Oh, I did didn't think you were carrying," said Cavendish. "Not in public."

Felix drank a little wine.

"But you have it?"

Felix waxed a little proud, *"Ah, oui, bien sûr!* It's safe. Beautiful, a Walther, like Bond. James Bond. PPK."

Felix was settling in, relaxing with the wine, becoming the voluble rascal Cavendish had befriended at a club near Porte St.-Denis called La Porte Jarretelle.

Cavendish slipped back to a near whisper. "I couldn't borrow it?"

"Borrow *mon bébé?*" Felix's voice rang out. "Nevair, *mon ami. Jamais!*"

Felix said this with a sly grin. He saw his straitlaced American friend going a little rogue. He enjoyed the sight.

Cavendish, meanwhile, wilted into a mixture of shame and disappointment. Felix noticed.

"*Mon ami*, you're a writer, an artist. Why do you need such a thing?"

Cavendish mumbled. "I don't really but, well ... I do. Sort of. There's this girl—no, woman."

"Ah, no! I see. A woman. *C'est clair!*"

"No, you don't understand," Cavendish replied hurriedly. "She's very nice. I wouldn't."

"No, no. *C'est très clair.* You're in love, but there's another man—"

"No, Felix, no. I'm not in love."

Felix laughed conspiratorially. "Oh no, of course not, you are not in love. Just jealous!"

"No!"

"So jealous you must shoot this man. Who is this villain?"

Cavendish sank his head. "It's not that, really."

"Ah, *oui*. Of course." Felix's tone was sarcastic.

"Really, Felix," Cavendish said. "He's violent. He beats her. I've seen."

Felix's face transformed, suddenly grim and sympathetic. "Ah, to beat a woman? No, *mon ami*. I hate that. I do not."

"I know you don't, Felix."

"You want to shoot this fucker?"

Cavendish paused to consider the thought of pumping Serge full of hot lead. "No, Felix," he said. "Scare him, you know?"

"Flash your gat?" said Felix, smiling impishly, delighted with his knowledge of movie slang.

"Yeah, I guess," said Cavendish.

Felix laid his hands flat and leaned toward Cavendish. "This I can do for you, *ami yank*. A gun to scare, not to shoot, *oui*?"

"You can do that?"

"*Ah, oui, pas de problème*," said Felix. "*Pas des balles*? No bullets?"

Cavendish considered this. He finished his wine.

"Maybe one," he said reflectively. "Just in case."

Another conspiratorial smile. "Just in case," he said. "*Je comprends*. This man, *l'autre homme*, he is *un peu dangereux*? A little dangerous."

"*Oui*," said Cavendish. "*Un peu.*"

"He beats his woman. He could beat you," said Felix. "But you shoot a bullet. At the sky, *peut-être*. He thinks, 'Whoa! This fucker means *les affaires*—the business,' *oui*?"

"*Oui*, yes, I hope."

"Okay, *ami yank*, I'll find you just what you need, A little gun, .22, .25. Small, okay?"

"Thanks, Felix."

"Hey, you need more wine!"

While they both had a second glass, they made arrangements for a rendezvous and Felix regaled Cavendish with the story of his recent three-month stretch at La Santé, the Paris prison off boulevard Arago.

"My God. Felix. You were in jail?"

"Historic jail!" said Felix proudly. "More *historique* than *la Bastille*! You know, Genet was kept there, in La Santé."

"Jean Genet? Really?"

"*Oui,* but Picasso? And Sartre. You know Jean-Paul Sartre?"

"Well, yes. Of course."

"They got M'sieur Genet sprung."

"Boing," said Cavendish.

Felix laughed.

CHAPTER 26
Les Noctambules

A pache Dance
by Raymond Cavendish
(From Chapter II)

    ... There was no beast prowling the murky corners and ravaged floor of Les Noctambules more monstrous and deadly than the one called Georges. He lurked behind chair legs and slipped between boots, hid in the ragged folds of the whores' skirts. He could see in the dark and move more quietly than the thick swirl of the brown air. He had lost an ear in a fight and one of his legs bent at an odd angle, rendering him oddly more agile moving sideways than straight ahead. His hair, in gray/black stripes, was patchy in places, but it blended into the crepuscular light at the edges of the room, making him almost invisible. It was those edges that he patrolled, in search of the rats who slunk from crevices and scurried, frightened of Georges but hungry for the crusts and spills that hit the floor, along the baseboards.

    Georges never devoured the rats he killed, but delivered them to the Boar, who sliced off, as reward, a morsel of moldy Cantal or disk of a saucisson sec. No rat long evaded the vigilance of Georges, except one who lived perhaps a charmed life, or—according to Maxim's theory—was the brainiest, cleverest rodent in all the 18th arrondissement. The rat's closest encounter with Georges had left his tail truncated and ragged at its new tip. Noting its half-tail, Maxim had begun to call the rat Demi-queue, eventually abbreviating to just Demique.

Demique's smartest insight was recognizing the loneliest and most melancholy among all the patrons in the boîte. Maxim was the rare human who could tolerate, even welcome, the company of vermin. After a period of adjustment between man and rat, Demique fell into the habit, once or twice a night, of crawling up Maxim's pants leg, perching on his leg and peeking over the tabletop at a bowl of bread.

Maxim never ate the bread. Legend says that, in Paris, it's impossible to find a bad loaf of bread. La Combe, proprietor of Les Noctambules, each day confounded that conceit by buying somewhere a half-dozen leathery baguettes—speckled with grit, rimed with mold, marbled with sawdust, spiced with the shit (or corpses) of an insect menagerie of flies, maggots, spiders, roaches, etc.—that were unfit for consumption by all but the most famished and desperate of humans. But, for an enterprising rat, the Boar's bread was a banquet. Understanding this, and feeling a natural brotherhood with Demique, Maxim had Valentin place on his table a few chunks of the establishment's wretched baguette.

Near midnight, Maxim could feel Demique sniffing at his shoes, preparatory to climbing up. Maxim scanned the room once again, to make sure Georges was not evident. Since arriving that night, Maxim had been warily watching the round table near the door. Usually, a sullen and contentious company of card players occupied the table, gambling for sous and accusing one another—sometimes coming to blows—of cheating. On this night, Nick had scattered the gamblers. He and his apaches hunkered together, whispering and drawing invisible maps on the tabletop with their fingers. This conference meant no good for someone unsuspecting somewhere in Paris, but it kept the apaches busy and so relieved everyone else, save the displaced card sharps, from the bullying of Nick and his boys.

Maxim felt Demique's claws through the cloth of his pants and, in a second, looked down to see the rat, standing on two legs, looking expectantly at the bread bowl. Maxim reached out, removed a thick slice and broke off a piece for Demique. Given his feast, Demique settled on Maxim's lap and nibbled away.

Maxim sensed movement close by. He looked up. Fifine had emerged from her hideaway, ready to sing her sad songs. But Gaspard, her piano player, was at the bar, clutching a full glass of gin and expostulating vehemently with the Boar. La Combe argued back, pointing a finger, bashing the bar. Fifine sighed, looked around and saw Maxim. She stood now, regarding him.

"Join you?" she asked.

Maxim's heart leaped.

"Oh, yes. Of course. Always."

Fifine found a chair that, miraculously, still had three legs. She settled across from Maxim. Her dress was filmy and tattered, her breasts only half-covered, her eyes like black jewels. Maxim had to remember to breathe.

Suddenly, Fifine gasped and began to stand up, poised to flee. "Look," she said, pointing.

Maxim's eyes followed her finger. "Oh," he said, "don't be ... This little fellow ... "

Demique tolerated Maxim's touch on his head (anything for another bit of bread) and peered up cautiously at Fifine.

"He's my friend," Maxim continued. "I give him a little bread. He keeps me company."

Hesitantly, Fifine returned to her chair. She watched, at first with disgust, then with a twinkle of amusement as Maxim broke bread and served the rat.

"Demique, that's his name. See the tail?" said Maxim. "He's the most intellectual creature in Les Noctambules, the only one to outsmart Georges. The only part the cat could catch was half his tail."

"Demique?" asked Fifine.

"Yes," said Maxim.

"That's funny." Fifine leaned closer, watching the rat. Demique took a perch on Maxim's sleeve, his half-tail switching back and forth as he ate.

"He trusts you,"

Fifine smiled.

This was the first time Maxim had ever seen her smile. It was beautiful enough to still his heart.

For a while, they didn't speak. Demique finished his crust of bread, twitched his whiskers, brushed his mouth and looked around.

"Oh, may I?" Fifine asked.

"Oui," said Maxim. "Gently, though."

She tore a bit of bread and, gingerly, in two fingers, offered it to Demique. The rat waved his paws cautiously, studying this unfamiliar hand but finally, too greedy to refuse, stretched and, quickly, snatched it away. Fifine smiled again, almost laughing.

"He trusts you, too," said Maxim.

She blushed and, suddenly, seemed almost embarrassed.

"I must go sing," she said, standing. She reached out and touched Maxim's hand, looking into his eyes. There was curiosity in her gaze but no hope of an answer. She bent close and whispered, "Adieu, petit Demique. Ne laissez pas Georges t'attraper."

A moment later, on the small stage, she tapped one of the piano's keys, rousing Gaspard from his argument. The piano player grumbled at the Boar and shuffled toward the stage.

As always, when she sang, her voice was like warm water poured into Maxim's soul. Was she watching him as she sang?

Maxim looked at the rat. Demique's glance said, "Impossible."

In the middle of her set, for a moment, a commotion in the back of the room drowned out the music. Nick and his apaches, rising from the table, shouting and clamoring, barged out the door, fired with some purpose that could only be guessed.

Safer, Maxim thought, not to guess...

JUNE

Le Fumoir
Sept. 22, 2006

CHAPTER 27

Le Fumoir

Steve fingered the rim of his wineglass while surveying the interior of Le Fumoir, a cocktail haven with clever food, whose windows faced the Cour Carré end of the Palais du Louvre.

"You know," Mie said, trying to break through Steve's reverie, "'Louvre' is from an old French word, *'louver,'* which meant 'stronghold.' The Louvre was built by King Philippe-August as a fortress to defend Paris from attackers entering Paris by way of the Seine."

Ignoring Mie's history lesson, Steve peered into the moody half-light of Le Fumoir and said, "I think we might be too old for this joint."

"Not me," said Mie. "Remember. You snatched me right from the cradle."

Steve ignored this, too. "I don't know. I guess it's me. Everyone here, the waitresses and bartenders, all these ... kids, eating, drinking, showing off, they're not just young. They seem to be expressing ... promoting the idea of being young, as a sort of ethos. I feel like I've walked into the middle of a Pepsi commercial."

Mie took a closer look. The wait staff, equally divided between male and female, were governed by a dress code of black and white. The men were uniformly fit and handsome, but they were only the *corps de ballet*. The waitresses were the ballerinas. They arrested the eye and held the gaze. Invariably brunette and suggestive of Asia, each wore a scoop-neck, skin-tight, long-waisted white leotard top that caressed her every curve and presented a torso, in profile, that would have plunged Rodin into his sketchbook.

"I could work here," said Mie.

"Yeah, you have the look. Thing is," said Steve, peering at the torso of the nearest waitress, "why am I thinking of Sean Young in *Blade Runner*?"

"You want to leave?"

"No, no. I like it here. I don't mind feeling old. People look at me here and they think I'm wise and crusty, maybe a little sinister."

He lifted his eyebrows in a sinister way.

"Steve, nobody's looking at you."

"Not even you, sweetie?"

"I have to," growled Mie. "And don't call me sweetie."

"Sorry."

A ballerina arrived, asking for their preferences. Steve ordered a bottle of Chateldon and the Popeye salad. Mie chose the risotto, a request that somehow drew an approving smile from the lissom *serveuse*.

"I guess she likes rice," said Mie as the waitress floated away.

Steve didn't hear this. His wineglass was frozen between tablecloth and lip. He was suddenly lost in thought.

"What?" said Mie,

Steve shook his head and sipped. He set the glass down.

"No," he said. "It's nothing. I just remembered something."

"Remembered? What?"

"Oh ... Uh, you remember the guy at the Petit St.-Benoit? You know, the sad guy?"

Mie rolled her eyes. "You mean, the dying nuclear physicist?"

"Well," Steve conceded, "he's not a nuclear physicist."

"Or Sherm Shaw, defrocked CIA agent?" said Mie, summoning up the alternative theory.

"No, forget that shit," said Steve. "I saw him."

Mie looked around. "Here?"

"No, no, no. At Galignani. The bookstore."

"The sad guy was buying books?"

"No, not him, not in person," said Steve. "I saw his book."

"He has a book?"

"Yeah, the sad guy's an author. A writer. His picture was on the back cover. I recognized him."

"The back cover of a book?"

"Yes."

"What book?"

"Wait, wait."

Steve dug into the shoulder bag he always carried.

"Here. See."

He held out a slightly battered hardcover book. A montage on the front cover showed two faces, a man and woman cunningly suggestive of Bogart and Bergman. They stood out in bold relief against a fifty-percent wash of chestnut leaves framing the fountain at place St.-Michel and the inevitable Eiffel Tower. Mie read the title aloud, "*Love and Death in the Latin Quarter,* by Raymond Cavendish."

"Yeah, Raymond Cavendish," Steve effused. "I've heard of him."

"Did you read the book?"

"I've started it. It's good," said Steve. "Y'know, it made the bestseller list. I remember."

While Mie paged through the novel, pausing to read a sentence here and there, Steve sank back into reverie.

"So, why's he so sad?" said Steve. "What happened?"

Mie looked up. "Uh oh."

Steve awoke. "What?"

"You're gonna talk to him, aren't you?" said Mie. "You're

gonna invade the poor sad guy's space."

"Um ... "

""You've already looked him up, haven't you?" asked Mie. "You already have a page full of notes, don't you?"

"Well ... "

"You have no respect for anyone's privacy, do you?"

"No, no," said Steve. "He's ... you know, a story."

"Oh my God. You know where he lives!"

Steve voice was meek. "Rue de la Harpe."

"Oh, for God's sake."

"No, really. Look," said Steve. "The book was copyrighted three years ago. By Little, Brown. Since then, nothing. No word from the publisher. No book review articles. He hasn't published an op-ed or a short story or anything. No interviews. I mean, c'mon. The guy had a bestseller. He was a hot property. They gave him a two-book contract. But he hasn't given them anything back. I mean, what the hell happened?"

"What happened?" Mie retorted. "Steve, why the hell should you care? You don't know this guy."

"No, we do," said Steve. "Sort of. I mean, we've seen him, three or four times. Jesus, that scene at the restaurant? With that other guy, the maniac in the leather jacket! ... And I've started his book. It's good. He sees Paris the way I see it."

"Really, Steve? How do you see Paris?"

This made Steve stop. "Well," he said. He paused to drink a little wine and welcome the arrival of the food.

"Okay," Steve started again, "you look at Paris through a window, clearly. It's beautiful, picturesque, photogenic."

"Uh huh," said Mie. She dug into her risotto.

"But then you look down," said Steve, "at the windowsill. The paint is peeling and the wood is chipped and gray. It's dusty and it's gritty and there are dead bugs. That's part of Paris, too. Not just the sights and the Seine and the beautiful churches. But the dust and the grit and the dead flies. This guy, Cavendish. He stirs that together. You stand in awe at

Notre Dame or Les Invalides, but then a rat runs across your shoe. Y'see?"

"That's why I don't wear open-toed shoes, Steve."

"You miss my point."

"No, I don't. I see your point."

"This guy, Ray Cavendish, has stuff to say about Paris—about life—that most people, most writers, don't even mention. He and I—"

"No, Steve, that's bullshit."

"What?" Steve tried to look hurt.

"You don't want to meet this guy so you can compare literary notes," said Mie. "You want to find out what's going on between him and the yummy waitress. And the crazy vandal in the leather jacket."

Steve suspended a forkful of salad. He cocked his head, "Maybe. A little bit. But … "

"But nothing, Steve," said Mie. "You're a voyeur. And a meddler."

Steve filled his mouth with salad and went quiet for a while. So did Mie. After a moment, a light reappeared in Steve's eye.

"Nah," he said. "You wanna know, too. You're itchin' to know what's goin' on with the sad guy and the waitress."

"No," Mie insisted unconvincingly.

"Oh yeah?" said Steve. He pointed his fork. "We hang around all these cafés and bistros. We watch people. We make up stories. I do. You do. For fun. But we're both reporters. We ask questions. We dig. We pry. We want a story. A real story. Right?"

Mie shrugged.

"We start out making up a story about the guy, the waitress, the crazy fucker in the leather jacket. It's just a story. Fiction. But then we see them again, and again. And then we find out, whoa, this guy's an author. He's got a bestseller but it's three years old and the guy is stagnant, sitting around, drinking, mooning over the waitress. This isn't just a story. It's not fiction. It's a *story*."

Mie sighed.

"You want to find out how it's gonna turn out, Mie," said Steve. "Just as much as I do."

Mie leaned forward. "Maybe I do," she said in her most dangerous voice. "But it's none of our business."

Steve backed down, an inch.

Mie pointed her spoon. "Leave the poor guy alone," she said, "or I'll use this to gouge out your eyes."

They froze that way, glaring at each other, 'til a smile curled the corner of Mie's lips.

"Okay," said Steve. "Hands off."

Mie watched Steve eat and knew he was lying. She didn't mind. She was curious about the next chapter.

CHAPTER 28

A *pache Dance*
  by Raymond Cavendish
  (From Chapter 12)

...*Stealing a pushcart was easy. Street vendors parked them overnight in the city's labyrinth of passages, cul-de-sacs and courtyards. Two of Nick's apaches had found one within a half-hour of their rendezvous at place St.-Georges and rolled it to the convergence of rue la Bruyère, rue Notre Dame de Lorette and rue Henry Monnier.*

Surrounded by four comrades and a woman named Odette, Nicolas scanned the locale. He muttered, "Good. This will work." Using tools brought by Denis, one of his crew, Nick stripped the kingpins from one of the pushcart's wheels. With a wrench and kick, the wheel would fall off.

Nick dispatched his crew to their posts and slipped into the shadow of a doorway. It was just past two a.m., late for most of Paris but still the shank of the evening in the sprawl of narrow byways that radiated around place Pigalle.

Odette, who had been for a while one of Nick's lovers, was outfitted like a slattern of the marché, a baggy dress beneath a stained apron, a moth-eaten shawl to hide the breadth and sinew of her shoulders. Odette was old for this business, but she had steel in her eyes, iron in her body and ice in her veins. Her face, for all her nearly forty years, was still arresting. When she smiled, she could light a room and disarm a mistrusting stranger.

And so, she was stationed at the borrowed cart, waiting for quarry.

Denis had been sent uphill on rue Henry Monnier, along with the hulking mec who was called Grosjean. They settled at the intersection of rues Henry Monnier and Navarin, where they could see all the way to rue Victor Massé and the spiderweb of little streets just north.

Two other apaches, Michel, nicknamed "Miko," and Stephan, had been sent down rue Laferrière to lie in wait. Miko was a plodder who took orders. Stephan, however, had talent. He was called Épée for his affinity with the long blade he tucked under his belt and for his lack of scruple for using it, in a pinch, against man or woman. Nick had told Épée, "Show it, don't swing it."

Clicking his teeth with the tip of his blade, Stephan had cocked his head and smirked.

The signal to Nick would be Denis, up the hill, lighting a cigarette. He and Grosjean fidgeted on the pavement, waiting and watching. Around three a.m., the big spenders and their tarts would begin to drift out of the cabarets and sex clubs that stretched along blvd. de Clichy from place Blanche to place Pigalle. Some of them, reluctant to retire so early in the evening, would venture south toward the all-night cafés around place de l'Opéra. Thenceforward, rue Henry Monnier was a favored route.

Twenty minutes passed on the quiet street before Denis spied the unmistakable four-eyed glare of a Peugeot 135 limousine, a gleaming land-yacht beloved of the high and mighty, as it topped the hill and headed toward rue Notre Dame de Lorette.

Denis grinned and stuck a cigarette between Grosjean's thick purple lips.

"Here we go," he said. He lit the match, fired up the cigarette and, for good measure, lit another match.

Nick caught the signal. He and Odette quickly pivoted the pushcart and lumbered it onto place, blocking rue Henry Monnier. Uphill, the Peugeot, a convertible, top up, with a melon-green body, black fenders, white tires and creamy leather inside, descended *toward Denis and Grosjean. It was twenty yards away when Denis slapped the cigarette from Grosjean's face and shoved him toward rue Navarin. Bristling with faux anger, he shouted at Grosjean. The big guy shouted back and they began a theatrical scuffle that served to discourage the car's driver from turning, toward the two obviously drunken brawlers, onto rue Navarin.*

Unaware that he was now boxed in, the driver of the Peugeot proceeded down rue Henry Monnier toward Odette and the pushcart.

As soon at the car had passed rue Navarin, Nick deftly kicked the wheel off the cart, which creaked and tilted onto its axle. The wheel spun once and settled on the pavement. Nick slipped back into hiding.

Rumbling cautiously down the ill-lit street, the Peugeot was within a few yards of Odette, in her street-vendor disguise, and the disabled pushcart when the chauffeur jerked the big limousine to a halt. For a moment, the car sat still, idling irresolutely.

Odette shouted. She waved. She half-smiled. She looked distressed.

A door opened. The driver's head emerged. He stayed half-inside the car, peering at Odette. She cried for help, pointing at the fallen wheel. A brief dialog followed. The driver had no wish to try repairing a goddamned wagon wheel. Odette countered by begging him to at least help her drag the busted cart out of the middle of the street. She claimed that then she could fetch her Uncle Hubert, who knew how to repair the wheel.

The driver seemed inclined until a voice barked from inside the car. The driver turned to speak to the occupant in the rear cabin. This went on for a moment. Odette crept toward the car. She was only a few feet from the glaring headlamps when the driver straightened, waving hands and shaking his head.

He said he was sorry. He couldn't get out of the car, not here, not at this hour. He had responsibilities. Odette, true to her imposture, flew into a rage, called him a bastard and a fucking lackey of the haute bourgeoisie, etc. This freed the driver to give her the finger, call her a slattern and a bitch, and climb back inside, slamming his door.

The car backed up a few feet and executed a loud, sharp left turn onto rue Laferrière—exactly according to Nick's plan.

As the Peugeot swung onto the narrow side street, where carts, parked jalopies and heaps of refuse left barely enough room for the big car to proceed, Nick emerged from hiding. Denis and Grosjean ran down the hill and joined Nick. Along with Odette, the three men followed the limousine.

The driver, seeing the four apaches in his rearview mirror and clearly suspicious, accelerated as much as he could. But after another thirty yards down this detour, rue Laferrière curved sharply. Beyond the curve, in the night, he could see nothing until, suddenly, Miko and Épée burst into the glow of his headlights. He slammed on the brakes. Before the chauffeur could gather his wits and plow through the attackers in front of him, Nick, Odette and the two other apaches were clawing him from the driver's seat and ripping open the doors.

A girl screamed.

The driver, a big man built for defending his passengers, fought valiantly, knocking Nick down and taking on Grosjean. While Odette clambered into the back seat to strip the young woman of her jewels and silken raiment, the other passenger, sixtyish, bald and seemingly corpulent, squeezed his way from the car. He stood outside, his face red and damp, a curl of smoke rising from his cigar, his eyes like pinholes. "Who are you? How dare you?" He said this in English. His companion, no more than nineteen years old, blonde and slim with bobbed hair and draped head-to-toe with clothing from rue de la Paix, whimpered and squealed in English as Odette methodically removed everything valuable from her person, from her pearl barrettes to her small, beautiful shoes and gauzy stockings.

After Denis struck the male passenger and knocked him away, the old man fought back, surprising Denis with a blow that staggered him. Then, forsaking his young consort, the passenger took flight, waddling downhill toward rue Notre Dame de Lorette. By this time, Nick and Grosjean had gotten the driver to the ground, where he lay in the gutter, bloody and dazed. Denis yanked Stephan by the shirt. "Come on," he said. "We can't let the fat fucker get away."

Nick looked up, anxious, as the two apaches pursued the fat man. "Don't—"

But they were already around the curve.

By the time Denis and Stephan strolled back to the car, Odette was holding the girl while Grosjean raped her against a fender. The girl was, by this time, battered and bloody-nosed, her makeup smeared, her clothes gone. Nick turned his attention from this scene and glared at Denis.

"The fat man?"

"Slit his throat."

"You killed him?"

"Not me," said Denis. "This psycho." He pointed at Épée. "With his fucking stiletto."

Grosjean paused in his activities, letting the girl slide to the pavement. "Merde!" he said, finding his pants and pulling them up. "Nicky, I thought we weren't supposed to ... "

Stephan, no regret in his attitude, held up his booty. "I got his purse. His watch. I got a ring, too, Diamonds! I had to cut off his fat fucking finger."

Nick rolled his eyes. "Where's the finger?"

Stephan looked anxious. "You wanted it?"

Nick's sudden rage darkened his face. He seized Stephan by his shirt and pulled him to his toes. "You dumb fucking asshole. Les vaches don't give a shit what we do, what we steal. But when we kill the rich people, moron, the other rich people panic. They want action, and they can pay the fucking flics more than we can pay the fucking flics."

"Ah, c'mon, Nicky. The fat fuck was askin' for it."

Nick hit Stephan hard enough to break an eardrum. Stephan crumpled to the street.

A light came on in a high window.

Denis said, "We gotta get outa here."

"Merde." Nick looked to Grosjean and nodded toward Stephan, the murderous Épée, who would have to be dealt with. But for now, Grosjean would carry him away, to a hiding place...

CHAPTER 29

Le Petit St.-Benoit

Cavendish strolled slowly toward rue Jacob. Given a gentle bum's rush by Mireille, he had left a half-bottle of wine behind at the Petit-St.-Benoit. Fearful of Serge's surveillance, Mireille had hurriedly served Cavendish his dinner—a lamb shank with a peppery sauce and boiled vegetables—and sent him away. But Cavendish was both sated and satisfied, He had accomplished his purpose.

As he was reaching for his wallet, Mireille had snatched up his check.

"No, *s'il vous plaît*, please, Cavendish," she'd implored him, "go. Please go, before—"

He silenced her with a finger on her lips. "I've decided I have to tell you this, Mireille."

Over Mireille's shoulder, Cavendish saw Patricia, the other waitress, watching. Her eyes twinkled with curiosity. In Patricia, Cavendish had an ally.

"What?" asked Mireille. "Tell me what?"

"I don't care any longer what you think, or anyone else," said Cavendish. "You can react any way you want. It doesn't matter."

Mireille, fuddled and troubled, said nothing.

"I've decided to admit this to myself," said Cavendish. "I

have to tell you. I can't go on pretending. I can't go on not saying."

"Cavendish," Mireille implored, "not saying?"

Cavendish smiled. He took her face in his hands. "That I love you."

Mireille gasped and pulled back.

Cavendish grinned. "It's a natural thing—"

"Oh, Cavendish!" Mireille's face was dark with fear. "You can't."

"Can't help it," said Cavendish. "It's like breathing. If you try to stop it, you turn blue and die."

"But you can't!"

"I know you can't," said Cavendish. "Or so you say. I don't blame you, Mireille. I'm not especially lovable. But I can love you. And I do. And I just thought you should know."

"Oh, Cavendish!"

And with that, saying no more. Cavendish had parted Mireille. He bade a conspiratorial adieu to Patricia and headed toward rue Jacob, where he intended to mosey westward, taking the air and thinking about the next chapter of *Apache Dance*.

His head was lowered, so he didn't see Serge 'til the two were literally nose-to-nose.

"Oh!" said Cavendish. He was suddenly staring into fierce, slitted eyes, listening to a low growl from Serge's throat.

It occurred to Cavendish to somehow relieve the tension. "How *you* doin'?" he asked, amiably.

No answer. He felt pressure on his chest. In Serge's fist, a knife, its blade at least six inches long, pointed toward Cavendish's chin. Cavendish immediately remembered the little gun he had bought from Felix. He was carrying it in his coat pocket, easily accessible with his right hand. He thought uneasily about James Coburn in *The Magnificent Seven*, and his deadly expertise in gun-vs.-knife showdowns.

Quickly gauging the difference between a lawless Mexican

village in 1879 and rue Jacob in 21st-century Paris, Cavendish decided to leave the gun, with its lonely bullet, where it was. While Serge seethed, Cavendish turned his head and saw that they were adjacent the arched entry to one of Paris' most charming hotels, the Maronniers. To be stabbed to death in front of this sheltered and lovely mecca for well-to-do tourists struck Cavendish as so absurd that he almost laughed.

He managed not to giggle in Serge's face. But he did smile, compelling from Serge a scowl of puzzlement. Slowly, Cavendish reached up with his gun hand and slid a thumb between the knife and his shirt.

"Mon ami," he said ever so softy. *"Pas ici. Pas maintenant."*

Serge grew more puzzled.

"Oui?" suggested Cavendish. *"Okay?"* He took a step backward. The knife remained stationary, pointing now toward the sky. Cavendish spread his arms at his waist and slouched in a gesture of surrender. Serge lowered the weapon and glared, but made no move on Cavendish.

Cavendish held his submissive pose. Serge remained a figure of menace, teetering on the brink of mortal compulsion. But, as must happen on a street as busy and fashionable as rue Jacob, the showdown collapsed with the sound of footsteps and tipsy voices. Cavendish saw behind Serge, approaching from the direction of rue des Saints-Pères, a Parisian couple, older man and dewy young woman, she combed and coifed, perfumed and cologned, silk and cashmere, laughing, touching and flirting, fit as a fiddle and ready for champagne.

Serge hastily hid the knife and turned, almost bumping into the woman, then stepped off the curb to let her pass. He turned once toward Cavendish, his stare black with warning—the predictable tough-guy cliché—that this wasn't over, not by a long shot.

"Yeah," muttered Cavendish. "I know."

He was tempted for a second to brace Serge, to tell him, keep your hands off Mireille. He held back, partly because his French wasn't good enough. But he understood, with sad acceptance, that the power Serge exerted over Mireille was beyond Cavendish's—or anyone's—effort to rescue her, until she decided to rescue herself.

Cavendish sighed once and turned away from Serge. He started in the direction of rue de l'Université, waiting for the clatter of Serge's footsteps and a blow to his back. But nothing happened and when Cavendish turned to look, Serge was gone.

In another block, he turned toward the Seine, thinking about knives, *apaches*, Nicolas and Fifine.

Steve Knight had almost panicked when he saw the maniac in the leather jacket pull a knife—Jesus, what a knife!—on sad, mild-mannered Cavendish. For one impulsive moment, Steve had been tempted to burst from the shadows and tackle the guy.

And probably, thought Steve, get stabbed himself. What did he know about disarming psychos?

Besides, even if he got involved, even if he saved Cavendish and came out of the battle unscathed—or merely bleeding— Mie would be ready to pull a knife of her own and finish him off. Choosing to shadow the American author, Steve had begged off dinner that night at Les Papilles—elegant and cozy—with Mie and Roberta, one of his oldest friends in Paris. Mie headed off to dinner, angry at Steve and spoiling for the chance to tell Roberta that he was a selfish, obsessive snoop.

Roberta already knew this.

Steve was still anguishing over whether to stay hidden or leap to Cavendish's aid when this gorgeous couple, a silver-haired patrician draped all over with a teenage fashion model in a red cocktail dress and no evident underwear, had made the scene, breaking the mood of malice and mayhem. Steve relaxed as the leather-bound Serge separated from the Yank and—after another moment of steely-eyed suspense—let Cavendish go.

Steve's next decision was to shift his surveillance from Cavendish, who was likely to just wander a while and go home, to the waitress' madman boyfriend. He followed the guy to, of course, the Petit St.-Benoit. Lurking across the street in a doorway, Steve awaited developments at the little bistro.

Serge didn't go inside. He peered through a window, fidgeted for a while, lit a cigarette and started pacing on the street. It was spring now, with lengthening nights and comfortable weather. There were people dining outdoors. They soon noticed the brooding, grumbling Serge as he spat smoke and marched angrily, back and forth, past their tables.

Finally, bearing a tray, the waitress emerged from the bistro's interior. Serge froze on the spot, staring at her. Paying Serge no attention, Mireille delivered plates and drinks to two sets of customers. Serge flung his cigarette down and crushed the butt mercilessly. Mireille finished her service and lowered the tray to her side.

For a moment, she gazed blankly at Serge. He glowered back, his body twitchy and electric with what Steve could only read as idiot rage. Steve knew he was being a selfish, obsessive snoop, but he had been sucked irresistibly into the sheer suspense of this triangle among waitress, sad guy and leather-jacket nutcase. Why was this guy always so pissed off?

How was it going to end?

This episode was over quickly. The waitress relented and stepped away from the tables, onto the cobblestones. In a heated stage whisper, the wacko in leather spoke angrily. The waitress, calmly, uttered what Steve guessed was a sharp rebuke that her violent boyfriend could not, would not let pass. So, he hit her.

The audience, on the *terrasse*, had been glued to the drama. They reacted with a wave of little leaps, lurches and gasps. They repeated themselves when the waitress, barely hesitating, slapped the lunatic in leather, shoved him violently backward and stormed back inside the restaurant.

"Holy shit," said Steve to himself.

He had a twinge of sheer terror when the seething psycho spun on his heels and glared into the dark doorway where Steve was trying to hide.

"Uh oh."

But Serge—beaten by a girl in public—was blind with anger and humiliation. He paused only a second or two before stomping away.

Steve was impressed with the waitress. She had spunk. But he also figured that she would pay a dear price for standing up to the bully in her life.

He looked at his watch. It was still shy of ten p.m. He had time, if he hurried, to have dessert with Roberta and try to make peace with Mie.

CHAPTER 30

Les Noctambules

A *pache Dance*
by Raymond Cavendish
(From Chapter 14)

... Maxim recoiled with alarm as Nicolas, in a crescendo of heavy footfalls, entered the subterranean bar by way of the little-used back staircase. Nick paused on the bottom step, peering wildly into the dim light. He was hatless. A sleeve was torn. A hand was bleeding, as though he had tumbled on coarse ground, scraping away skin as he broke his fall.

La Combe, "the Boar," stepped out from behind the bar, swelling to his full girth and pointing a thick finger at the newcomer. "Out!" he bellowed. You can't come here. Les vaches, they're all around, hunting. Hunting you!"

Ignoring this, Nick staggered toward the publican. He did not halt 'til his chest was pressed against the Boar, his eyes glaring upward, the heat and rank smell of his body enveloping both men. The Boar, ready to raise his fist—as big as Nick's head—and crush the intruder, heard a metallic click and paused. Lightly held in Nick's hand, hanging beside his leg, was a stiletto. Its blade had snicked from its sheath with the pressure of Nick's thumb.

Nick smiled joylessly. "I borrowed it from Stephan. You know, l'Epée. He doesn't need it anymore."

Valentin, the gossipy waiter, was crouching beside Maxim. He whispered, "They shot 'im. The cops. Stephan got away, but he died at Odette's. The cops followed him there, took Odette away. They got them all, except Nicky."

The Boar, sliding gingerly, retreated behind the bar.

"Give me a drink," said Nick, leaning on the bar. La Combe wiped clear a space. Nick laid down the knife he had taken from Stephan's body, fleeing before the police broke down Odette's door. Odette, who loved Stephan, crazy as he was, had stayed behind.

Nick slumped against the bar. He drank down a glass of the Boar's harsh cognac in a gulp and banged the glass for more. All the drinkers who had been clustered on the bar had backed into the shadows.

"They've been here, Nick," said the Boar. "They'll be back."

"Fill the fuckin' glass."

The Boar poured, his hand now trembling, his eyes wandering to the doorway.

Reluctant to enter Nick's vicinity, Valentin slipped into the chair beside Maxim.

Maxim had heard about the carjacking on rue Laferrière. Everyone in Paris knew the story. But Maxim hadn't followed the aftermath. He had worked, he had slept a little, he had spent hours in his dark corner of Les Noctambules drinking, waiting for Fifine to sing, hungering for a smile, or just a glance. Two nights before, police had burst into Les Noctambules, rampaged, searched and then departed. Maxim had barely noticed.

"I don't understand," he said to Valentin. "Nick's apaches, they robbed a car. It happens every night. The cops shrug at such things. They don't care."

"Maxim, mon ami," said Valentin, suddenly a brother to the drunken romantic he normally disdained, "don't you know? Haven't you listened?"

"Huh? Listened to what?"

At the bar, Nick nursed his second cognac, looking warily over his shoulder, left, right and behind his back. He was a black cat on *a fence.*

Valentin nudged Maxim's arm. "It's on everybody's lips. Over this robbery, the vaches are on the warpath."

Maxim shook his head. He looked down at his empty glass. "I don't see why."

As though by magic, Valentin produced a bottle and filled the only glass on the table. He drank down half and passed it to Maxim. "The car was no ordinary car."

"What's so extraordinary?"

"Do you know the name Speer?"

"Speer?"

"The American," said Valentin. "Cicero Speer."

Maxim's eyes fluttered open a little wider. "Famous, yes? A rich man?"

"Rich? Hah!" Valentin rolled his head and went saucer-eyed. "Rich as a Rockefeller! Richer!"

"So, this Speer. He was in the car?"

Valentin laughed raspily. "In the car, yes, Maxim. In the car. Out of the car. Dead. Killed, stabbed, stuck like a pig! By l'Epée, with that knife you see, on the bar."

Maxim was fully awake, but skeptical. "Valentin, this doesn't explain why the police—"

Valentin knew what Maxim was going to ask. "Oui, bien sûr, Maxim," he broke in. "Even if you kill a rich man, the police go, 'So what?' They go through the motions. They arrest some miserable mec who's been arrested a dozen times. They pin the crime on him, the press goes along, they print his picture, they scream for blood. A month later, Monsieur de Paris drops the blade. The crowd cheers. Justice is triumphant."

Maxim nodded gloomily.

"But this one—you should know this, Maxim. It was in all the papers. Nick's gang, they killed a friend of M. Roosevelt."

"Roosevelt? The American president?"

"Yes, a friend of the president, this Speer. For good measure, they raped his daughter. Sixteen years old—a virgin, they said. Her first

time in Paris, she begs her daddy. She wants to see the cancan at Le Moulin Rouge. Afterwards, eh. Her father dead. She, stripped, fucked and naked in the street."

"And the American president," said Maxim.

"Really pissed off."

Maxim whistled softly. "The crime of the century."

"So, suddenly, a thousand flics are combing the city. In two days, they catch them all," whispered Valentin. "Stephan and Denis shot dead. Miko, beaten so badly he will never speak, never walk. They'll carry him to the guillotine. Grosjean locked up in Santé, also certain to lose his head."

"Odette?"

"Tore away from the cops and threw herself out the window."

"Only Nick," said Maxim.

"Oh!" Valentin wax staring at the bar. "Look!"

While Nick was drinking, La Combe had sidled along the bar, reaching beneath. He came up with the hand ax with which every regular patron of Les Noctambules was familiar. In his younger days, the Boar had hunted wild pigs with this weapon. He would face a boar like a bullfighter and split its head as it charged.

He returned to Nick and lay the ax on the bar, beside Stephan's stiletto. La Combe kept a hand on the ax. A voice near the doorway broke the silence. "I hear them. Les vaches!"

"Leave. I mean it, Nicky," said La Combe. "I'm not getting mixed up on your shit. Get out!"

Beyond the door, feet were thumping on the cobblestones.

Nick and the Boar glared into each other's eyes. After a moment, Nick moved his hand to the knife and slid it, slowly, off the bar. He stepped back. He turned to look toward his only possible escape, the stairway to the back alley. Between the bar and the stairs was the bibine's sad little stage. Cowering there, trying to hide in the dark from Nick, Fifine sat. She wore a small black shift with thin straps and a slit at the hip. Her legs were exposed, eggshell white and beautiful. Her face was lowered, her arms crossed, her legs pressed together.

It took an instant for Nick to lunge toward Fifine, to snatch her up, wrap an arm around her waist and press the blade to her throat.

Fifine cried out weakly, trapped, terrified.

Nick walked his captive back toward the bar.

"Hide me," he said to the Boar.

"Fuck you."

"I'll kill the bitch."

La Combe was holding the ax at his shoulder, as though to strike. But he was frozen in place. His eyes were distant.

The sounds of the police were louder. They were grouping outside Les Noctambules. They could be heard now, faintly, in the alley. Nick's last avenue of escape had closed.

"I'll kill her."

The Boar's eyes scanned the interior of his assommoir. Its every denizen—the regulars and strangers, the cripples and pickpockets, muggers, pimps and whores, sabouleurs and piètres, hooligans, hubains, coupe-gueules, clochards, gamblers, grifters and slatternly vulvivagues—had retreated into shadow, leaving a semicircle of filthy floor. They watched, with rapt fascination, fear and a frisson of bloodlust. Whether Fifine lived or died, whether Nick was caught, killed or somehow got away, was all the same to them. They would be entertained. If the girl were cut open like a fish and left in a lake of blood, the only victim would be La Combe, who might be closed down by the city for harboring the most hunted criminal in France. And he, the Boar, would be back on the streets among the scum and canailles who had been, days before, his clientele and livelihood.

"C'mon," said Nick, pressing the blade. He jerked his head toward a curtained space behind the Boar. It was just large enough to fit two people. "Back there."

La Combe hesitated. There was a thump against the door. A voice, "Who the fuck locked this door?"

"I'll kill her." A thin line of blood appeared on Fifine's neck.

"Open up!" came a roar from outside.

The Boar laid down his ax. He bowed his head. Swiftly, Nick dragged the limp, weeping Fifine behind the bar.

The door crashed in. The drunks, burnouts and sluts of Les Noctambules scattered like cockroaches, seeking darkness and backing to the walls. Police swarmed.

Concealed by the broad body of the bartender, Nick shoved Fifine behind the curtain and followed her, crushing her into a dirty wall, pressing her to a neglected floor strewn with rat turds. He covered her mouth with his bloodied hand and pressed the point of the knife to her cheek. She wept silently, her eyes wide, imploring but also, insanely, trusting.

The lead cop, a sergeant named Sorel whom La Combe knew well, rushed to the bar, hitting it hard enough to knock over a bottle and raise dust from its crevices. "La Combe, you fucking degenerate, is he here?"

The Boar assumed the calm and ingenuous demeanor that every seasoned petty crook assumes in the presence of the heat.

"Nice to see you, too, Sorel. Your children are well? How's the little woman?"

Behind Sorel, two dozen rampant gendarmes were tossing people hither and thither, shining lights in their faces, rifling their stinking clothes, shoving their fists up the skirts of the whores. They shouted and stomped, swinging clubs. The thunk of polished wood on skulls was a ragged drumbeat.

"Where is he, Boar? You know. You always know!"

"Who do you mean?"

Three cops had burst into the little closet where Fifine slept. Her every pathetic possession flew out from the room.

Sorel conceded to La Combe's reticence. "Nick," he said. "Nick. Nicolas Mercier. You know who the fuck I'm talkin' about!"

To punctuate his demand, Sorel slammed his nightstick on the bar.

"Ah, Nicky," said the Boar. "Used to be a regular here. I admit that. But since that ... tragic incident, with the American. And his little girl, poor thing. I told him begone. He's not welcome here."

"Begone? Shit, you lying son of a bitch," blubbered Sorel.

"I think he left town," said La Combe coolly. "If I were in his *shoes, that's what I'd do."*

"Fuck you, Boar."

Sorel leaned across the bar, studying the shelves and bottles, a cracked mirror, stacks of crates on the floor, the soiled curtain, a two-legged stool on which the Boar now and then rested his bones.

Sorel peered. "How do you sit on that?"

"I balance," said the Boar.

Sorel scowled. Pandemonium still reigned in the boîte, but Sorel was deaf to his troop's depredations. La Combe, stone-faced but terrified, sidled a few inches to hide the curtain.

"My father was a farmer," he said, conversationally, as though this was a normal evening at Les Noctambules. "To milk the cows, you used a stool like that. Shorter legs. You balanced."

Sorel shook his head. "Why not one more leg?"

La Combe smiled and shrugged. "Tradition?"

"Farmers are morons," said Sorel sourly.

The Boar shrugged. "A drink?" he said. "On the house?"

Sorel surrendered. He nodded. The Boar poured. The clink of glass and the bellowing of the police covered a whimper from Fifine.

After the police had broken a few tables, drunk their fill and gone, Valentin helped Maxim off the floor, where a burly flic had thrown him. Valentin's bottle had survived. He and Maxim shared another loving cup.

Nick emerged with Fifine. He clutched her in his arms and kissed her brutally. "You saved me, babe," he said. She pulled away, stumbled to a chair and crumpled into it, hiding her face in her hands.

Overwhelmed with shame, Maxim sank into the shadow of the staircase. He had done nothing to help the woman he worshipped. Nick would have slashed her throat, tossed her down—and Maxim? What would he have done?

He wept and drank.

Gaspard tinkled the piano keys. Maxim could not look up even as, somehow, like a sparrow in a distant tree, Fifine began to sing...

La Gare
6/18/06 11/32

La Gare
19 chaussée de la Muette

CHAPTER 31

Au Général Lafayette

When the *maître d'* led Mireille and him to a prime two-top beside a window looking out upon the confluence of rue La Fayette, rue Druout and rue du Faubourg Montmartre, Cavendish had hesitated—fearful of being seen from outside by the lurking Serge.

Mireille had sat quickly, leaning toward the window, captivated by the bustling parade of Parisians, chic and ragged, rich and wretched. "These are my neighbors," she said, touching Cavendish's hand and guiding him toward his seat. "The tourists don't come here."

Cavendish sat, warily. "Besides, it's Thursday night," said Mireille. "The bully's in Belleville with his buddies and *belote*."

Cavendish laughed at the alliteration. "Poetry," he said. "Can I use that?"

They ordered kir and looked around while they settled. The view of the bar is reason enough to dine at Au Général Lafayette, a classic brasserie in the unfashionable ninth arrondissement. Asymmetric double arches of dark woodwork, guarded by silvery beer taps, framed tall mirrors lined with shelves of bottles. Overseeing the bar is a giant Guinness toucan, beneath whom two bartenders in white shirts and black bowties officiate genially.

Sprawling outward from the bar, arches and pillars in matching oakwork shelter an interior of bentwood chairs, palm fronds, art nouveau lamps and lush brown leather banquettes.

The drinks arrived. The waiter left menus behind and receded. Over his kir, Cavendish regarded Mireille, curiously. It had been two weeks since he had ambushed her with his confession of love. When he invited her out this night, he was uneasy. He expected refusal. But she had smiled and accepted, almost eagerly. On route to the Général Lafayette, Mireille had been quiet, linking her arm into Cavendish's but distracted, looking into shop windows, peering at passersby. Now, she laid a hand—long, pale, delicate fingers with hidden strength—on Cavendish's.

She held him in her gaze. "Serge was surprised," she said.

"Surprised?"

"He said you have a gun."

Cavendish started. "What?"

"You don't?"

Cavendish didn't answer this. "What makes him think ... "

Mireille smiled. "He thought he saw ... " She paused, searching for a word. *"Un renflement?"* She remembered. "A bulge! In your pocket."

The waiter returned, sparing Cavendish from answering Mireille. They hadn't studied the menu. So, they sent him away. Mireille picked up the bill of fare and read. Cavendish did the same.

They decided to start with fish, herring for Cavendish, *tataki d'espadon* for Mireille. Then, grilled *onglet* and *saucisson de Lyon* (speckled with pistachios). The waiter was ready as soon as they rested their menus. He complimented Mireille for choosing the *saucisson*, but he meant that she was beautiful. To drink, Cavendish ordered a surprisingly inexpensive Saint-Estèphe.

As the waiter backed away and turned, Mireille sank the

hook back into Cavendish. "So?" she said.

"So?"

"Is there a gun? Cavendish, are you crazy?"

Cavendish began to explain that he had bought from an old friend a very small gun, with one little bullet, that he never intended to shoot. He wanted it only to frighten Serge.

"Frighten?" replied Mireille with so much emphasis that she spilled a drop of kir. "Frighten Serge? Do you frighten a mad dog, Cavendish? Do you point a toy gun at … at… " Her eyes widened. " … Darth Vader?"

Cavendish couldn't help but laugh.

Mireille clutched his hand, her face stern. "What if you had pointed this stupid gun? What would happen?"

Cavendish knitted his brow, trying to conjure the scenario. Mireille didn't wait.

"Serge, I know Serge," said Mireille. "He would walk right up to you, 'til the gun is in his face, *devant son nez!* And he would say to you, Cavendish, sweet Cavendish, he would say, 'Go ahead, fockah!' He would say, 'Shoot! Shoot me!' But you, sweet Cavendish, would you shoot?"

Cavendish blushed.

"No!" Mireille kneaded his hand and looked tenderly into his eyes. "You wouldn't shoot. And Serge, ah, *mon Dieu!* He would take your silly gun, he would hit you, on *your* nose, with *your* gun! And he would keep hitting you. *Il casserait le pistolet sur ta tête!* On your stupid head! You know that, Cavendish?"

Cavendish sighed. "Well, yeah, I know. I guess."

"He would have hurt you terribly. He is so angry, so strong. so fierce." Mireille laid her palm on Cavendish's face. "Serge could kill you, Cavendish."

"Well, not much of a loss."

Both hands now. Again, she almost spilled the wine. "To me," she said intensely. "To me, a loss. You are so stupid, Cavendish … "

Suddenly, Mireille seemed to realize she was halfway out of

her chair in a crowded restaurant, clutching the stubbly face of a funny, middle-aged American man. She released Cavendish and settled back. The waiter broke the mood efficiently by arriving with *hareng* and seared swordfish.

"Ah, looks great!" said Cavendish.

Mireille scowled across the table. "The gun," she said. "You will throw it in the river."

Cavendish nodded enigmatically and ate quickly.

After a while, Cavendish asked, "Mireille, are you angry with me?"

Mireille's fork clanked, "Oh no, Cavendish. No!"

"But you were," he said. "About the gun."

"Well … "

"But why? Serge, that night, he was angry, yes. And fierce. But he was just," Cavendish used a word he didn't think Mireille would understand, "bluffing."

Mireille didn't hear the word. She stared at her plate. "I shouldn't be angry at you, Cavendish. I shouldn't … "

She didn't finish the sentence. She was silent for a while, finishing her *entrée*, drinking her kir and watching as Cavendish poured the red.

"Cavendish?" she said softly.

"Yes?"

"The way I am," said Mireille. "Am I sick?"

"Oh no, not even a little bit. You are wond—"

"Am I crazy?"

"Not that, either."

"Oh."

Before they spoke again, the waiter had cleared the table and delivered their *onglet* and *saucisson*.

"Beautiful," said Cavendish.

A moment later, Mireille said, "If I'm not crazy … "

"Well," ventured Cavendish, "you just might be in love."

Looking into Cavendish's eyes, imploringly, Mireille said, "But … with who?"

Cavendish smiled. "Whom."

Mireille wrinkled her brow and then understood. "Oh, Cavendish! Who, whom. Shut up!"

And the subject passed.

But that night, after parting with Mireille at the Métro, Cavendish walked home with a spring in his step.

JULY

CHAPTER 32

Chez René

Steve and Mie's frequent visits to Chez René had conferred a sort of status. They were familiar enough to the owners that they dared to reserve a particular table, in the corner on the side of the restaurant that overlooked the blvd. St.-Germain. Moreover, there was at least one waiter who recognized them. He had greeted them with the hint of a smile and hurried to serve their aperitifs.

"That waiter. He's not as bone-chillingly terrifying as he used to be," said Mie.

On the walls above Steve and Mie were old posters of art exhibitions—Calder, Kandinsky, Jean Dubuffet—from thirty years before. They were seated on the banquette, facing the salon, all the other diners in view. Also visible was the bistro's "bridge," where the bartender reigned and the cashier calculated each "*addition.*"

While he sipped kir, Steve laid a hand, beneath the concealment of the tablecloth, on Mie's thigh. His fingers inched upward. Mie squirmed but did not resist.

"Theoretically," she said, turning to peer into Steve's eyes. Steve's hand stopped moving. He flinched beneath her gaze.

"Theoretically what?"

"A couple breaks up."

Steve responded warily. "Uh huh."

"The woman moves on."

"Woman," said Steve. "She have a name?"

"Er ... " Mie paused to think, then smiled. "Renée."

"Uh huh."

"She finds another guy. They fall in love. They get married."

"Name?"

"Oh, well, let's see ... Bob."

"Dull."

"Now, the man, the ex-husband ... " Hurriedly, Mie scanned the posters on the wall. "Ah," she said. "His name is Fernand."

Steve laughed. Mie continued.

"Fernand also finds someone, a woman—exotic and beautiful. He's in love. She feels the same about him."

Steve, silent, cocked his head expectantly.

Peering over the rim of her glass, Mie saw a vintage poster that dated to the 1920s. "Josephine."

"Exotic and beautiful," Steve prompted. "But ol' Fernand isn't quite as hasty, on the rebound, as his ex-wife. Fernand isn't sure he wants to marry Josephine?"

"Oh no, he does," said Mie. "But he won't. And Josephine can't understand why."

Steve leaned toward Mie, his hand squeezing her leg significantly. "How old are they?"

"Old?"

"Yes. Twenties, thirties, sixties, eighties?"

"Ah, hm. Josephine's young, twenty-five, twenty-six."

"A mere child."

Mie scowled at this.

"And he's what?" asked Steve. "Forty?"

"Okay."

"So, he—Fernand—he might be thinking that they're too far apart. He doesn't want to trap her into a life, later on, of caring for a senior citizen while she's still young enough to kick up her—"

"No, no, no, Steve." Mie planted a hand on Steve's mouth. "They blend."

"Blend?"

"They work in the same ... office. They do the same work. Fernand and Josephine have everything in common. Their age doesn't matter."

"Well, then," said Steve, "what does?"

"Theoretically?"

"Uh huh."

"Fear."

'Fear?"

"Yes."

"Fernand is afraid?"

"Yes."

"Of what? Of Josephine? She's a domineering termagant?"

Mie shook her head. She laid her hand on Steve's and guided it further up her thigh. "You tell me," she said.

Steve let out a sigh.

"Okay, Josephine, look," he said. "When Eileen left me, I was shook. But I got over that. I mean, I could understand. Before she broke off, I'd already left her, in many ways. Too much work, all that traveling. Eileen hated that. She was always ... rooted. She liked being at home and she wanted me there with her. I was—I am—a goddamn nomad. I pretty much ushered the other guy into her life."

"So?"

"So, I'm not afraid—I mean, Fernand's not afraid of losing Josephine to his job, because it's her job, too. She's there, right? Working side-by-side with Fernand. They're a team. They have shared interests."

"And they love each other."

"Yeah, right," said Steve. "Fernand is not, mark my words, afraid of commitment, especially to a cupcake like Josephine." Steve ventured further up Mie's thigh. She purred. "But ... "

"But?"

Steve departed from the theoretical. "There's this Cavendish guy."

"Cavendish?" asked Mie. "We're leaving Fernand?"

"We're leaving theoretical."

The waiter arrived, peering down owlishly and wielding his order book expectantly. Steve snatched his hand away from Mie's goodies and assumed an obedient pose. Mie, decisively, ordered sautéed *cèpes* and the *onglet de boeuf "Bercy."* After dithering long enough to set the waiter's foot tapping, Steve asked, as always, for the *blettes au gratin "René"* (a dish unique to Chez René), followed by the bistro's peerless *boeuf bourgignon*.

The waiter also agreed to bring a bottle of the Beaujolais that has been Chez René's house wine for the better part of a century.

"The sauce for the *boeuf bourgignon*," Steve speculated. "They never turn off the heat. It's been simmering since World War I."

Mie smiled indulgently. She said, "Cavendish?"

Steve nodded reflectively. "Look, Cavendish and me, we both feel the same pressure, to get up every day, stare at the keyboard, riffle through our notes, squeeze blood from our brains, and then write."

"So do I," Mie protested.

"Yeah, but you haven't been at it for twenty-some years. You're fresh and eager."

"And you're not?"

Steve let this pass. He said, "Cavendish is a good writer. I've read half his book. He sees into people. He captures the feel of Paris, the bent light and the street smells as you walk along. He's good."

"Okay, but ... "

"But suddenly, after one novel, it all stalled. His pen dried up. His vision went blind. He burned out in his forties. I'm in my forties, for Christ's sake. You see what I'm sayin', Mie?"

"So," said Mie. "You're saying that Cavendish will never

write again? He's hopeless? He's the living dead?"

"Well, no."

"Couldn't he just be temporarily stymied?"

"I don't know, but that's what scares me. What if he is, as a writer, dead? In his forties?"

"Like you?"

"Yeah, like me." Steve said. "What if, suddenly one day, the fire flickers out? I can't push myself on to the next story. I can't find the angle. I bury the lead. I don't even write the lead. There is no lead. And I just get fucking tired of calling strangers and begging them for an interview, for one lousy frigging quotable comment ... "

"Steve, I don't think—"

Steve was rolling. "How long can a guy go on, grinding it out, hammering away, stringing together words 'til the words run out? Jesus, chasing the same goddamn rabbit without ever catching it, like Elmer fucking Fudd?"

Mie smiled sardonically. "Steve, wow. Elmer Fudd? Are you sure you're only forty, old-timer?"

Steve slumped, exhausted by his tirade. Mie consoled him by replacing his hand on her leg.

She spoke. "You're working on a false parallel here, whitey."

When Mie called him "whitey," he knew he was in trouble. He stayed silent.

"Cavendish, obviously, is not you."

"Well, no," Steve attempted. "He writes novels, I write—"

"No, that's not what I mean."

"Oh."

"Cavendish," said Mie instructively, "is rootless. He's alone in a foreign city with, apparently, no friends. He's in love with a woman who's in love with another man who's violent and dangerous. How does this situation compare to you, whose friends are myriad, whose daughter's crazy about him, who's in love with a woman who loves him?"

"Um, well, this *is* a foreign city."

"Steve, did you file a story today?"

"Well, two actually."

"Good copy?"

"Jeez, I think so."

"I read it. It's just fine," said Mie. "So, you feel like quitting? Are you all dried up? Have you gone the way of all Cavendishes?"

Steve hung his head in surrender, his parallel shattered.

"Steve, stroke my leg and quit worrying."

"Well ... "

"Mm, feels good. A little higher, big boy."

They finished their kir. The Beaujolais had arrived. Steve poured.

"So," said Steve, suddenly suffering a brainstorm.

"So?"

"To get the girl—"

"Wait. Are we back to Fernand and Josephine?"

"No, no," said Steve. "Cavendish and the gorgeous waitress. She's drawn to violent, dangerous men."

"Aren't we all," said Mie.

Steve pressed on. "So, to compete for the woman, does Cavendish have to resort to violence? Should he beat her up?"

Mie shrugged. "Maybe so. There are some women ... "

The arrival of *blettes* and *cèpes* interrupted her thoughts. For a while, Steve and Mie just ate and drank. Mie's thigh went unfondled.

"So, unless he's ready to administer a few bruises and concussions," Steve asked with food in his mouth, "Cavendish doesn't have a chance with the yummy waitress?"

Mie set down her fork. "Seriously?"

Steve nodded.

Mie thought for a moment. "We don't know," she said. "We really don't know either of them. We just watch and make up stories. We're voyeurs. But if I were that woman, my God, I would do whatever I could, I'd grab any other guy, to get away from that great-looking gorilla in the leather jacket. I think she wishes she could escape him. She should. There's something about her—something better and finer. She's got class."

"She's got Cavendish," said Steve.

"Hm," said Mie, "if she wants him."

"I hope she does."

"Me, too, but," said Mie, "she'd have to walk away from … the gorilla, from her life's greatest passion, from the violence that might be the thing that makes her feel more alive than anything else."

"And might kill her," said Steve.

"Oh, she knows," said Mie. "She's afraid, but not afraid enough. Danger can be like a drug. You know it can kill you but you can't resist just one more fix. You want to quit. But you can't just go cold turkey."

Steve looked up from his *blettes*. "What about you, babe? Do you crave a little danger? Violence? Lacerations and contusions?"

Mie shook her head. "We've been there, Steve," she said. "In Tokyo? The bombs, the guns. The girl with the knife."

Steve reached out and touched just above her breasts, where she still bore the scar. "I don't want you going through that again."

"Me neither." Mie smiled. "But it was exciting."

"Yeah, and I gotta admit," said Steve, "I like your scar. It's sexy as hell."

"And me?"

"You?"

"You like me?"

"No," said Steve. He paused. "I love you."

They stopped eating for a kiss that lasted long enough to gain the attention of a dozen other patrons. The waiter, at a discreet distance, watched approvingly and estimated the time needed to elapse before serving the beef.

Steve worked on Mie's thigh, pushing her skirt upward,

breaching her lingerie.

"Steve, we're in public."

"And your point is?"

CHAPTER 33

Les Noctambules

Apache Dance
by Raymond Cavendish
(From Chapter 16)

When old Silvére's hair went white, the apaches who bought his goods began to call him Le Renard Argenté, which was soon reduced to Renard or rendered in English, easily heard from a distance, "Fox." Silvére was weak and feeble, and he always had money, which made him an easy mark. But there was not a truant or coupe-gueule who would lay a finger on the Fox. His inventory was too rare and precious, and he always carried a few samples, close at hand and primed for action.

He was waiting at Maxim's table before he crept down the alley stairs and slipped into his chair in the shadows. Maxim, barely taking note of Silvére, scanned the room fearfully.

Silvére relit a half-smoked cigarette and squinted through the flame of the match. He said, "Take it easy, mon ami. He won't be here."

Maxim caught Valentin's eyes and nodded at him to bring drinks. Valentin responded with a rude gesture, but turned to speak to the Boar. Maxim looked at the Fox.

"Did they catch him?"

Silvére snorted. "They never will. They've given up."

Maxim understood. Every member of the gang that had killed the bloated American tycoon and raped his little girl were either dead or doomed to the blade. The police had fresher quarry to hunt than Nicolas. Worse, Nick's elusiveness had worked to his advantage. His hair-breadth escapes had been reported, exaggerated and glamorized in the penny press. He had become for the moment the dashing, defiant Geronimo of the Paris apaches.

As long as Nick was at large, Maxim was haunted. His life revolved around Fifine. To win her over, to rescue her from this hellhole, to save her from Nick's cruelty was Maxim's sole purpose. She gave him hope, now and then, by coming to his table, talking and pouring out her pain, drinking and weeping. She would let Maxim hold her hand. Once he caressed her cheek and she had put her hand on his. She had kissed his palm. But afterward, nights passed 'til a week had gone by, ten days. She barely looked in his direction. And one night, suddenly, she was back at his table, looking into Maxim's eyes, remembering when she was a girl, talking about a dream mother baking bread in an imaginary kitchen—instead of her real mother.

Maxim would interrupt by begging Fifine, again, to let him take her away, buy her a dress, many dresses, silken slippers and beautiful bonnets. They would walk together arm-in-arm, on rue St.-Honoré or the Champs Elysées, nodding to strangers, stopping for tea and cake, making plans for the future. As he spun his fantasies, she would listen to his pleas, staring past Maxim wistfully, almost believing. Eventually, her gaze hardened into a cold stare. She would smile bitterly, shake her head, pat Maxim dismissively on the hand and return to the stage, to awaken Gaspard and sing her sad songs of broken dreams and shattered hope.

... Malgré les blessures
Malgré les larmes, je souris ...

It was hope that had drawn Maxim to Silvére.
"Do you have it?"

The Fox opened his mouth to answer, but clammed up as Valentin materialized, bearing two cloudy mademoiselles of brownish fluid.

Silvére considered it. "Your best brandy?"

Valentin grinned. "Our worst," he replied. "Our only."

And he left. Cautiously, Maxim and Silvére lifted their drinks and tilted the glasses. Silvére drank his down in a gulp and winced afterward. Maxim, who was at Les Noctambules for the night's duration, sipped. And grimaced.

Silvére, at long last, answered. "I have it, yes. It's not cheap. I don't dicker."

Maxim shrugged. "Let me see."

Silvére made a production of surreptitiously slipping a cloth sack from a pocket inside his coat and sliding the object into the shadow that darkened half the table. He let it lie, still covered. Scorning Silvére's caution, Maxim lifted an end of the sack and dropped, with a clunk, the gun. Three bullets also escaped, rolling in little circles before Silvére, anxiously, snatched them up and held them tight in his hand.

"You are careless, friend," said Silvére.

Maxim laughed icily. "M'sieur, look around. All you see here are cutthroats, thieves, gangsters, whores. No one to be shocked at the sight of a little pistolet like this. No one dumb enough to interfere with your business, knowing that this isn't the only gun on your person. Everyone here knows you, Renard. Half of these canailles are your customers. Some no longer here have died with your bullets in their guts."

Silvére scowled as Maxim examined the gun, a "Lebel revolver," with a six-round cylinder designed for eight-millimeter rounds. He looked on top of the barrel, where an inscription read "Mle 1892."

"How old is this?" he asked warily.

Silvére was amused by the question. "How should I know. It belonged to a drunk soldier who got rolled. Or maybe a cop left it on his kitchen table for his kids to steal while he went to take a shit. These weapons come to me second-hand, third-, tenth-hand. I take them apart, look at every piece, clean them and oil them. I'm a conscientious merchant, my friend. This gun shoots, I promise."

Maxim felt its weight, held the curving grip, set a thumb on the hammer and fingered the trigger, gingerly. He felt a surge of energy that shocked him, because he had been so long without it. He laid its full length across both hands, studying its shape, admiring its intrinsic sense of menace, appreciating its finality.

"Well?" said Silvére. There was a trace of impatience in his tone.

"Hmm," said Maxim. He was teasing. Something about the gun in his hands made him cool and discerning. The world around him, the roaring, grunting din of Les Noctambules, seemed somehow less chaotic and threatening. His fingers, now shiny with gun oil, seemed to be gaining a hold on things perpetually beyond his reach. The knot in his stomach, which never went away, which often doubled him over in fear, pain and confusion, felt suddenly, miraculously looser.

He asked, "How many bullets?"

"It holds six—"

"I know that." Maxim's voice was impatient and virile.

"Um, eighteen," said Silvére. "I can get you more."

Maxim pictured himself reloading twice, firing all eighteen rounds into Nicky's face 'til it was mangled beyond recognition.

"This is enough," said Maxim, feeling suddenly sheepish. He couldn't seriously imagine himself shooting at anyone even once, much less eighteen times.

Silvére named his price. Maxim nodded. The transaction was done in seconds. Silvére was uncomfortable with his back turned to this mob of pickpockets, arm breakers and sicarii. He stood, looked around, nodded to Maxim and edged backward to the alley stairs. Then he was gone.

Maxim tucked the gun into one coat pocket, the sack with bullets into the other. He sat back, sipping his rotgut, awaiting Fifine's first songs. She would emerge from her little closet, near his table. She would not look at him as she passed.

After five minutes, Maxim couldn't shake an odd restlessness. In ten, he couldn't sit still. He felt prickly and jumpy. Valentin arrived with a fresh drink. Maxim stood, took the glass and drank down the dram. He handed Valentin a coin and headed for the door—not the alley escape but the main door. He pushed past bigger, menacing men who stepped in his way but then, hastily, stepped aside. A tough named Baptiste, known for his skill with the sap that always hung from his wrist, smiled at Maxim's approach, spreading his legs and hunching his shoulders. But something in Maxim's demeanor changed his attitude. Smirking curiously, Baptiste let Maxim pass. There was a huge whore named Zelda who would lift a man by the waist, throw him to the floor and sit on his face. She intercepted Maxim, exposing her breasts, ready to flatten him. Maxim planted a hand between her mighty tits and pushed her away. Backpedaling and stumbling, she screamed in maidenly affront. But no one came to her aid and Maxim was out the door before her tantrum had been drowned out by shouts of hilarity and surprise.

Outside Les Noctambules on the damp cobblestones, Maxim paused, wondering where to go, suddenly thinking to return inside. Fifine had yet to sing. He could go back to his table, soak up the Boar's bitter booze and slip into a familiar languor. But his mind was made up when he saw, approaching the pothouse, a familiar trio of apaches, their boots yellow, their eyes as red as their scarves.

Maxim felt not the usual prudent urge to skulk away. He straightened his back and walked—no, sauntered—toward brutes who could happily render him little more than a stain on the cobbles, men who, until this moment, made him look for a hole in which to crawl and cower.

"Who's this?" shouted one, whom Maxim knew as Marteau. "Our little friend, Maxie." His tone was not friendly.

"The one," said another, known as the Butcher, "who moons like a calf over Fifi."

"The cunt who sings," added the third apache, who had named himself Cochise after a real red American Apache.

"Gentlemen," said Maxim.

The apaches closed in. The Butcher had unsheathed a knife, Cochise was carrying an iron rod. Marteau, unarmed, had fists like anvils. Six feet from his antagonists, Maxim drew the revolver from his pocket. The three apaches stopped, looking to one another, staring at the gun.

Coolly, Maxim felt in his other pocket. While the others hesitated, he removed a handful of bullets, flicked the revolver's cylinder and—slowly, staring into Marteau's eyes—loaded three chambers. Lowering the barrel, rolling several rounds in his left hand, he smiled grimly.

"Who's first?" he asked. He pointed the barrel at Marteau's heart.

"Wait a minute," said Cochise.

"Merde," said the Butcher. "Where'd you get that?"

Maxim didn't answer. He waited, watching for Marteau, the leader, to deflate and relax. Because Marteau's mind tended to work in slow motion, this took another minute. It came to him, as it must, that the body of a known criminal, found in the street, would trigger no sympathy from his fellow crooks and no curiosity among police. No family would come to take it away. Eventually, the enterprising owner of a cart and horse would hear of it and haul it off to one of Paris' medical schools to be used for anatomy lessons.

Finally, Marteau's tone turned conciliatory. He said to Maxim, "Maxie, friend, mind if we go inside?"

Maxim took a hospitable step back and waved the gun casually. "Be my guests," he said.

The three apaches sidled submissively past Maxim, who kept the barrel pointed at the tender area just below their belts. Marteau, last to enter Les Noctambules, paused to scowl at Maxim. He began to speak. "We ... "

He didn't finish. He saw something in Maxim's eye that told him a threat of revenge would have no force. Marteau knew how a man looked when he had nothing to lose.

"Bonne soirée," said Maxim genially.

"Yeah, right," muttered Marteau, barely audible above the roar from the open door.

Maxim stood rooted for a moment, still pointing the gun, perhaps ready to shoot any head that poked itself outside the bar. But none *appeared. Eventually, carefully, he unloaded the gun. He put revolver and bullets in their separate pockets and headed up the street, toward the top of Montmartre. He paused after a dozen steps and stood on tiptoe.*

He raised his arms. He thrust out a leg, threw back his head, laughed out loud and spun in a circle 'til he was dizzy. Maxim danced then, a soft-shoe step that scuffed along the cobblestones, up the hill, by the light of an apache moon ...

SEPTEMBER

Le Petit Pontoise
8/18/06

CHAPTER 34

Rue de la Harpe

Cavendish spun on his heel and glared. He fumbled in his coat pocket for the gun he had bought from Felix, forgetting for a moment that it wasn't there any longer. He had obeyed Mireille. The silly pistol was at the bottom of the Seine.

He strode toward the man he suspected of shadowing him.

"Who are you?" he demanded. There was something familiar about the stranger. "Do I know you?"

"Um, well, no," mumbled Steve. "You might have noticed me, I guess."

"Where?"

"Well, we eat, my ... um ... "

What was Mie to Steve?

"Your what?" Cavendish's nose came an inch closer to Steve's.

"I've seen you," Steve said, "at the, uh, Petit St.-Benoit."

Cavendish cast his eyes upward in a remembering gesture. "Oh," he said.

Steve waited. Cavendish pointed a finger, "Yeah," he said. "With the Asian woman. She's hard not to notice."

"Well, yeah, she's my ... uh ... "

Cavendish bypassed the issue of Mie's status. He leaned forward. "Are you following me? Who are you?"

Steve sighed, looking around. Rue de la Harpe is one of the rare narrow streets on the Left Bank that evaded the bulldozers dispatched by Baron Georges-Eugène Haussmann, Napoleon III's merciless czar of urban renewal. Running through a jigsaw of lanes between the Seine and blvd. St.-Germain, rue de la Harpe has turned into a tourist mecca, touted by guides as the last living relic of medieval Paris. Steve and Cavendish stood on a cobbled pavement surrounded by budget restaurants from which importunate "hosts" emerged to buttonhole passersby and boast about the sumptuousness of their establishment's "authentic" French—or Italian, Greek, Swiss, Middle Eastern, North African, Auvergnate, Belgian—cuisine.

It was five in the afternoon, too early for natives to dine, but "suppertime" for the Americans who milled and blundered among rue St.-Severin, rue de la Huchette, rue Xavier Privas, rue de la Parcheminerie and rue de la Harpe, eventually succumbing to the lies of this or that barker.

Above the hubbub, Steve explained that he was a journalist who had noticed Cavendish at the bistro on rue St.-Benoit and later saw his photo on the back cover of *Love and Death in the Latin Quarter*.

"This neighborhood"—Steve waved an arm, almost striking a large-bosomed woman in brand-new University of Paris sweatshirt—"is where your novel takes place."

"Some of it," Cavendish allowed. With this, he was silent again, forcing Steve to keep talking.

"Well, I sort of followed you," Steve lied, "because I'm interested in, um, what you're working on next ... and, y'know, the American in Paris thing. The life of the expat writer?"

"Sort of a tired story line, isn't it?" said Cavendish.

Steve wobbled his head in surrender. "Yeah," he said. "But I've read most of your book. You don't see Paris the way others do. You're not ... um ... "

"Starry-eyed and romantic?" suggested Cavendish.

Steve sighed with relief. "Exactly."

Again, silence from Cavendish. A group of gabbling Italians, sixteen strong, flowed around them, like the tide around beached tugboats.

"So," Steve finally managed, "I wonder if—"

"An interview?"

"Yeah, would you?"

"I'm disinclined," said Cavendish.

"Oh."

"But," Cavendish said. "My agent has been bugging me, for something like that."

"Ah," said Steve. He was reluctant to press, lest the author retaliate with a refusal.

"We can't talk here," said Cavendish. "This is a friggin' zoo. And, I have to be … "

A wave of his hand denoted "elsewhere."

"Ah, right," said Steve, denoting empathy.

"Tell you what," said Cavendish. "You know the Rosebud Bar?"

Steve did a quick map search in his head. "In Montparnasse?" he guessed.

"Yeah, rue Delambre," said Cavendish. "You can look for me there."

"When?" asked Steve eagerly.

Cavendish smiled wanly. "I go there now and then," he said. "Look for me."

"Right."

Cavendish turned to go. Looking back at a perplexed Steve, he said, "And stop following me."

Steve met Mie an hour later at Maison Peret, purveyor of voluminous salads and earthy *tartines*, near Denfert-Rochereau. As they took their seats at a terrace table, Steve said, "Looks like we have a new joint to hang out at."

"Really? Where?"

"The Rosebud."

"Oh, I love that place."

"Good."

"But why?" asked Mie.

"How about we eat first?"

They ate. Mie dropped hints about getting married. Steve beat around the bush, and they never got back to discussing the Rosebud Bar.

CHAPTER 35

Belleville

Apache Dance
by Raymond Cavendish
(From Chapter 17)

... he was waiting for her.

The dawn pierced a space between the buildings across the alley, filtering through a greasy window and rendering Nicolas a silhouette, slumped in a chair beside his kitchen table, scratching inside his pants.

Fifine was exhausted, her body wilted and clammy from the overheated confines of La Combe's dive. She had ventured to Nick's two rooms for the first time in weeks, hoping he was gone, hoping to be alone.

Nick stood, his arms hanging, like some beast in the jungle. His hair stood up. His belt buckle clanked.

"Nicky," she said wearily. "They didn't find you."

"No thanks t'you, bitch."

Fifine flinched as though bee-stung. "Nicky, I didn't—"

"So, have you been fucking him?" Nick took two large steps toward Fifine. in this tiny space, it was enough to put them face-to-face.

Fifine was bewildered. "Who?"

Nick curled a lip and growled. "Don't you bullshit me," he said.

"The little bookkeeper. the one who sits mooning at you in the corner, playing with his dick."

Fifine shook her head.

"So, you were fucking the bookkeeper?"

"No, no—"

"If you can fuck him," snarled Nick, seizing Fifine by the throat and lifting her to her toes, "you can fuck me, too."

Fifine, choking, couldn't answer, save with a rasping note of panic and terror as Nick dragged her to the kitchen, into the sunlight. While all but strangling her with one hand, he tore at her with the other, ripping away her clothes, gouging her skin. Blood mixed with sweat between her breasts.

He pressed her against the dirty window, so hard that the glass cracked and spidered. Below, feeding her chickens, Mathilde Moreau heard the noise and looked up. Through the cloudy glass, she could discern Fifine's tattered shift and the skin of her buttocks, bleeding where she had cracked the glass. Mme. Moreau watched the girl as she writhed in Nick's steely grasp. She took note of the unsteady rhythm of the man's struggle to impale the girl while fighting her resistance and trying not to kill her. The broken-window tableau was, in its way, a remarkable performance, especially so early in a dull, quiet spring morning in the slums of Paris, as though life and death themselves were dancing to a tune no one else could hear. Mme. Moreau observed it passively, but with fascination.

Here was a rare moment for her to lament the death of her husband, a man almost as violent as Nicolas. Xavier Moreau, who one day fell from a scaffold and dashed out his inadequate brains, would have gaped, licking his lips, at the sight of Nick and Fifine and, as soon as the show had finished, would have screwed his Tilde up against the chicken wire.

When Nick had spewed his spoonful, he let the girl sink to the floor. He backed away and sat, wincing from the discomfort of a penis chafed by an unwelcoming womb. As Fifine gathered the remnants of her dress to cover herself, she didn't take her eyes off Nick. Her gaze was angry and accusing.

"What's your problem?" Nick muttered.

Fifine shook her head.

"You asked for it, bitch," said Nick.

Fifine got to her feet, nude but for the shreds of her dress. Blood was smeared on her body. It trickled down one of her thighs. She went to the outer room, where a woolen winter coat, long enough to cover her, hung on a hook. She took it down, wrapped herself and hurried barefoot out the door. She didn't utter a word. She didn't look back at Nick, who had stood—still holding his penis—to watch her go.

"She'll be back," he told himself.

He wondered if there was any food ...

CHAPTER 36

Vaudeville

Weaving their way home from *salade de homard* and *rognons de veau* at Aux Crus de Bourgogne, a favorite vestige of the old Les Halles district where waiters still wear white shirts and black ties, Steve and Mie stopped for a midnight drink at Vaudeville, with its long, elegant, covered terrace and a dessert menu that periodically incites the pyromaniac excess of *crêpes Suzette*.

Steve, who felt like lingering, ordered a half-bottle of Chablis with Perrier Rouge on the side. Before the fluids arrived, Mie put on her interrogatory face.

"What?' said Steve.

"Today," said Mie, "you were hanging up your phone as I came in."

"Can you hang up a mobile phone?" asked Steve.

"Don't do that."

"What?'

"Don't divert the subject."

"What subject?"

"I heard you say a name."

"A name?"

The waiter impinged. He set down four glasses and the water bottle. He went stoically through his routine of uncorking the wine and pouring a few drops into Steve's wine glass. Steve quickly sniffed and nodded. The waiter poured and departed.

"It's nice wine," said Steve.

"You're diverting again."

"Oh no, not me," said Steve, looking attentive and cooperative. "You heard a name. Are you sure? You were barely in the room."

"Hanratty," replied Mie, crisply.

"Well then," Steve conceded. "I guess you heard right."

Mie passed her glass under her nose, then consumed an infinitesimal sip of Chablis. Her face softened.

She returned to Steve. "So, who is he?"

"Would you believe he's a jeweler," said Steve, "who specializes in engagement rings?"

This question gave Mie pause. She peered at Steve, intimating surprise, then hope, then skepticism. Finally, she said, "No."

Steve smiled. "You're right. When I buy the ring, it ain't gonna be over the phone."

"Out of the trunk of a car?" asked Mie.

Steve laughed. He touched Mie's hand and gazed blearily into her eyes. Mie studied his face. Steve had drunk quite a bit of wine at Aux Crus de Bourgogne. How much of this seeming moment of romance was true love, and how much was grain alcohol?

"I've been doing a little window-shopping at place Vendôme."

Mie scowled, "Oh, Steve, that's too much."

"For you?"

"For us. You could buy a house for the kind of money you'd—"

"Just window-shopping."

"So, the trunk of a car."

Steve smiled. "Would it matter?"

Mie raised her eyebrows and changed directions. "Who's Hanratty?"

"Ah," said Steve. He drank a little wine. "Back to the third-degree."

"Hanratty."

"He's a literary agent, in New York."

"You're not writing a book, Steve."

"No, but Cavendish is."

Mie fluttered her fingers and sat back. "So, you keep hounding the poor man."

"I'm not hounding anyone. I was curious. You saw him, too. You were curious. We cast him as a scientist, a failed spy, whatever. We wondered what was going on with him and the waitress. Did you know her name is Mireille? And there's that desperado in the leather jacket. C'mon, babe. You want to know, too."

Mie shook her head. "Maybe I'm curious, but not enough to invade someone else's privacy."

"I did not invade," Steve insisted. "I introduced myself. I—"

"No, he caught you following him. He asked you who the hell you were and what the hell you wanted."

"Well ... " Steve assumed a sheepish expression. This was usually effective.

Mie relented. "How did you find out the woman's name. From the author? From Cavendish?"

"No, I asked Patricia."

"Who's Patricia?"

"The other waitress. At the Petit St.-Benoit."

Mie's face sank an inch. "You interrogated the other waitress?"

"I didn't interrogate," Steve said. "I just asked. I said to her, that woman waited on us several times and she was great. And Patricia—I asked her name, too—she said, oh, that's Mireille, there's nobody better. Patricia loves Mireille. But she worries about her."

"Worries?"

"Because of Serge."

"Serge?"

"The guy. The bruiser in the leather jacket. He's Mireille's boyfriend. But Patricia says he's *fou dans la tête*."

"Crazy in the head."

"Right," said Steve. "But Patricia also said Serge is steamin' hot sexy. But scary. Possessive. Impulsive."

"Yes, well, we've seen that," said Mie.

"Mireille with this Serge guy, It's one of those love 'im-hate 'im sort of things," said Steve.

"Like you and me?" asked Mie.

Steve ignored this. "Patricia told me more."

Mie tried to resist asking, but failed. "What?"

"Well, it turns out that Serge isn't exactly Mireille's first rodeo."

"That's not a surprise, Steve. She's not exactly a girl."

"Right, well, when she was a girl, she studied at the Sorbonne."

"Really?"

"Yeah."

"Patricia told you this?"

"Yeah."

"I thought you just asked her for Mireille's name," said Mie. "How long did you talk to this woman?"

"Well ... " Steve paused to regroup. "We, uh, sat down, had a glass of wine."

"Oh, for God's sake. Did you ask her out to a movie?"

Steve recoiled. "C'mon, Mie. Patricia just wanted to talk, about her friend. She worries about her."

"I heard that part."

Steve pressed on. "Okay, right. So, Mireille's a young girl at the Sorbonne, beautiful, impressionable. She gets seduced by a professor."

"Of what?"

"Huh?"

"What did he profess? His subject."

"Oh, dunno. Patricia didn't say."

"You didn't ask?"

"Well, no."

"My guy, the investigative reporter."

"Can I go on?"

Mie waved Steve forward.

"Anyway," said Steve, "sweet, young, naive Mireille falls in love with the professor, and pretty soon, she's pregnant and the professor's no longer smitten. Or even available."

"Of course," said Mie.

"She has the baby—"

"Boy or girl?"

"Um ... "

"Never mind. Go on."

"Well, doesn't matter. 'Cause the baby dies."

"Oh," said Mie, dismayed. "Shit."

"Yeah, just like Anna's little Misha in the pirate raid."

"Who?"

"Never mind," said Steve. "Anyway, Patricia said losing her baby just about crushed Mireille. She didn't finish school. she had no job and her baby's gone. So, she took off. She got as far as St.-Malo, where she worked in a café by the sea, slinging fish and shucking oysters. Of course, inevitably, she married a fisherman, who beat her."

"Oh," said Mie. "Shit."

"But happy ending," said Steve. "A big storm came up, sank the bastard's fishing boat. He was drowned, never to be seen again."

Mie's glass was empty. She waggled it. Steve poured more Chablis.

"Anyway," Steve went on, "the fisherman's family blamed Mireille."

"For what?"

"Her husband's death."

Mie waxed angry. "What? They thought she started the storm?"

"Actually, sort of," said Steve. "They said she was bad luck. She was a jinx. She cast an evil spell that kills fishermen."

"Oh, for Christ's sake," said Mie. "Is this the 21st century?"

"Apparently not in Brittany," said Steve. "Pretty soon, it was all over St.-Malo that Mireille was death to fishermen. People crossed the street when they saw her coming. Little boys threw stones at her. She lost her job."

"She had to get outa that place."

"She did," said Steve. "Back to Paris."

"Where she ends up with this caveman Serge."

"Yeah, well, it was a kind of reunion. They'd been an item when they were in high school. But then Serge dropped out, got in trouble, did a little jail time. They lost touch."

"Lucky for her," said Mie.

"Yeah, but then, after Mireille got back to Paris, she bumped into ol' Serge again, at some market way up in the Eighteenth."

"The *marché de la Butte*, probably."

"Oh," said Steve. "Really?"

"Yes, I know most of the markets in town."

"Yeah, you do."

They paused, looking around at the other customers. It was past eleven p.m. and Vaudeville was no longer serving food. But drinks were flowing and desserts abounded.

"It appears," said Mie, "that Mireille has bad taste in men. The professor who knocked her up and left her to twist in the wind. The fisherman who beat her and died and then his family drives her away. And now this Serge asshole, who looks like he might kill her any minute."

Steve nodded. "He might. Patricia says Serge knocks Mireille around. He carries a knife and, apparently, he's jealous of Cavendish. If ol' Serge up and kills anyone ... "

"It's Cavendish?"

"It's Cavendish."

"Shouldn't somebody warn the guy?"

"Mireille's done that, again and again. But, according to Patricia, he won't give up."

"He loves her?"

"That's what Patricia says," said Steve. "She said Cavendish went through this big transformation after he started hanging around the Petit St.-Benoit. When he first showed up, he just sat there, moping and drinking. But Mireille can't resist a stray puppy. She started talking to Cavendish, listening to his troubles, asking about his writing. Patricia said she could see the spark come back into his eyes."

"Uh huh," said Mie dubiously. "Does Mireille love Cavendish?"

"Well ... "

"Does she love Serge?"

"Yeah ... "

"Not good for Cavendish."

"But she definitely likes him. They get together. They talk."

"She likes him."

"Yeah."

"Just enough to make Serge blind with jealousy," said Mie, "and get Cavendish killed?"

Steve knocked his head. "Well, killed? I don' know."

"Steve, he's a crazy Frenchman who carries a knife, right? He beats women. He's an ex-convict. Come on!"

"Jeez, it's not as though I can do anything about—"

"Steve, you met him."

"Who? Serge?"

"No, Cavendish."

"Oh. Well, yeah."

"You talked to him?"

"Yeah."

"So, he might listen to you, if you tell him to back off from this girl—woman—who might get him killed."

"No. I don' know."

"What do you mean, you don't know?"

"Well, Patricia said Cavendish sort of depends on Mireille."

"Depends?"

"Yeah, remember, he had stopped writing for almost a year. But he had a book due, a follow-up to *Love and Death in the Latin Quarter*. I talked to his agent."

"Hanratty" said Mie, nodding.

"Yeah. Well, poor old Cavendish used up most of a year trying to get started on the new book. But nothing happened 'til he met Mireille. Something about her ... inspired him. He gets energy from her. He writes for her, because of her."

"Do you write for me?"

Steve looked up. "Uh ... yeah."

Mie laughed.

"So," Steve began.

"So," Mie broke in, "if Mie breaks it off with Cavendish. If she stops seeing him. If she breaks his little heart in two, she breaks Hanratty's heart, too."

"And there's no book."

"And Cavendish falls apart, ends up in the gutter and slashes his wrists with a rusty corkscrew."

Steve sighed. "Shit, I hope not."

"You should talk to him," said Mie.

Steve scowled. "I thought you told me to stop following him and *not* talk to him."

"I did," said Mie. "But that was before I knew there was a jealous boyfriend dead set on murdering him."

"Well, murder might be a little bit of an overstate—"

"You know where Cavendish lives, don't you?"

Steve made a face. "Look, he comes and goes at all hours. I've knocked on his door but I'm not sure he ever answers the door. I can't just stand for hours in the street hoping to see him show. I did that once. I don't have time—"

"Maybe we can find him at Mireille's restaurant."

"He hardly ever goes there now. Because of Serge."

"Right, the lurking maniac," said Mie.

"Well, I guess," said Steve, "there's the Rosebud Bar."

"The Rosebud, yes. Let's go."

"You love that joint."

"'Deed, I do."

CHAPTER 37

Le Singe Doré

Apache Dance
  by Raymond Cavendish
  (From Chapter 21)
  ... had been holed up in Marseilles, sweltering in the Mediterranean heat.

After returning to Paris, he laid low for two months, but sent emissaries into his old haunts, searching for Fifine. The Boar still reigned over his menagerie of louts, sluts and fripouilles at Les Noctambules, but Fifine had fled, leaving no word behind. The Boar, who knew where she had gone, feigned ignorance and, if asked twice, brandished his hand ax.

Nicolas knew that if he were to visit Les Noctambules, he could have squeezed Fifine's wherabouts from Valentin or simply pounded the truth out of Gaspard the piano man. But the Boar's domain was off-limits to Nick. The police had lost interest in him—the city had a surplus of fugitive murderers—but they might reinstate the dragnet if he were to announce his return to Paris by knocking heads at La Combe's bar, an oasis where cops could always drink and fornicate for free.

But Paris is a small town. Its "wrong side," as Balzac called it, is shrunken, teeming and incestuous. No secret lasts long. No hiding place is safe.

On a chill and drizzly evening in November, Nicolas pushed his way inside and surveyed the layout of a bal-musette at the top of rue Mouffetard called Le Singe Doré. The clientele were a strange, volatile mix. There were thugs, thieves and hustlers of a slightly higher order than Nick's apache gang. Nick noted a sprinkling of swells and nightclubbers who had ventured into Paris' poorest precinct for a crawl through the wild side. Clustered at the bar were figures familiar to Nick, high-toned gangsters and pimps who bribed the concierges at only the better hotels. He spotted a renowned cracksman called Doigts de Velours and a well-preserved dowager, in wig and organdy, who had lost her virginity—it was said—to Louis Napoleon. A pickpocket called Verdi, his eyes huge and his fingers as slim as a girl's, slithered along the bar. Two men looking arrogant and austere in black were, Nick realized, members of the Bonnots, the most feared gang of political terrorists in France. Nick came to understand that he had entered the current capitol of the Paris underworld when he spied the notorious Count Pierre, engaged in whispered conversation with La Mère Dubossie.

Le Singe Doré had sprung up from the muck of the Paris gutter while Nick was on the lam. Although called a bal-musette, it was styled after the music halls of London. Rows of seats flanking a central aisle were packed full with every sort of boulevardier, rubbernecker, night owl, grifter, slummer, flirt, hooker, mark and drunken student. At the far end of the aisle, musicians—guitar, piano, violin, bass fiddle and accordion—were tuning in an orchestra pit, barely audible above the roar of the mob. Above the band, a stage, not large but vast compared with the slivered slab at Les Noctambules. There was no curtain.

Nick muscled his way past the bar and through the standing crowd to the top of the aisle. By the time he had cleared a space, he was damp with spilled booze. The hall stank of soured alcohol, sweat and unwashed bodies.

Beside Nick, a woman labored, with one hand, to keep her breasts inside her dress while managing a drink with the other hand. She nudged Nick.

"First time here?" She grinned salaciously.

"Yeah."

The woman waved her nondrinking hand, exposing a blue-veined breast. "Pretty fuckin' posh, eh?"

"Yeah," replied Nick. Le Singe Doré was, indeed, the fanciest joint in the precinct.

Nick held his spot. The woman tucked in her tit and shoved her way back toward the bar. Nick waited. In ten minutes, with a fanfare from the band, a cadaverous gent in a tuxedo, with a pencil mustache and brilliantined hair, took the stage and stepped forward. Aided by the band and several "ushers" who circulated among the audience with an air of menace, he reduced the prevailing roar to a grumbling undertone.

Nick could barely discern what this maître des cérémonies was saying until, raising his voice to a sort of vulpine yelp, he introduced the "chanteuse bien-aimée du Singe Doré, the bitter fruit of Montmartre, Mademoiselle Montmorency."

The singer, slight and brunette in a black silk slip and tall heels, her hair lank, her skin white as fromage blanc, her head down, wandered as though lost and aimless, toward center stage. She stopped, chin sunk to her chest. She waited a minute, two minutes, 'til, at last, the hall had fallen silent, 'til even the falling-down drunks had been quietly lowered to the floor. A tap of her foot, at last, cued the violinist to insinuate a forlorn dirgelike tune that faintly stirred Nick's memory. The other musicians took another moment to join the melody and repeat the motif.

Still not revealing her face, this Mlle. Montmorency sang soft and low a lament that seemed to bleed from the scabbed fissure of a broken heart.

Le sang sur mes lèvres
Est l'amour de mon homme
La plaie de mon coeur
Est son âme dans la mienne...

Nick knew this song.
She lifted her face and sang.

Il voit mon visage
En chacune de ses amantes
Malgré les blessures
Malgré les larmes, je souris...

Nick endured, somehow, through the end of the song, through the bridge and the repetition of the last lines.

À la vie, à la mort
Je serai sienne
Il sera mien
De l'amour à la mort
Il sera mien

The crowd of dipsos, criminals and libertines exploded into raucous shouts and thundering applause. Fifine stood motionless, head back, eyes closed, as though transported somewhere else. Her very attitude, her distance from everyone, her languid indifference had captivated Paris' vast insomniac throng and brought them to Le Singe Doré to share her pain and absorb the anguish in the raveled thread of her voice.

The glad ruckus had settled back to reverent silence and the band had just struck the first notes of Mlle. Montmorency's next song when Nick could no longer stand back.

Breaking from the crowd, he sprinted down the aisle, vaulted the orchestra, clambered up the apron of the stage, tearing open a hand on the zinc edge.

Suddenly, he loomed over Fifine, glaring down, working his fists, one of them dripping blood. Here was an unscripted tableau that stunned and bewildered the audience. Was this some new wrinkle in the show?

Fifine gazed up frightened, trembling before the man she had escaped. A sound deep in her throat was the murmur of a dove with a broken wing.

Nick seized Fifine, fragile, slender, feather-light. He held her up and faced the puzzled throng. "Mine!" he shouted.

"She's mine! Not yours! Mine!"

The audience was now convinced, this was part of the show. The jilted lover returns! They began to applaud.

Nonplussed, Nick staggered back. Losing his balance, he set Fifine down, She stumbled sideways, wild-eyed, hugging herself. Freed from Nick's grip, Fifine spun toward the wings. She tried to run but faltered as one heel caught between floorboards. Reaching down desperately, she tore off her shoes. Barefoot, she began to flee. But Nick had regained his footing. Catlike, he extended a claw, snatching Fifine by a shoulder.

She staggered and fell, elbow banging the floor, head down. She began to cry. The crowd gaped in silent, cathedral fascination.

Suddenly, helplessly, she was on her feet, on tiptoes, pressed against Nick, her breasts crushed, her breath gone. With more strength than she imagined she had, she planted both hands on his chest, inhaled violently and pushed away. Surprised, Nick let go, raising his hands above his shoulders. Freed unexpectedly, Fifine flew backward toward danger she could not see. Crying out in fear, she reached out.

Nick swept a hand, catching her by the wrist and spinning her in a circle that neither could control. A shout went up from the throng. The band leader motioned for music. In a second, the musicians were accompanying the struggle onstage with knife-edged jabs of tuneless rhythm.

Fearful of tumbling to the floor, Nick released Fifine. She careered backward, lost her feet and fell, rolling 'til she slapped her hands down and stopped, her slip bunched at her waist, her legs exposed. Dizzied and bruised, she peered down sightless at the gaping crowd.

She heard his footsteps. She gasped. He seized her by the waist, lifted her again, held her above his head. The musicians followed, flowing together, rising, soaring, drowning out Fifine's scream.

He loosed his hold, letting Fifine's body slide downward, her feet touching the floor, then her knees. She slumped on the stage, breasts to her thighs, hair brushing the floor, tears dripping ... until, like a storm rising violently from the clash of music, his thick hands seized her arms, lifted her and pushed her brutally away. She flew backward, felt his hands slipping along her arms. She could not stop herself!

Nick, suddenly, clamped her wrists, jerked her headlong flight to a cruel halt that seemed to tear her shoulders from her body. Pain radiated into her neck and turned her vision red as she spun, held by her wrists, her toes skimming the stage, her voice keening.

Nick let go. Fifine rolled away, her slip tearing, her skin raw. Her hands burned. Before she could shake the fog from her eyes, look up and find her legs, he had pounced again. Nick snatched her by the waist, lifted her to a shoulder and then, snapping her neck, thrust her above himself like a prize doe, impaled and gutted.

Nick froze in this pose, displaying his fickle woman, regained, disgraced and half-naked. The frantic music jarred his ears. The thudding bass matched his heartbeat. He glowered past the stage lights at a thousand wide, wondering eyes and open mouths. Above him, Fifine wept and dared not move.

"Mine," he said softly.

Then he shouted, "I'll do what I want!"

And Fifine knew.

He was lying.

Yes, he could hold her in his grip, squeeze the breath from her lungs and the blood from her heart. But he could not have her, not again. She would not go back. She could not go on with Nick. Overnight, the breathtaking scene at Le Singe Doré would be talked about in every precinct. Nick would be forsaken by confederates, fingered by foes, hunted again by the police, chased and hounded. Joined to him, there was no hope. If he would die, then she would die.

"No," cried Fifine.

Nick tensed. She could feel it. She knew what he was about to do. No one else. The music screamed and guttered. This, for every hungry eye in the house, was a show. For the finale, Fifine would be flung down once more and broken.

"No!"

The voice was not Fifine's. She saw, standing in the aisle, Maxim. In his hand, what? There was a gun?

"Let her go!"

Audience members, near Maxim, closed in on him. He swung toward them, flailing with the gun. They backed away.

Maxim aimed at Nick. "Let her go!"

Nick sneered. "You won't shoot me, you fucking pipsqueak."

Maxim fired a bullet that passed Nick by inches. The music stopped. Contempt faded from Nick's face, replaced by puzzlement.

"Let her go." This was neither outcry nor appeal. It was an order.

"Maxim," cried Fifine. "Oh no. Please."

Nick read Maxim's eyes. He took in the steady hand that held the gun. Slowly, his gaze fixed on Maxim, his face suddenly bland and timid, he lowered an arm and let Fifine slip down his body. Her feet brushed the floor.

Overcome, she sank down, collapsing. Her legs curled beneath her, one hand holding her up, she peered out past the lights, her eyes imploring Maxim to drop the gun, to leave, to spare himself Nick's revenge. Before a thousand mocking spectators, Maxim had risen up to shame Nicolas. Now, Fifine knew, nothing mattered in Nick's existence but to make sure that, though he might die tomorrow in a hail of police bullets, he would, tonight, deal mercilessly with Maxim.

Fifine cried out, "Maxim! Please, go!"

Nick's hand still clutched Fifine's wrist, still kept her bonded to him.

"Let her go!"

Nick's hand tightened.

"Oh no," said Fifine. She understood.

"No!" said Nick. "Go ahead. Shoot me, you chickenshit bookkeeper."

It had dawned at last on the audience that this standoff, with a real gun, was not a show. The band trailed off and a low murmur replaced the music.

"You don't have the balls," taunted Nick. "You little coward."

"No, Nicky," gasped Fifine, "don't."

Nick slapped his chest. "Come on, Maxie. Do it."

Maxim pointed the gun. He thumbed the hammer back.

Fifine whispered desperately. "Nicky, he will. He'll shoot."

Nick squeezed her wrist. He nodded. He looked down at Fifine, with eyes that seemed almost loving. "I'll be dead tomorrow," he said. "What's the difference?"

Nick released her hand. He swept his hair away from his face and glared defiantly at Maxim.

Hurriedly, Fifine rose, to whisper that oh, yes, there is a difference, that life must must be clung to, if only for one more dawn. Tenderly, forgivingly, she reached up to touch Nick's face.

The bark of the gun startled even the coolest heads among the profligate sinners in the smoky hall. The bullet entered just below Fifine's shoulder...

OCTOBER

Michel

JAMESON

Rosebud Bar

CHAPTER 38

The Rosebud Bar

After splurging on *os* and *escargots, sole meunière* and *filet de bar,* with a piquant Sancerre at Le Select on blvd. Montparnasse, Steve and Mie skirted around the block to the Rosebud Bar. They settled into a corner banquette beneath the little effigy of Jean-Paul Sartre. A lively, bilingual waitress hurried over and took their order for the overpriced house specialty, the *pick-me-up du Rosebud.*

They had hit a quiet spell at the Rosebud. Two solitary drinkers, well separated, occupied barstools. A half-dozen theatergoers, spruced-up and middle-aged, were clustered volubly in the rear salon, beneath art by Steinlen and Giacometti and a fiercely nostalgic Mistinguett poster. With a panoramic view of the serpentine mahogany bar, Steve and Mie could watch the doorway.

The musical motif of the Rosebud's sound system is jazz. A Ben Webster composition ended, giving way to Art Tatum.

"Did I ever tell you," Steve asked, "what Dick Hyman said about Art Tatum's left hand?"

Mie lifted a slender, pale, immaculate hand. "At least four times."

"Ah," said Steve, swallowing his anecdote.

The white-jacketed bartender, backed by mirrors and

rows of exotic bottles, fashioned their drinks with a deftness and dignity that bespoke a lifetime of sacerdotal mixology. As he stirred, he cast an approving glance toward Mie, who was exceptional in red silk with a bare shoulder, her lipstick matching her shoes, and a slit in her skirt that didn't quite reach her waist.

"This is the third time we've been here in a week," said Mie.

Steve cupped Mie's chin, drew her forward and kissed her lingeringly.

"Steve!" said Mie.

"This joint brings out the romantic in me," said Steve. He caressed her thigh.

"Steve!"

"*Voilà!*" said the genial waitress, who was dirty blonde, fit and over forty. She set down their drinks, along with ramekins of olives and potato chips.

Steve thanked the waitress. He clinked glasses with Mie and, summoning his inner Bogart, said, "Success ... to crime."

"Uh huh," said Mie. She peered, past a trio of tables, toward the entrance. "This is not a nightcap. It's a goddamn stakeout."

Steve rolled his eyes.

"Hardly," he said. "If this were a stakeout, we'd be stuck side-by-side in a musty Crown Vic, smelling each other's BO and peeing into a jar."

Mie sighed. "You watch too many cop shows."

"Besides," said Steve, "This is one of the nicest watering holes in all of Paris. It's the Buddha Bar without the Asian kitsch. It's Harry's without all the Americans."

"Steve, you're American."

"Yeah, but the only one. Look around."

Mie paused the argument, sipping her drink. "Well, I do like it here," she said. "But they'll never show."

"Yeah, probably," replied. "The guy said that they only come here, like, once in a while."

"And why, again, do we care where they go, what they do?"

"Pure morbid curiosity."

"Journalists are supposed to be above vulgar voyeurism."

Steve tilted his head. "Well, sometimes I'm a journalist. Other times, I'm just a reporter."

Mie considered this. "And what am I?"

Steve thought for a moment. "Yummy?"

Mie pinkened but responded sharply. "Professionally."

"Smarter than me," said Steve. "Prob'ly gonna be better than I ever was."

It was Mie's turn to kiss Steve.

"You keep this up," said Steve after catching his breath, "you and me are gonna end up hitched."

This prompted a minute of contemplative silence, as they sipped and avoided eye contact.

"Besides," Steve began again, "this is one story that's not the usual bistro bullshit."

Mie wrinkled a brow. "Bistro bullshit?"

"Yeah, look at us. We amuse ourselves by speculating," said Steve, thoughtfully, "about the lives of strangers we see across the tables in a crowded restaurant."

Mie nodded.

"We make up stories. We never see these people again. We forget the story the next day."

"Oh, before that," said Mie. "We've forgotten by the time we walk out the door."

"Well, there you have it, babe. We haven't forgotten. That's why this story is different."

"It's different," said Mie, "because you won't let it go. You've been snooping into these people's lives."

"No, no," insisted Steve. "These people, Ray Cavendish and the beautiful Mireille—and then the maniac boyfriend— we didn't find them. They found us. They wouldn't leave us alone."

"Leave us alone?" Mie scoffed.

"Look, we had a perfectly good yarn about this guy. He was

a dying physicist. And she was, what, just a waitress, right? But then, there she is again. We didn't go looking for her. She popped into our lives and … I mean, how big is this city? You never see a stranger twice!"

Mie nodded. "Steve, she waits tables at a bistro. We keep going back to the bistro."

"Oh no, we saw her elsewhere," Steve said. "She insinuated herself."

"Oh, for God's sake."

"So, we gave her a story. Princess of Monaco."

"Monaco?"

"San Marino. Sorry," said Steve. "I get my postage stamps mixed up."

The door opened. Steve looked up hopefully. A couple came in. They were strangers.

Mie spoke. "We could've left it there. We could've left these people alone."

"Yeah, and we probably would have. But then, Leather Jacket comes along," said Steve. "Reality rears its ugly head. Suddenly, the real story is better than fiction. Suddenly—"

"Suddenly, you get snoopy."

They exchanged a meaningful look. They sipped their pick-me-ups. Each one ate an olive.

Mie relented. "Okay, I give. I admit it. I'm curious, too. Otherwise, we'd be drinking someplace where we could actually afford the drinks. But it's a wild flamingo chase, Steve. There's almost no chance they'll suddenly walk through that door … "

Suddenly, Cavendish and Mireille walked through the door.

"Holy shit," whispered Mie.

As soon as his eyes adjusted to the low light in the Rosebud Bar, Cavendish recognized the reporter he had met on rue de la Harpe. He pretended not to notice. This was his first night out with Mireille in almost a month. He had finished his draft of *Apache Dance* and wanted to tell her about it. He wanted to reveal how it ends and somehow—subtly—intermingle Fifine and Nicky and Maxim with Mireille and Serge and Cavendish. Turning his back on Steve and Mie, Cavendish guided Mireille to a corner of the banquette, closest to the doorway. He positioned himself so that the other couple could not see Mireille. He was being rude and he didn't care. He wanted all of Mireille's attention and none of anyone else's. Things were happening to Mireille's feelings. He could sense her turmoil but he didn't know what it meant.

"Well, that's odd," said Steve. "The guy's giving us the cold shoulder."

Mie smiled. "Do you blame him?"

"Well, I mean," Steve muddled. "He told me he'd be—"

"Hush," said Mie. "Something else is going on."

"Where?"

"Here, Steve. With them."

"Yeah, what?"

Mie rolled her eyes. "Men."

"Whaddya mean by that?"

"You're staring at those people, Steve. Stop it," said Mie. "Look at me."

"Look at you?"

"Look into my eyes."

Steve groaned.

Steve obeyed Mie only until the waitress swept by. He watched as Cavendish ordered drinks. For an instant, Mie caught Mireille's eye. Mireille recognized her and nodded almost imperceptibly.

"Ah," said Mie.

"What?"

"This is a heart-to-heart."

"What's a heart-to-heart?"

"Them," she said. "They have a lot to talk about."

"Yeah, but what?"

"Well, we'll never know, will we, Steve?"

Steve glanced at the other couple and grasped his curiosity's futility.

Mie put it into words.

"You can watch them all night and you won't find out anything," said Mie. "They will lean close and talk low. You could slide over there and eavesdrop on their conversation, but you won't do it. I wouldn't let you. Their lives are none of our affair."

Steve slumped and exhaled. Mie was right.

"Besides," she went on, "lives are messy. Even if you could hear every word they're saying, you'd get just a snapshot. We could shadow him, or her, or both of them together—if they are together!—for ten years, and we might never see how their story comes out. Real life isn't a story—you know this, Steve—it isn't something you can tie up with a bow and run the credits to the tune of 'As Time Goes By.'"

Steve crooned softly. *"You must remember this. A kiss—"*

"Hush!" Mie wasn't finished. "Now, you've met the guy. Cavendish. If you made a sincere effort to get to know him, you could maybe—some day—sit down with him, ask questions, make friends, eat out together with me and the beautiful waitress. We could babysit each other's kids. We could plan vacations together. We could—"

"Jesus Christ!"

Steve clutched Mie's arm as he stared at the door.

"It's Leather Man."

"Oh my God."

Just inside the door, Serge stopped spraddle-legged, swiveling his head, impatient for his eyes to adjust. In the startled bar, every eye turned toward him. In the air around them, Tatum ended "Without a Song" with a little dance on the keys and a somber bass note. A moment later, the first percussive trill of Duke Ellington's "C Jam Blues" stabbed the Rosebud silence.

Serge shifted, squinted and saw them. He shouted in French. Mireille snapped back. Cavendish turned to face Serge, planting his hands on the table, poised to stand and confront him.

The bar's ambience, sepia and softspoken, evaporated. The Rosebud took on the feel of a pothouse in the wrong neighborhood, where every look was a taunt and every drink an aperitif to violence. Sensing this, the bartender inched along the bar, eyes fixed on Serge. The merry group in the rear froze in place, wary of drawing Serge's attention but straining to see what next.

The bartender edged further, to the end of the bar, and opened his mouth to speak. Serge sensed movement. He turned. Quickly the bartender backed up a step and made a gesture of surrender. His eyes flickered, judging the distance to the telephone.

Serge spun back toward Mireille and Cavendish. He loomed over them. Mireille gripped Cavendish's arm, pulling him toward her. She glared angrily at Serge.

Cavendish spoke warningly to Serge. "I have a gun." He plunged a hand into his pocket.

Mireille responded in near-panic, seizing Cavendish with both hands and forcing him to look at her. Their faces were inches apart. "No, Cavendish!"

She turned to Serge.

"It's not true. There's no gun."

Cavendish tried to protest. "No, no. I have—"

There was a knife in Serge's hand.

"He threw the gun in the river!" Mireille said this, in French, too fast for Cavendish to understand.

Cavendish's hand dug into his empty pocket. Serge pointed the thin blade at Cavendish's nose.

"J'ai un couteau, sheet-'ead."

Cavendish's face reddened but he dropped the pretense. He showed Serge his empty hand and curled it into a fist. He scowled up at Serge.

Suddenly, as Ray Nance's trumpet pealed through the bar, Serge had Mireille by the arm, snatching her from the banquette, almost toppling the table. Instinctively, Cavendish reached out and rescued one of the drinks. The other slid away. The glass clanked on the floor, its contents splashing Cavendish's shoes.

Mireille was against Serge's chest, his breath in her eyes, pushing to escape his grip. The knife handle, blade pointing up, pressed on her backbone. She stabbed his foot with her heel. He cried out. Mireille pulled away, spinning back and stumbling. She would have crashed into the table, falling onto Cavendish, but Serge lashed out with an arm and took her back, by the waist.

The bartender cried out in alarm. The waitress rushed back behind the bar, clinging to the bartender. Pummeling Serge's arm, Mireille broke away again. She lunged toward the door. Serge stepped in her path, snatching her wrist and swinging her toward the bar's interior.

Serge let go. Mireille's momentum carried her violently backward. She struck a table, pushing back into the next table and the next. Chairs tumbled. Mireille fell hard, sliding on the floor. She lay still for a moment, leaning on an elbow, her jaw taut, pain in her eyes, her skirt torn, her stockings ruined.

She looked up at Serge. *"Tu es ... lâche,"* she muttered.

"Salope!" Serge snarled back.

Cavendish pushed away a table and rushed to Mireille. As he reached out to stroke her face, Serge swung a leg, kicking the other man's ribs. Cavendish tumbled away, gasping for breath, rolling 'til he hit a barstool. It tipped onto him, banging his head.

The bartender shouted again. Serge feinted toward him,

knife foremost. The bartender backed off, trapped in the embrace of the terrified waitress.

Crushing her arm, Serge snatched Mireille to her feet. She cried out.

Mie looked out over the jumble of tables and chairs piled up in front of her. Under her breath, she said to Steve, "Are you gonna do something?"

"Like run?"

"No, like help that woman!"

"Did you notice the knife?"

Mie nodded.

Steve said, "And how big that sumbitch is. You see that?"

"I see," said Mie. "But ... "

"Look. The bartender's afraid to move," said Steve. "Dig around in your purse. Find your phone."

"Phone! Oh! Yes."

Mie began searching her handbag.

Mireille clawed at Serge's face, gouging two red streaks into his cheek. Serge roared in surprise. Mireille broke free, but reacting in rage, he pounced on her. They staggered together toward the bar. Knocking a stool aside, Serge pinned Mireille against the bar. The waitress bleated in fear. The bartender brandished a bottle, twelve-year-old whiskey pouring down his arm and drenching the waitress.

Serge slipped the knife under his belt, freeing both hands.

Locking his fingers in hers, Serge backed from the bar, drawing Mireille. She writhed and resisted but could not break away. Beneath her feet, Cavendish rolled to a sitting position. He shook his head, spraying drops of the blood that was running from his nose.

"What's the police emergency number?" Mie whispered.

"Jesus, I don' know. Try 911."

"Shit."

"What?"

"I can't."

"Why?'

"I don't know the Wi-Fi password here."

"Oh, shit."

As Serge pulled and spun Mireille, she tried to kick him. Nimbly, he avoided her feet. She only succeeded in losing her shoes. Serge drew her back and held her 'round the waist, spinning her, burying his face in the curve of her neck as she turned in a circle, again and again 'til she was dizzy. Her toes barely touched the floor.

Cavendish shook his head, trying to focus, gazing up at Serge and Mireille. Serge lurched to a stop, bending Mireille backward, his face between her breasts, 'til her hair touched the floor. She gasped for breath.

"Jesus," said Cavendish. "It's the dance."

Serge, as though suddenly caught in the fluid force of Johnny Hodges' sax, swirled Mireille and lifted her. Helpless, she bent over Serge's shoulder, the lights above her blurring and blinding her.

"It's on the menu," said Steve. "Here."

Mie read the Wi-Fi password and thumbed it onto her screen.

"Ah! Got it!"

"Great. Call the cops."

Mie dialed a number.

"Shit."

"What?"

"Nothing."

"What?"

"911 doesn't work here. All I get is beep-beep-beep."

"Shit."

Cavendish wiped the blood from his nose with a sleeve. He reached up, clawing for a hold on an upright bar stool. Serge flew past, clipping Cavendish with a knee. Cavendish sank back to the floor. Cursing, he shook the cobwebs, spreading more blood. He gripped the stool with both hands.

Ellington jammed on.

Serge slid Mireille down his body, bringing her face opposite his. He stared and studied her. She fixed him in a tight, icy gaze. *"Lâche,"* she whispered coldly. *"Bâtard."*

"Tu es à moi," he growled, desperation in his voice. *"Seulement."*

Gritting his teeth, he crushed her arms in his fists and shoved wildly, letting her fly away, but snatching her wrist as she stumbled toward the cellar stairs. She cried out in pain. He yanked and spun her, her head back, missing the end of the bar by an inch. He would have killed her—his alone, his forever. Nance screamed. Hodges moaned.

Cavendish saw. He embraced the bar stool, pulling himself up. Pausing, nauseous, he bent over the stool. His head spun. He felt blood running in his hair.

"Hey!"

Mie shouted across the bar at the bartender. She was ignored. Both the barkeep and the waitress were transfixed by the scene unfolding before them.

"Hey! *M'sieur!*"

No luck.

"Shit!"

"Hey, goddammit!" Steve tried. "Bartender! Hey!"

As though waking from a sound sleep, the bartender craned his neck and squinted toward Steve.

"Hey!"

The bartender spread his hands, palms up, looking at Steve inquisitively.

"The emergency number!"

The bartender, one eye on Serge and Mireille, looked puzzled.

"Shit," said Steve to Mie. "What's 'emergency' in French?"

"Um ... "

Cavendish, on his feet but wobbly, staggered along the bar, dripping blood. The waitress, seeing Cavendish's distress, awoke from her own shock and rushed toward Cavendish with a bar cloth. Cavendish, pressed it to his nose and turned, looking for Mireille.

She was pressed to a table, Serge between her legs, the front of her tattered blouse balled in his fist. His other hand held the knife.

Steve stood. "Fuck it," he said.

He shouted at Serge. "Hey, you son of a bitch!"

Holding his pose, Serge turned his head toward Steve. Mireille, exhausted, whimpered softly.

"Whot de fock?" said Serge in his best English, glowering at Steve.

"That's enough, goddammit," shouted Steve. He was hemmed in by a wall of upset furniture, but he pointed a finger accusingly.

"What's the hell's wrong with you?" Steve yelled.

"Steve," Mie whispered. "Don't. You can't."

"I have to," Steve replied.

"No. I have to," said Cavendish. He was upright, standing in the middle of the floor, facing Serge.

Serge released Mireille. She teetered on the table, slipped to one knee and breathed hard, staring at the floor. Serge moved swiftly on Cavendish, leading with his knife. His charge would end with the blade plunged to the hilt in Cavendish.

"Oh my God!" cried Mie.

A foot from Cavendish, Serge stayed his blade, pointing it

up so that he came to a halt with point beneath Cavendish's chin.

"What's going on here?" Mie said, wilted and bewildered. "This kind of Wild West crap doesn't happen in Paris."

"Yeah?" said Steve, as he poised to leap the pile of tables and chairs, steeling himself to tackle the Frenchman in the leather jacket with a knife.

Before Steve could leap, Mireille rose. She rushed toward the two men, pressed together in the middle of the bar, glaring at each other. The bartender had slipped out from behind the bar. The crowd in the back might have moved a few inches. The stool drinkers had slipped behind the bar and taken refuge near the kitchen door.

Oblivious to the knife, Mireille threw herself at Serge and Cavendish, bouncing away once and returning, pushing and grunting. Stubbornly, in an effort that seemed strangely comical, she wedged herself between the two men 'til, at last, she had room to push at Serge's chest and edge him back. Straining for breath, she gazed up at Serge, tears smeared on her cheeks.

"C'est assez." She breathed heavily and coughed once. "Serge, enfin. Assez! S'il tu plaît. Please. Please ... "

Serge's eyes turned inward. He seemed to shrink. He let Mireille, gingerly, take the knife. She wrapped Serge's hand in both of hers. Their eyes met. Mireille talked softly.

"What's she saying?" Steve asked.

"Shut up. I'm trying to hear."

Steve clammed up.

"I wish my French was better," Mie grumbled.

Cavendish backed away and leaned on a barstool. Mireille and Serge were in the middle of the bar. Duke Ellington had given way to Jim Hall's gentle, conversational guitar.

"I can't hear," said Mie. "She's whispering in French."

"Whatever she's saying, it seems to be working."

Serge had lowered his chin, listening to Mireille, offering brief, meek replies. After a few minutes, Mireille waggled a hand at Cavendish. He approached, pausing uneasily beside Mireille.

Mireille, looking into Serge's eyes, spoke in English. "Until he loved me, you know," she said to Cavendish, "he never hurt anyone."

"What? It's your fault?" ventured Cavendish. "You made Serge crazy?"

Serge understood this. He tightened.

Cavendish looked at Serge. "Mireille, ah." His smile was ironic. "She would make any man crazy."

They kept their eyes fixed on each other. For a while, the music was the only sound.

"No?" asked Cavendish.

Serge tilted his head. His body relaxed. He lifted Mireille's chin and asked, *"Aimes-tu vraiment cet mozzafockah."*

Mireille kept her eyes fixed on Serge. She signed and paused. With a half-smile, she said, *"Ah ... je suppose."*

Cavendish seemed to shudder. "Really?" he said.

Mireille was still locked in Serge's gaze. *"Oui,"* she said. *"Vraiment."*

"What was all that?" Steve asked Mie.

"The fight's over," said Mie.

"Yeah? Who won?"

"The woman."

"Oh."

Steve broke the spell by climbing noisily out of the jumble of bar furniture. Serge turned on him and spoke irritably.

"Who za fock a' you?"

"What? Who? Me?" Steve muddled. "Oh, I'm just passin' through here, pardner."

Mie joined Steve. "He's with me." She caught Mireille's eye. *"Comment dit-on* 'nosey'?" Mie asked.

"*Curieux*," said Mireille.

"Ah, well," said Mie, "this is Steve. *Il est trop curieux.*"

This got a laugh from Mireille, which allowed everyone in the Rosebud to do the same, excessively, in a wave of relief.

Steve spotted the bartender. "Drinks for everyone," he called.

Mie responded instantly. "No!" she called out. "Just us."

"Aw, come on, Mie."

"Steve, look around. Fourteen twenty-euro cocktails?"

"Oh." Steve blanched. "A little steep, huh?"

Steve wanted to sit together with Cavendish and Mireille and find out more about them. But Mie pulled him away. From the end of the bar, they watched Mireille kiss Serge goodbye, chastely and consolingly. He tucked his knife away and shuffled out the door.

"Jesus," said Steve. "Suddenly, I feel sorry for that psycho."

Cavendish and Mireille went back to their corner and huddled together, talking inaudibly. They held each other's hands and kissed frequently.

"Everything about them," said Mie, "has changed."

"Yeah," said Steve. "When they came in—"

"When they came in," said Mie, "the sad author didn't know the beautiful waitress was in love with him."

"Did she know?"

"No," said Mie.

"So," said Steve, "just like that?"

"When you know, everything changes."

The Rosebud waitress, her insouciance restored, gamboled over to them and delivered a round of pick-me-ups, along with more olives and chips. "*Service,*" she said, smiling and patting Steve on the cheek. "On ze 'ouse."

"*Oh, merci!*" said Mie.

"What's an 'ouse?" said Steve.

Mie ignored the question.

The waitress lingered, looking over at Mireille, who was nuzzling Cavendish's nose.

"C'est amour," said the waitress.

"Oui," said Mie a little enviously. *"C'est doux."*

"Et," asked the waitress, looking Steve up and down, *"vous?"*

Mie laughed and rolled her eyes.

Steve observed the girl-talk suspiciously.

Mie clinked Steve's glass and brushed her lips on his. She guided his hand to a bare spot high on her thigh.

"Let's," she said breathily, "talk about us."

LA FIN

LA CHANSON DE FIFINE

(TRANSLATION BY ANNE-FRANÇOISE PELÉ)

Le sang sur mes lèvres
Est l'amour de mon homme
La plaie de mon coeur
Est son âme dans la mienne
Il voit mon visage
En chacune de ses amantes
Malgré les blessures
Malgré les larmes, je souris
Chacun de ses gestes
Qu'il soit doux ou vigoureux
Exprime un amour
Qu'il ne peut nier
Atteste qu'il est à moi
Dans la joie, dans la peine
Par-delà l'amour et la haine
À la vie, à la mort
Je serai sienne
Il sera mien
De l'amour à la mort
Il sera mien

The blood on my lips
Is my man's love

The ache in my heart
Is his soul in mine
He sees my face
In his every lover
Through every bruise
I smile through tears
His every touch
Though soft, though hard
Reveals a love
He cannot deny
Confesses he's mine
Through pain, through joy
With love and hate
In life and in death
I will be his
He will be mine
In love and death
He will be mine

ON TERMS IN FRENCH

When an author contrives to speckle the text of a novel with foreign words and phrases, there are four approaches to conveying English equivalents to the reader. One is to immediately follow the foreign term with a translation. This is effective but, in my view, an annoying narrative tic.

The second is to trust the reader to deduce the word's meaning from the context, which is hit and miss, and a frequent source of frustration. The third is to apply to one's reading the method I used while writing this novel. Since I'm not remotely fluent in French, I either used translation sites online or riffled through my copy of Larousse.

The fourth approach is a variation on the latter. The author scours the manuscript for troublesome snatches of *Français* and tucks them into a little lexicon at the back of the book.

One of the complications of compiling the glossary below is that many of the words in the *Apache Dance* passages derive from slang and argot common among the criminal classes and the Paris demimonde of the early 20th century. Never common in polite speech, many of these terms have disappeared from the vernacular. My richest source for these *gros mots* from the demimonde of yore is Luc Santé in his captivating history *The Other Paris*. If you're curious, for example, about synonyms for prostitute, well, here's an instructive passage from Santé': "... the actresses and dancers and models, the kept women, the courtesans, the grandes cocottes, the demimondaines, the *horizontales*, the *amazones,* the *lionnes,* the 'marble girls,' the 'man-eaters'... *lorettes*, an elastic designation for courtesans and kept women whose relative fortunes could be determined by their address...". Of course, he goes on.

The glossary below covers most of the French words and idioms that pop up in *Bistro Nights*, plus a sampling of "underworld" terms bandied among the denizens of Les Noctambules. Any term that appears in the book but isn't defined below is either so obvious that even I could figure it out, or you can just pass right over it without losing the thread.

GLOSSARY

l'addition: the check, in a restaurant

amoureux (m.): lover

apache: a street thug, gangster (inspired by the appearance of Buffalo Bill in the 1900 exhibition)

argenté: silver

asperge: asparagus

assiette: plate

assommoir: a dive, pothouse, speakeasy. "Its squalid walls sweat misery and stink; its crippled tables and spavined benches serve as a dormitory for a stunted population of beings no longer conscious of their own existence and who retain no human qualities." (Alexandre Privat d'Anglemont)

attraper: to catch

bal-musette: a dance hall with origins in an Auvergnat bagpipe called a *musette*

bar (various names): *boc, bibine, boîte, cabremont, caboulot, cargot, abreuvoir, assommoir, bastringue, boucon, bouffardière, bousin, cabermon, troquet*

bar (fish): bass

bien-aimée: beloved

bien sûr: of course

bistro: from the Russian word for "quickly," introduced during the Russian occupation of Paris in 1814, "the kind of no-nonsense restaurant favoured by Cossacks" (Andrew Hussey)

blettes: chard

la bohème: the underworld, underbelly, demimonde — "the other Paris," home to "… vagabonds, discharged soldiers, escaped galley slaves, swindlers, mountebanks, lazzaroni, pickpockets, tricksters, gamblers, *macquereaux* [pimps], brothel-keepers, porters, literati, organ-grinders, ragpickers, knife-grinders, tinkers, beggars—in short, the whole indefinite, disintegrated mass thrown hither and thither…" (Karl Marx)

bouquiniste: a seller of books from stalls along the Seine

cabillaud: cod

canaille: scum, scoundrel

capon: a gambling shill

casser: to break

cèpe: a variety of mushroom

c'est assez: that's enough

chanteuse: singer (f.)

chouchou: pet

clochard: bum or hobo. "… a sleeping *clochard* always looks like a corpse, ideally a headless corpse…" (Robert Giraud)

cochon: pig

comment dit-on: how does one say

confit de canard: preserved duck

coques: small clams from Brittany

coquille St.-Jacques: scallop

cornichon: small, tart pickle

cote d'agneau: lamb chop

coupe-gueule: cutthroat

cour des miracles: an encampment of beggars, whores and thieves

couteau: knife

daikon: large, white radish (Japanese)

la danse apache: a violent dance unique to apache culture. "...one of the apache dances for which they were famed, and in which the man, with fierce grimaces, often looked as though he intended his partner grievous bodily harm..." (Netley Lucas)

la danse macabre: an image of skeletons cavorting over the dead to the tune of the Grim Reaper, first depicted during the Black Death of the 14th century

daurade: sea bream

desolé: sorry

devant: against

doigt: finger

doré: golden

doux: sweet

écorcheur: a denizen of ramparts and ditches near the 14th-century walls, "an underclass of desperate peasants, army deserters, whores, pimps, touts, thieves and professional assassins" (Andrew Hussey)

écrivain: writer

espadon: swordfish

estaleur: street merchant

étranger: stranger

flaneur: a wanderer through the streets of Paris, a vagabond observer and a connoisseur of the human comedy. "The crowd is his domain, as air is that of a bird, as water is that of a fish. His passion and his profession is to *marry the crowd*. For the perfect *flaneur*, for the passionate observer, it is an immense pleasure to make a home in the multitude, in the flux, in the motion, in the fleeting and intimate." (Baudelaire)

flic: cop

fougueux: fiery

franc-mitou: a fake leper

fripouille: scoundrel, blackguard

fromage blanc: cream cheese

fruits de mer: seafood

gigolette: female lover, prostitute, slut

grisette: a young working woman who is coquettish and flirtatious

homard: lobster

hubain: a beggar claiming to be cured of rabies after a dog bite

ici: here

je me demande: I wonder

je sais: I know

lâche: coward

laisser: to let, allow

mademoiselle: a medium-sized drink served in a bar

maillotin: war hammer, violent troublemaker, from *maillets*, or mallets used by angry rebels in the 14th century to smash statues and heads

maintenant: now

mais: but

maquereau: mackerel

Le Marais: "the marsh"

mascaron: mask

matraque: bludgeon

mec: guy

mère: mother

merlu: hake

millefeuilles: a "thousand-sheets" layered pastry

Minitel: A pre-internet, telephone-based business and personal directory, unique to France

misérable: the smallest drink served in a bar, a thimble's worth

monsieur: the largest drink glass served in a bar

Monsieur de Paris: the executioner

Mort au Vaches!: Death to the cops. "… In wishing death to the *vache*, in other words, gendarme, the apache is making no extravagant threat out of mere bravado; the dealing of a death blow is almost as much a part of his life as is the ardent love-making of his dancing…" (Netley Lucas)

Ne pense pas: Don't think

nez: nose

onglet: hanger streak

os a moelle: bone marrow

parigot(e): a native Parisian "whose dry black humor constantly and consistently works against government and state" (Andrew Hussey)

"Parmerde": Rimbaud's word for Paris, "a disease-ridden place that smelt of shit both day and night."

perdre la tête: to lose one's head; go crazy

Petit Poulet: Chicken Little

peut-être: perhaps

piètre: a fake amputee

plouc: a gormless or oafish outsider to Paris; tourist

porte jarretelle: garter belt

pot au feu: beef stew

Le Pré aux Clercs: bank of the Seine once favored by students of the Sorbonne for fishing parties and general revelry

pression: draft beer

prix fixe: fixed price

prochain: next

ravacholer: to wipe out, after anarchist François-Claudius Ravachol *ravalement*: facelift, renovation of a building facade

rifodés: beggars posing as a burned-out family

rodeur de barrières: an urban highwayman, mugger

rognon: kidney

sabouleur: a fake epileptic

salope: slut

sans-culottes: lowest of Parisian working-class, who wore long trousers rather than breeches (*culottes*)

saucisson sec: dry sausage

savate: a form of kickboxing favored by *apaches*

sein-pourçeau: pig's breasts

serveur/ serveuse: waiter/ waitress

seulement: only

shoyu: soy sauce (Japanese)

sicarius: A knife-wielding killer (Latin)

singe: monkey

souteneur: a pimp

suprême de volaille: roast chicken with mushrooms and a mustard sauce

tapis-franc: thieves' den; a dive in which everyone present could be assumed to be a criminal

tarama: cod eggs (Japanese)

tataki: seared raw meat or fish (Japanese)

tartare: raw

tartine: an elaborate open-face sandwich, with a vast repertoire of ingredients, usually served on a slab of rustic bread called *pain Poilâne*

travers de porc: short ribs of pork

trop: too

truant: criminal

trublion: disturber of the peace

Tu es à moi: You belong to me

les vaches: the cops

veau: veal

velour: velvet

villa: a narrow residential side street, often a cul-de-sac with rowhouses

villon: a "cousener, conycatcher, cunning ot witty rogue; a nimble Knave; a pleasant theefe" (Randle Cotgrave)

vin chaud: mulled hot wine

voyous: hooligan

vrai de vrai: the real thing, original gangsters, true tough guys

vraiment: really

vulvivague: prostitute, literally "itinerant vagina"

zarin: a long, thin, sharp knife favored by *apaches*

ON BISTROS

The restaurant scene in Paris is both timeless and ephemeral. Over the past three decades, my wife and I have frequented bistros, some nearly a century old, that haven't changed since we first dined there. Others have transformed radically, sometimes for the better, often so much worse that we stopped going there. A few of our favorites—afflicted by hard times, old age or the vicissitudes of culinary fashion—have simply perished, leaving behind an empty storefront or a brand-new nail salon.

The restaurants that appear in this story are mostly real places that can still be found and patronized. Several, including the venues in Cavendish's *Apache Dance*, are fabricated. All the real restaurants introduced to readers by my characters are places where my wife and I have dined or imbibed. These locations do not represent the *avant garde* of Parisian dining. None is a gourmet mecca populated by celebrities and dignitaries and requiring reservations weeks—or months—in advance. They are joints we chose because they are eminently accessible, serving excellent—often imaginative—dishes at reasonable prices.

Paris has dozens of similar bistros, bars, cafes, restaurants, brasseries and even humble neighborhood tabacs that we have yet to discover (we're always looking), but which provide a sublime dining experience with genial service that's true to a culinary tradition unlike any other city in the world. Below are thumbnails of the locations—from a "restaurant list" I regularly update—that play a role in Bistro Nights. If you try one out and find that it's either not there any longer or has been overrun by the slobs and dilettantes unleashed by online "influencers," please accept our condolences and move on to the next adventure on the list.

(Ch. 1) **Le Petit St.-Benoit** (4, rue St. Benoit, 01 42 60 27 92). Simple but excellent food, tightly packed tables, congenial staff, comfortable atmosphere. Still quite cheap but not as cheap as once it was. One of those rare restaurants where you won't get hassled if you don't reserve. A classic Paris experience!

(Ch. 2) **Le Pré aux Clercs** (30, rue Bonaparte, 01 43 54 41 73). You don't go here primarily for the food, which is standard café fare, prepared well but not distinctive. You're here to linger on one of the Left Bank's busiest corners, where the parade along the streets, and the clientele on the terrasse, are as entertaining as a night at the Moulin Rouge, without the cover charge. Come late, order cognac, enjoy the show.

(Ch. 3) **Pâtisserie Viennoise** (8, rue de l'École de Médecine) is possibly the most "authentic" little hole-in-the-wall bakery in Paris, or at least on the Left Bank. We have our morning café crème there, served by a welcoming and cheery staff, in a drafty little salon that has not been redecorated since the place opened in 1928. The pastries stacked in the window are magnificent. Every morning, right around nine, a garbage truck plays a concert just outside the window.

(Ch. 4) **La Quin Cave** (17, rue Bréa, 01 43 29 38 24). Nothing much to eat here. This is just one of the best joints to drop in for a glass of wine after dinner in Montparnasse. Its founder, Frederic, who loved drinking with the clientele, started it as a wine shop, then put out a barrel and a couple of stools, and pretty soon, he had a bar. Kill a bottle, buy one for the road.

(Ch. 4) **Le Bistrot du Dôme** (1, rue Delambre, 01 43 35 32 00) has the best, freshest fish in Paris, a wonderful atmosphere, charming waiters, Paris' most intelligent wine list. We've experimented with other fish joints but always return here. It's adjacent to the famous Café du Dôme.

(Ch. 5) **Les Deux Magots/ Café de Flore/ Brasserie Lipp.** These three restaurants are the foundation of nightlife and social style in the St.-Germain-des-Prés area. The Magots (6, place St.-Germain-des-Prés) and the Flore (172, blvd. St.-Germain) have battled to be the "place to be seen" sipping champagne and dining al fresco on the terrasse. They're too expensive to be a habit for most people, but they're a stop on the Tourist Trail as important as the Eiffel Tower. Across the street, the Lipp (151, blvd. St.-Germain) is the hearty, snooty, costly German restaurant that has hosted every famous gourmand from Balzac to A.J. Liebling. Too expensive to be a hangout (and be prepared to get lip from the Lipp waiters) but a premier bucket-list checkpoint.

(Ch. 7) **Le Quartier Vavin** (18, rue Vavin, 01 43 26 67 47) is all about location. It's a serviceable café, always busy because it sits halfway between an afternoon of sunshine and people-watching at the Luxembourg Garden and an evening of feasting and imbibing at one of the restaurants, bistros, bars and celebrated cafés of Montparnasse. Very often, you know you've arrived there because a magnificent vintage car is parked out front.

(Ch. 8) **Le Closerie des Lilas** (171, blvd. du Montparnasse, 01 40 51 34 50). Famous and expensive. We've never eaten there but we tend to drop in for a late drink at the bar where Hemingway hung out and picked fights with Morley Callaghan (and got beat). The atmosphere is old-school Paris, classic and opulent. This is one of the five great literary hangouts of the Lost Generation. Perfect for a bottle of champagne at two in the morning.

(Ch. 8) **La Grivoiserie** (3, rue St.-Beuve, 01 45 49 10 40). Once known as Le Timbre because it's barely bigger than a postage stamp, it has sustained the quality of its cuisine under new ownership. The pleasure here is the elbow-to-elbow proximity of your sympathique neighboring diners, the intelligence of a constantly changing menu and a wine list that's both unpretentiously brief and eminently drinkable.

(Ch. 11) **Clamato** (80, rue de Charonne, 01 43 72 74 53) is the most creative seafood purveyor we've found (so far) in Paris. You can't reserve, but you can usually squeeze in at the counter, the best place to sit because you can watch the chefs at work. We recommend lunch rather than dinner. Clamato's strength is small dishes featuring crab, squid, calamari and other delicacies often served cold or raw. Even if something seems weird, order it. It's hard to go wrong here.

(Ch. 13) **Café de la Nouvelle Mairie** (19, rue des Fossés Saint-Jacques, 01 44 07 04 41). A wine bar near Panthéon unfortunately featured on the TV series "Emily in Paris," the Nouvelle Mairie remains, bless its heart, a little too hard to find for most tourists. The clientele are largely Parisian, the wine is hearty, the entrées are fresh and generous. Dinner choices, chalked on the ardoise, are dependable. Good conversation and friendly service on a quiet street.

(Ch. 14) **Le Bon Saint Pourçain** (10 bis, rue Servandoni, 01 43 54 93 63). Tucked into a little street near the church of St.-Sulpice, this is a somewhat obscure (you'll never find it in a guidebook, or unless you're looking for it) local hangout, now under new and trendier ownership, with dishes more creative than those served in the past by Mom and Pop. But it's still a cozy hole-in-the-wall away from the madding crowd.

(Ch. 18) The best soup in Paris is the Soup with Shrimp Dumplings and Noodles, at **Mirama** (17, rue St.-Jacques, 01 43 54 71 77), the unlikely-looking Chinese joint just behind the eglise St. Séverin. No reservations; just go. Stand in line if you must. Don't leave Paris without tasting it.

(Ch. 20) **Les Éditeurs** (4, carrefour de l'Odéon, 01 43 26 67 76) is a fashionable café that serves one of Paris' best breakfasts, and the second best pain au chocolat in the whole city. (The best is at Isabella, a boulangerie in place Maubert.) We usually economize by buying one petit dejeuener (café crème, two pastries and O.J.) and then just one more café au lait—plenty for two. But the big breakfast is wonderful.

(Ch. 25) **La Tartine** (24, rue de Rivoli, 01 42 72 76 85) has been here forever. Originally a family-owned wine bar that specialized in Loire vintages and open-faced French sandwiches on pain Poilâne, it went through a few owners and a renovation before settling into its traditional menu of simple plats and bar food and a slightly expanded wine list. It remains a soothing refuge on a hectic thoroughfare.

(Ch. 27) **Le Fumoir** (6, rue de l'Amiral de Coligny, 01 42 92 00 24). One of the best lunches in Paris, just behind the Louvre. Le Fumoir is popular with the yuppies who work in this area, so reservations even for lunch are recommended. The interior is cool and dark. The cuisine has Asian influences. The waitresses—who outnumber waiters—are all slim and comely in white blouses and black skirts, and they all seem to be brunettes. Our favorite dish is the Popeye Salad. Despite the name, there's no smoking inside.

(Ch. 29) **Les Papilles** (30 Rue Gay-Lussac, 01 43 25 20 79) has one of the heartiest lunch menus on the Left Bank, in a setting surrounded by shelves of wine and delicacies and a grand zinc bar. It's close, cozy and congenial. Dinner here is also excellent but always limited to two main dishes.

(Ch. 31) **Au Gênêral Lafayette** (52, rue La Fayette, 01 47 70 59 08) serves standard bistro food, well-prepared—at exceptionally thrifty prices—in one of the loveliest dining rooms in Paris. You're surrounded by auburn woodwork, graceful arches, art nouveau flourishes, brass fittings, Chinese wallpaper and greenery. The bar, backed by ten-foot arched mirrors, has ten beers on tap and a giant wood-carved Guinness toucan. A classic Paris experience in an out-of-the-way neighborhood.

(Ch. 32) Our favorite hearty restaurant is **Chez René** (14, blvd. St.-Germain, 01 43 54 30 23). Follow rue St.-Jacques away from the Seine, turn left, walk about fifteen minutes. It's not open on Sundays and Mondays. Order beef, chicken or charcuterie. But beware, the charcuterie "starter" is enough to serve a full meal to a hungry family. Under new ownership in the last few years, it's still a lovely, classic bistro. The house wine has always been a modest, fruity cru of Beaujolais.

(Ch. 36) **Aux Crus de Bourgogne** (3, rue Bachaumont 01 42 33 48 24) is one of our "home" bistros, where we go for warmth, friendship, comfort, familiar surroundings, dependably superb cuisine. It has changed owners and staff since we first went there, and prices have gone up, but it's still a first-rate bistro. They specialize in foie gras and serve a lovely boeuf bourguignon.

(Ch. 36) **Vaudeville** (29 Rue Vivienne, 01 40 20 04 62) is a sprawling brasserie/bistro just up rue Vivienne from Le Grand Colbert and Palais Royale, with a reliable menu of thoughtfully prepared familiar cuisine. It supposedly closes at eleven p.m., but we got served drinks on the terrasse at midnight while watching, indoors, a waiter playing with fire and dishing out crêpes Suzette. This dessert alone, now hard to find in Paris, is worth an evening at Vaudeville.

(Ch. 38) **Le Select** (99, blvd. du Montparnasse, 01 45 48 38 24). One of the four great literary cafés on this historic boulevard— along with Le Dôme, La Rotonde and La Coupole—Le Select is old-fashioned and ornate but steeped in Parisian elegance and surprisingly friendly. The menu is traditional and scrupulously prepared. An evening here summons up ghosts. If you can find a copy of Noel Riley Fitch's Paris Café: The Select Crowd, read it before you come.

(Ch. 38) **The Rosebud Bar** (11, rue Delambre, 01 43 35 38 54) is an art deco refuge near blvd. du Montparnasse, reputed as a late-night hangout for the theater crowd. It's a superior alternative to Harry's Bar, which nowadays epitomizes the lament of Yogi Berra: "It's too crowded. Nobody goes there anymore." The drinks cost too much, but the atmosphere makes it worthy of a splurge.

BIBLIOGRAPHY

Marcel Allain & Pierre Souvestre, *Fantomas*, William Morrow, New York, 1986

Honoré de Balzac, tr., Jordan Stump, *The Wrong Side of Paris*, New American Library, New York, 2003

Marie-France Boyer, *The French Café,* Thames & Hudson, London, 1994

Noel Riley Fitch, *Paris Café: The Select Crowd*, Soft Skull Press, Brooklyn, 2007

Janet Flanner, *Paris Was Yesterday: 1925-1939*, The Viking Press, New York, 1972

Andrew Hussey, *Paris: The Secret History*, Bloomsbury, New York, 2006

Maurice Leblanc, tr., George Morehead, Alexander Teixeira de Mattos, *The Lupin Collection*, M.A. Donahue & Co., 1910; W.R. Caldwell & Co., 1913

Netley Lucas, *Criminal Paris,* Hurst & Blackett, London, 1926

Stanley Meisler, *Shocking Paris: Soutine, Chagall and the Outsiders of Montparnasse,* St. Martin's, New York, 2015

Elliot Paul, *The Last Time I Saw Paris*, Random House, New York, 1942

Luc Santé, *The Other Paris*, Farrar, Straus & Giroux, New York, 2015

Eugene Sue, *Les Mystéres de Paris,* Penguin Classics, New York, 2015

François Thomazeau, *Au Vrai Zinc Parisien,* Editions

Parigramme, Paris, 2004

William Wiser, *The Crazy Years: Paris in the Twenties,* Thames & Hudson, London, 1983

ABOUT THE AUTHOR

David Benjamin is a lifelong storyteller, dating back to Mrs. Poss' second- grade class at St. Mary's School in Tomah, Wis. His loosely told memoir, *The Life and Times of the Last Kid Picked*, was originally published by Random House and has been reprinted in a revised version by Last Kid Books. His Last Kid Books include a collection of his essays, *Almost Killed by a Train of Thought*, and thirteen novels, *Three's a Crowd, A Sunday Kind of Love, Summer of '68, Skulduggery in the Latin Quarter, Black Dragon, Jailbait, Bastard's Bluff, They Shot Kennedy, Fat Vinny's Forbidden Love, Woman Trouble, Witness to the Crucifixion, Choose Moose* and *Dead Shot*. As a journalist, Benjamin has edited newspapers, published and edited several magazines, and authored *SUMO: A Thinking Fan's Guide to Japan's National Sport*.

Since its launch in 2019, Benjamin's publishing imprint, Last Kid Books, has won twenty-eight independent-press awards. These include, for *They Shot Kennedy*, the Midwest Book Awards' 2021 grand prize for literary/historical/contemporary fiction, and a 2022 Silver Medal to *Fat Vinny's Forbidden Love* in the Independent Book Publishers Association's prestigious Benjamin Franklin Awards. His essays have appeared in publications that include the *Philadelphia Inquirer, San Francisco Examiner, Minneapolis Star-Tribune, Los Angeles Times, Chicago Tribune* and Bill Evjue's *Capital Times*.

Benjamin and his wife, Junko Yoshida, have been married for ages. They live sometimes in Madison, Wis., and the rest of the time in Paris.